Western Novels by G. R. Howe

No Time To Trust

Crow Woman on Deadman

Short Stories Out of Kane

Dragons Of Fire

G. R. Howe

ISBN-10:0985040718
ISBN-13:978-0-9850407-1-0

For Joy

Acknowledgments

I would like to thank the following people, who took their valuable time to read and edit this manuscript. Their comments and suggestions were invaluable. Thanks especially to my chief critic and grammarian, Joy Howe, who has lived with every word. Special thanks as well to Martha Howe, Rachel Montgomery, Diane Halsey, and Glenn Halsey.

Foreword

Fifty-three years hence, accompanied by his grandson, he would show up at a confessional in the Catholic church on the Isleta Indian reservation and visit the only priest with whom he would ever speak. When asked if he was seeking absolution, he would say to the priest, "Hell no. Don't want none of that. Too damn old for one thing and too damn forgetful for another." Looking at the man of God, he would think this man dressed in black skirts had one worthless, thankless job listening to people "whining" about the life they made for themselves. The old man would volunteer that one of the most difficult things he had done was bury a friend, a man he'd known, a gypsy by birth.

Having heard this statement, the priest would glance at the old man's grandson and be told that the non-confessor was eighty-three years old and grouchy, not to mention hard of hearing. So the priest, out of kindness, would raise his voice and ask if burying the gypsy was the most difficult.

"No, it wasn't," the old man would reply, appearing to think before he answered the question. "The most difficult was buryin' my wife."

Out of respect for the dead and the old man the priest would pause, hesitating, and ask if his wife was old when she died.

"No, she was twenty-six," he would answer.

"Twenty-six? Oh my. So very young."

The priest would offer his sympathy. Then the old man would nod in understanding and lean forward and whisper, telling him "not to worry about neither one." The priest would ask why not.

"Because I kept the law," he would reply. "Because, I took an eye for an eye. Because vengeance was mine."

The priest would look at the old man and say, "Vengeance belongs to the Lord God, my son, and none other."

And the old man, knowing who he was and what he had become, would say to the priest in his rough, gravelly voice, choosing his words carefully, "Who else? I was just borrowin'."

CHAPTER ONE

John Jacob Hannon awoke with a start. He dared not move. In the darkness, in the musty dank smell that surrounded him, he held himself still, listening. Stillness was his training. Instinctively he went there when the world around him was thunder and lighting, when nothing made sense, when the very ground under his feet shook and moaned.

In his confusion, hidden somewhere between night and day, he was unable to distinguish between dream-thinking and the reality of the cold, damp floor against which his face was pressed. He remembered someone striking him behind his left ear, smashing him hard with clenched fists, stars lighting up his head. He'd fallen to the floor. Someone held him, kicking him, busting his ribs, beating him until he could no longer move. He remembered a knife at his throat. Later when he had regained consciousness, he strained against ropes that bound his arms, hands, and feet. But he didn't remember how he had come to be tied so tightly he could hardly move.

Oh Lord, he thought. His head ached like black, black sin. Taking a breath, he listened. He sought to ground himself, to find something familiar.

He heard a creaking groan and tried to place the sound. It reminded him of damp saddle leather, how it creaked in the morning after a hard rain--or worn boot leather after the dew soaked into the sole, swelling the underslung heel. He tried to categorize sounds. It occurred to him that what he heard was not unlike the sounds of a log house creaking in the quiet of night, or the sound of a pine forest in the dead of winter. He recalled tall pines standing in heavy, wet snow, their branches bent toward the earth. Inevitably they would crack and pop under the weight, releasing the snow. But this wasn't it.

Something was wrong. *No! Everything was wrong.* He spread his fingers slowly, expecting he didn't know what, feeling the deep grain in the wood. The place smelled of rotting, stale water. *Not swamp water, not . . . what was it?* The floor seemed to vibrate, tilting, moving, then righting itself more or less, again and again until his stomach grew queasy. He couldn't place it; he'd never experienced it before.

He tried to concentrate, fighting through his aching head, jumbled thoughts, snippets of conversation, smells, and sounds. Some of the memories were pleasant. He remembered his sister: the way she smiled, the long billowing blue dress with white lace about the neck, and the smell of her. He remembered the smell of breakfast, the aroma of sourdough biscuits, bacon, and gravy, and the sea breeze wafting through the open window.

"Happy birthday," she had said. "Where are you going this morning, little brother?" Without waiting for an answer, she continued, "Don't forget dinner . . . at seven." She leaned over the kitchen chair where he sat and kissed him on the cheek. "Your friend, that old Chinaman, what's his name? He will be here. Peter's off work. He's coming home early. So you come home early. Hear me, Jake? We're all expecting you. Please be on time." She had hugged him, throwing her arms around his neck, saying, "Oh Jacob, it's so nice of you to come all this way just to see me."

He remembered he was forty years old, that it was August 13, 1873, that he enjoyed rye whisky, and 1861 model Navy colts. Oddly, he knew they weighed forty-two ounces and were thirteen inches long. He knew it had a brass trigger guard, that the barrel was seven and one half inches long.

Gingerly he touched the skin behind his ear, exploring the cut then rubbing his thumb and forefinger together. Blood. He could feel it on his fingers like thick grease, the sort used on the hubs of freight wagon wheels. He could smell its coppery smell, and wondered about the extent of his head wound.

He concentrated on remembering a short walk he took on a breezy coastal day. After biscuits and gravy, after the plates and forks were washed, dried, and put away, he'd walked down to the sea, then down to the harbor to watch the ships. He'd fed the seagulls crumbs of old bread, then he'd stopped by a saloon–a bar. He remembered a mirror. It was dark inside and cool. The thick plank flooring was solid and didn't creak when a man walked its length. Behind the bar was a picture of a beautiful, scantily clad vixen. He remembered her long, long legs, and bare feet, her face hidden behind a fan. Her eyes peered at everyone no matter where they stood in the room. Behind the bar tall, dark bottles sat on shallow shelves.

The long mirror hung behind a long mahogany bar with no stools, its dark surface smooth to the touch. Men stood leaning against it, talking, laughing, asking the bartender to set up one more round.

Had he been waylaid? Robbed? Where was he now? It was so dark. There was no natural light. Could it be night? It had been day when he'd left the cottage on the hill for his stroll down to the harbor. Sensing no immediate danger, he started to rise.

Just as he was getting his knees under him, a narrow, dark door opened, partially framing three men. One held a lamp in his right hand. He looked up as the dull yellow light flooded the small room, illuminating every corner, chasing the shadows behind stacks of wooden boxes and fifteen gallon barrels. The man holding the lamp moved through the door, stepping to his left, holding the lamp high. In that instant Jacob Hannon realized he was not alone; he wasn't the only man whose red blood dripped onto the wood floor. With the opening of the door he realized he was a prisoner. A cold anger seized his heart, constricting his throat until it ached, making it hard for him to breathe.

"What do we have here?" The man in the middle spoke rhetorically, holding a cocked hat tucked under his arm, the gold buttons of his tunic shining even in the dull light. He wore shoes polished black, with gold buckles. His leather soles were neatly trimmed. Jacob watched the dandy survey the room, his eyes bouncing from one man to the next, finally coming to rest on him.

"Get up, you," he demanded. It was an order. The man wasn't asking.

In that instant Jacob Hannon decided he did not like him. Hannon was good at first impressions; usually they were lasting. He started to get up. Before he could rise to his feet, the man standing to the right of the black shoes and cocked hat grabbed him by the arm, jerking him up. The man was very strong, effortlessly lifting Jacob's one hundred ninety pounds. Jacob made a mental note. This was someone to avoid, someone to respect.

"Stand when the Captain orders it," he said. "Be at attention while he speaks. Eyes straight ahead. All of you."

Jacob heard the rustle of clothing as the men behind him stood. No one talked. Someone groaned.

Disdain colored the Captain's voice. "You men," he said, "have volunteered to sail the *Rake*. We are at sea, half a day outside of Frisco. The First Officer will see to your needs. Do as you're told. Maybe you'll live. Disobey an order and you'll have a cat of nine tails on your back. Trouble me and you'll spend your time in this hole, company for rats, starving to death. You don't work . . . you don't eat. The pay is eleven dollars a month. You'll get paid when I decide you've earned it. From the looks of you, that will not be any time soon. Do not look for shore leave. There won't be any." He paused in his speech.

When the Captain spoke again he spoke slowly, his voice resonating in the small room. "You'll be divided into the starboard watch and the larboard watch. The Second Mate is in charge of the starboard watch. The First Officer has the larboard watch. This is he. " The Captain pointed to the brute standing on his right, the very man who had jerked Jacob to his feet. "He'll answer any questions. Listen and learn. Do it quickly and live. Ignore him and die."

The Captain turned on his heel and exited through the doorway. The lamp holder followed him, leaving the lamp with the First Officer. Without further discussion the First Officer divided the six men into two groups of three. The first group was assigned the starboard watch, the second the larboard watch. The man's instructions were short, not giving even lip service to the "volunteer" nature of their presence onboard. It was clear he backed his orders with sheer force. Of the six, no one spoke; no one offered resistance. The First Officer looked them over as he spoke. "There's no talking on deck except at breakfast and dinner. Below deck it is permissible. Breakfast is at seven bells. On deck you will work. Sundays is the exception. Sunday is for reading, writing, and dressing your best. It is for sitting on the windlass or forecastle telling stories, singing, and praying if you have a God. Every other day starts at first light with washing down, scrubbing, and swabbing the decks. The rest," he said, "you will learn as you go. Do as you're told. Do it quickly. Questions?" He asked in a menacing tone, not wanting any.

No one spoke.

The Second Officer arrived to claim and collect his crew. The First Officer pointed out the three men assigned to him. Once they were gone, the First Officer took the remaining three, including Jacob Hannon, up on deck.

Thus began the first day. It was followed by a thousand more, all onboard the ship though not all at sea. Each day was a continuous round of grueling work, bare feet, and grub not worth eating. The experience was harsh, punctuated by a cat of nine tails on bleeding backs when the First Mate determined that their obedience was not fast enough, or accomplished with the proper urgency, or done properly. At times punishment was wrought "just because."

From his first conscious moment escape was all Jacob Hannon thought about. He made his plans early and waited. He changed his plans often and waited. He tried to remain unobtrusive. For a big man that was difficult, if not impossible. He was the example no one wanted to be. He began a studied practice in staying small, of hiding in plain sight, of only being partially seen, if at all.

In order to escape he had to arm himself. A traveling drummer on his way to the Orient presented him with his first opportunity.

It was three weeks out and a Sunday. The crew had gathered about the forccastle. Aft of the mainmast the gun drummer was speaking with the First Mate, his voice carrying. He'd opened his traveling case. "Take a look at this one here. It holds six shots. This particular revolver? Never been fired. Gonna sell it to Chinese royalty. The big man himself. Sort of a king. This one here was made by a fellow by the name of Sam Colt. We owe him the Navy. This one is better. Look at this. Ya just slide the brass cartridges into this here cylinder, fire away and when you're done you throw the spent cartridges away. It is much quicker than a Navy. That's for damn sure. No paper cartridges. No cap, no primer. Get 'em wet, they still fire. Doesn't take long to reload. Fact is, you can reload in a fraction of the time. Nice idea I'd say, these here brass cartridges are. Gonna save a lot of lives and get some non-believers killed."

The crowd that sat about the forecastle watched the First Mate as he hefted the revolver, sighting down the barrel at the grey horizon. He smiled at the drummer and said something that was unintelligible.

"Here, my man. Take this one here and give it a try." The drummer pulled another pistol from his case. It was of the same design only with a dark wood grip. "This one was made for the army trials," he said. "It's a single action. You pull back the hammer 'til it locks, then pull the trigger. I've run several rounds through it myself. Drop the hammer on a couple. See what you think." The drummer pulled some brass casings from a box. He was smiling, ever in his element, selling.

From his perch in the forecastle Jacob guessed they were .44s. He was wrong. They were .45s.

The First Mate took the revolver from the drummer, sighted down the barrel at nothing but rolling seas and white caps, then rolled the cylinder with his fingers. All eyes were on him as it clicked repeatedly. There is something about someone playing with a pistol, tossing it about, working it, rolling the cylinder, letting the hammer drop on an empty chamber. Invariably it attracts attention. Perhaps the very air changes. Something and everything gets charged up. Attention is drawn like evening fire-light draws big, blood-sucking mosquitoes in the swamps of

North Carolina. Death seems to wait on one more click.

Jacob Hannon listened, watching, sitting way back and out of the way in the forecastle. He'd seen this before. The conversation around him dropped to a whisper, ebbing away into silence but Jacob Hannon's mind raced. In the evening he stole the pistol with the wooden handle along with a partial box of cartridges, wrapping them in oil cloth. The difficulty and the key was hiding it. And that, as they say in northern Arizona Territory, was not "a piece of apple pie." It was entirely a matter of hiding it where the Captain would never think to look. Because look he did.

Minutes after Jacob Hannon procured the weapon he took the Captain his mess. Today it was served in his cabin. He delivered it early while the Captain was still on deck. In his absence Jacob hid the Colt and the cartridges, wrapped in oil cloth, in a cabinet behind the bottom drawer where it butted up against the wall. He'd just picked up the platter bearing the Captain's dinner as the Captain walked into his cabin.

"Put it on my table," he was instructed.

Jacob Hannon replied, "Yes, sir" and left, closing the door behind him.

Two days later the drummer discovered his pistol was missing and all hell broke loose. Every inch of the vessel was searched and re-searched. Every inch except, of course, the Captain's cabin. Nothing was ever found. A man's back was laid bare. No grog was served, no food eaten. And so it continued until men started dropping. Jacob Hannon remained stoic. He had no choice to his way of thinking. After spending a day and night locked in darkness with his fellow "conscriptees" his conscience bothered him some for he was the cause of much sorrow, pain, and anger.

Everyone was a suspect. One individual got right in Hannon's face, nose to nose. "You steal that pistol, Arizona? You did, didn't you? You better find it, you know what's good for you."

Jacob Hannon just looked at the man and shook his head. "Where would I hide it? In my boot? If I had it, I'd use it on you and then I'd kill the Captain. Remember that."

The man was suddenly silent.

From another traveler he stole a blade, eleven inches of folded steel. The previous owner had disclosed this information as he brandished the blade in the Sunday evening sun. Again, as in the first instance, the pilgrim was discussing it with the First Mate.

A man called Buck had been sitting in front of Jacob Hannon watching the immigrant from the forecastle. "See that, Jake? See that knife? You watch. It will disappear just like that pistol."

Jake looked over and saw blade reflecting sunlight as it flashed in the sun. There was irony in those words; the very telling led to its theft.

As before, the blade's disappearance caused a second search. Every bunk was disassembled, the contents of every seabag dumped and inspected. The Captain stalked the quarterdeck in anger, waiting for the culprit to be caught, waiting for someone to be punished, and, undoubtedly, die. Both times some poor seaman was beaten senseless for a perceived affront. Another was banished to the hold in chains to starve with the roaches and rats. It was a month before that man saw daylight again. By then he'd have said anything, except he knew nothing. Yet he admitted to the crime hoping, perhaps, for death. Jacob Hannon and the others were ordered on deck and found him hanging from a yard arm, a lesson to all would-be thieves. Every man was forced to stand for two hours staring at the corpse swinging back and forth in the wind.

Hannon never said a word. He was too shocked and too late. But the man's death galvanized his thinking. This was going to end, and so was the life of the man who walked the quarterdeck in his shiny black shoes and polished buttons. The sailor's body twisting in the wind was never forgotten. Had Hannon known that the death of another would result, he most probably would have given up the weapon and his life, killing the Captain first. At least he'd like to think so. But he didn't know and the rage within him boiled endlessly.

It was hard as all "billy-hell" to hide weapons successfully on an one hundred fifty-eight-foot sailing vessel. But he did it. First he hid them behind a drawer in the Captain's quarters. Then he moved them to another hiding place, also in the Captain's quarters. Their final resting place was in the decking itself. It was a hiding place that had existed undisturbed since the keel for the *Rake* was laid in Norfolk, Virginia. He hid them under a false board of a drawer that was hardly ever opened, in a space between the deck and the hull. The drawer itself contained odds and ends of the Captain's personal property: a sack of six marbles, a handleless blade never used, silver buttons for a tunic, the log book that for six years tracked the voyages of the *Rake*. There was a colored sea shell from New Zealand's Christ's Church, a piece of teak wood from the wheel of the Captain's first ship, and a compass that no longer worked, its needle bent. The space was hidden beneath teakwood strips that fit together perfectly. The small cavity was just large enough for the knife and the pistol. Jacob stuffed it with oil cloth to keep them from rattling and rusting. Additionally he kept them oiled, wiping them clean, then oiling them again when he could.

Nearly two years later he stole a second pistol. Ironically, it was from the same drummer, once going to Hong Kong, once returning. In addition to the two pistols he had twelve .45 caliber rounds and a half empty box.

Each theft was met by a stoic, angry Captain striding back and forth across the quarterdeck. Sailors' backs were laid bare by the whip, rations withheld. The men grumbled and swore. Everyone looked for the culprit who had brought such misery into their already miserable lives. Even Jacob Hannon looked, suggesting places where the weapons might be hidden, finally suggesting they could have been thrown overboard. No one believed him.

When he was punished, he bore it stoically for he knew he was going to escape and the Captain was going to die. The pain would pass. His tormentor's pain would not. At least no one died following the third theft. The Captain had one more nail pounded into his coffin.

Every single Sunday his prayer was exactly the same. "God bless Colonel Colt, his wife, and all of his kids." Thus he would pray, saying the same words to a

God that he did not know while watching the First Mate walking the quarterdeck. Jacob Hannon would examine his bare toes, rub his calloused feet, and think about the fact that one day someone was going to die and it wasn't going to be him.

His life was intolerable. Upon each arrival in a new port, Jacob Hannon and each of the shanghaied men were ordered below deck. There they were held behind a locked door by a stone faced guard, with no light, no water, no heat, and little or no food. When they did eat, the grog was cold, the bread, mealy, and no one dared to hazzard a guess as to what swam around in the green soup. Sometimes they were incarcerated for a week--sometimes longer; time enough to unload and reload the hold, time to find new passengers going to new destinations with old trunks and great expectations.

Jacob Hannon waited.

Any other time he was below deck, he learned how to take all of the doors off of their hinges from the inside. He made a skeleton key for the pantry and discovered a second hiding place for his second pistol. For the room of incarceration he made several keys using a butcher knife and a fish bone. He hid one inside the room in case he was locked inside with a need to get out.

He prepared. He waited. No one would say that he waited patiently. There was nothing patient about Jacob Hannon. Port after port he was jailed in the room where he kept the key for its door. Still, he waited. Three years he waited until he heard talk that the *Rake* was headed for San Francisco. Hope began to stir inside him. He cleaned the decks, fed canvas to the wind, watched, and listened. Time was winding down. He could feel it.

Based on this feeling, he moved the two pistols and the knife to a new hiding place inside the wall in the room of incarceration. As he expected, the very next day he and his fellow captives were herded below, down the long hallway, and locked securely in the "room." In the darkness he smiled. Years had now melted into hours, hours into minutes. Jacob Hannon's waiting was over.

Once in the room he listened as the door closed behind him, the lock turned, and the tumblers fell in place. He hoped he heard footsteps fading. After several minutes had passed, he said to his companion, "Buck, I figure it's about time I get off this tub. I reckon I'll be leavin' today. Think you might want to do a little gettin' away yourself? Take a vacation?"

There were scoffs in the cramped quarters. Buck laughed at the comment. It was hard to get excited in pitch darkness in a locked room with an armed guard pacing outside. Hannon hoped he wasn't outside and convinced himself that he couldn't hear him.

"You'd be dreamin', Jake," Buck replied, his voice low. "Suicide, that's what you're thinkin'. I'd say you ain't goin' nowhere! None of us are."

"You think the Second Mate's outside or maybe someone else?" Hannon asked.

Buck shook his head, though no one could see him. He answered, "Probably the steward. The Captain will want someone that he can trust. We'll be here till we weigh anchor." His voice carried a feeling fraught with discouragement and hopelessness. "From the feel of it we're takin' in sail. My guess, another hour we'll be droppin' anchor."

Jacob Hannon smiled. Relief washed over him. "Buck, wake me when you hear the anchor chain released. And you be thinkin' about gettin' off this tub with me. The rest of you boys, too."

He heard some grunting as he stretched himself out atop three flat traveling trunks that lay side by side. He lay next to another disbelieving soul, already asleep. Minutes later he was drifting, feeling good about himself and the callouses on his hands and feet, knowing what he was going to do, knowing the time was at hand.

It seemed to Jacob Hannon that Buck's nudge came within minutes, yet he'd slept for an hour and a half. When he awakened, the ship no longer moved beneath his feet. She was quiet, her beams no longer singing their song, no longer groaning under weight of sail and endless wind. He was greeted by an unearthly quiet.

It was time.

Buck nudged him again. "Anchor's down," he said.

Jacob Hannon stretched in the dark, stood up, and went searching for the tallow candle he'd hidden behind a trunk. Striking a match, he lit it, to the surprised faces of his fellow prisoners. "Gents," Hannon said, greeting the five men. From a sea bag he drew pants and socks and began changing his clothes. After buckling his belt he sat down and pulled on his boots.

No one said a thing as they watched.

In the dim candle light he found the shirt he'd worn three years ago; pulled it on and buttoned the sleeves. He paid the spectators no mind. Finished, he looked at Buck.

"You ready?" he asked.

Someone else answered, "Yeah. We're all ready."

Jacob listened to the voices, wondering if there was going to be a problem.

Buck's voice was hopeless yet he was alarmed. "What's got into you, Jake?"

"Buck, I'm leavin'. Gonna have a talk with the First Mate and the Captain before I do."

Buck did not reply.

And Hannon didn't wait. To everyone's surprise he moved to the door and tapped on it, pressing his ear against the wall. Someone moved behind him but he heard not a sound from beyond the door. The bastards were trusting rusty hinges and an old lock. *A mistake*, he thought. *A bad mistake for I got the key.* He repeated the maneuver, listened, heard nothing. Unless Hannon missed his guess, no one was waiting on the other side, at least not right now. But soon.

On bended knee he worked on the wall board that held the hinge side of the door, pushing it, pulling it twice, until it moved up and in. From inside the wall he retrieved the Bowie knife, sheath and all, laying it on the floor in the dim candle light. Quickly he unbuckled his belt and slipped it through the sheath loop, rebuckling it. Then he found the key.

"What's he doin'?" someone whispered.

Reaching farther inside he laid his hands on the pistol wrapped in oil cloth and brought it out, laying the bundle beside the key. He reached inside again, bringing out the second oil cloth bundle. Jacob Hannon unwrapped the pistols, shoving the first in his belt.

"You!" someone exclaimed.

"Me," Jacob Hannon replied. "You boys need to decide. Ya' stayin' or comin' with me?"

He removed the oil cloth from the second pistol, checked the loads, and prayed a silent prayer to all that was holy that all six would work when he required it. He then checked the first pistol, placing it behind his belt buckle.

Hannon inserted the key and knocked on the door as he turned it. If someone was there now, they would respond. He waited. There was no response, not yet, but the absence of a guard worried him. Without hesitating, he yanked the door open and stepped into the hallway, a pistol in his right hand. No one. Not yet. *Someone was sleeping on the job,* he thought. It left him wondering if that fact was going to raise up to bite him. He dismissed it immediately; he didn't have time to give it another thought.

Turning to the men inside the room, candle light flickering off their faces, he said, "Gents, I'm now goin' ashore but first I'm goin' to have a short discussion with the Captain and the First Mate. If you're of a mind to go ashore, make yourselves available to row when I call for volunteers. Either way it makes me no never mind. Suit yourselves."

"Jesus, Jake! You're gonna get us killed."

"Maybe. Someone is goin' to die. That is certain." He stared at Buck. "Buck? Are you comin' or goin'? You're welcome to stay here for the rest of your life. Make up your mind."

Buck nodded. "I'm right behind you."

"Good."

To the other four he said, "If you want to go ashore with me, be topside. I ain't askin' for no favors."

From the dim hallway Hannon said to Buck, "Stay close. This shootin' could get a little tricky." He saw Buck nod. The man's breathing was quicker then ususal. Hannon turned to the business at hand.

He thought of the twelve rounds sitting quietly in the cylinders and reminded himself to make every one count. "Buck I need you to watch my back. Yell if I have a problem, then hit the deck." He paused, "Buck. If you want to stay onboard and avoid trouble tell me now. I will understand."

The somber man nodded, nary a word passing over his lips. Sweat glistened from his forehead. Finally, he said, "No one will be sneakin' up on you, Jake."

"Good. Make damn sure."

"I will, Jake."

Hannon came up on deck on the starboard side, away from the harbor activity, his boot heels clicking on the deck's teakwood planking. It was simply unbelievable how good it felt. Three years without boots. As he moved aft he was conscious of Buck's footfalls and of the pistols' weight in each hand. He walked erect, purposefully, moving toward the quarterdeck--that no man's land where no common sailor was supposed to walk. Ever. Mentally he pictured what he'd find. The First Mate would be on the port side. The Captain--the beater of men, the punisher, his jailer, the man who'd stolen three years of his life–he would be on the starboard. Hannon thought of some other words for him, imagining the pistol the Captain carried in his waist belt.

As he suspected it would be, it was the same today. Except today Jacob Hannon had a Colt in either hand: both loaded, cleaned, oiled, the hammers pulled back, each waiting on the trigger.

As Hannon walked past the main mast, a path opened before him. Surprised, sailors stepped back. Others stepped aside. All moved out of the way without being asked. Inside Hannon smiled. *You gotta love a brace of pistols for shorting a conversation.* Jacob gave them no time to focus on him. Someone stood, blocking him, and did not move. Without hesitation Hannon struck him over the head with a 7½ inch pistol barrel, knocking him to the deck. The feelings inside were electric, like an afternoon thunderstorm rolling off the Grey Ridge at the west end of the Cooley. It was time and he had waited so, very, very long. Those sonstabitches who hit him over the head and dragged him into this rat hole were going to pay. *You boys better be gettin' out of the way.*

The sudden movement caused by Hannon crossing the deck disturbed the general order. The First Mate saw the confusion; then he saw Jacob Hannon striding toward him, pistol grips in either hand. He yelled a warning just as the pistols came up, just before Hannon shot him through the chest twice. Each round caught him, pushing him backwards. Before the First Mate's body hit the teakwood deck, the hammers were pulled back and locked.

It was a cathartic experience for Hannon. He shot the First Mate for his imprisonment, for the thousands of hours of his bare feet running in the rigging overhead, for the salt beef and pork he'd been forced to eat or die. He shot him for having to sleep in the forecastle with the rats, for the lashes across his bare back for nothing more than a glance. He shot him for the cold damp and unbearable sea, for the moldy, weevil infested bread, for every single day of his imprisonment. And he shot him because he stood in his way of going ashore.

Everyone but Jake and Buck was diving for cover.

In the ensuing melee, the Captain heard the First Mate's warning, and he heard the blast of the .45s. He saw the First Mate tumbling backwards, his body rolling, then sprawling on the quarterdeck. Stepping quickly backwards, nearly tripping, the Captain pulled his pistol from his waistband, cocking it, certain he could restore order. After all, he was the Captain. He had to be obeyed. His very thought was law.

It was then that Jacob Hannon shot him through the heart, through the head, and through the abdomen, pulling the hammers back on both pistols, fully intending to shoot him again. The Captain's bleeding body had crumpled to the quarterdeck. When Hannon ran up the steps, he found the steward bending over the body.

"He's shot. He's dead," the steward said. "You've killed . . . "

"I sure as hell hope so," Hannon replied.

For the first time in his life, Jacob Hannon stood on the quarter deck of the *Rake*, his booted feet spread apart, one pistol pointed at the steward, the other covering the crew. "I'm goin' ashore," he announced. It was then that he recognized that he had happened to come on deck in the middle of payday. He saw the steward's strong box sitting on a small table with the lid open, a chair now vacant, a book of reckoning at hand

"But first I'm bein' paid," he said. "Mr. Steward, I'll be drawin' for three years," No one moved. "Mr. Steward, sir, I'll be wantin' my pay. Buck, he'll be wantin' his pay. And you'll be wantin' to give it to him." He paused, staring at the steward. "That will be now, Mr. Steward. Count me out three hundred and ninety-six dollars. Then I'll be takin' my leave."

The steward returned to his chair, staring anxiously at Jacob Hannon. He began counting out bills as Hannon turned his attention to the crew.

"The steward is itchin' to finish payin' you folks whatever you got comin'." Hannon raised his voice. "I'm not sure what'll be left but this mornin' it was the Captain's dyin' wish that you all be paid. He owed me three years. Buck, too. Me and Colonel Colt are takin' any objections."

There were none.

Jacob Hannon glanced at the ship's complement: the crew, the six passengers, three men in black suits and top hats, three women with worried expressions, their eyes dark and hidden under wide brimmed hats and scarves. He looked them in the eye, with a pistol in each hand daring anyone to stop him.

He spoke to the passengers and crew.

"Listen to me," he said. "Nearly three years ago I was shanghaied and forced to sail by these bastards that lie dead behind me. I did not take my imprisonment kindly. Far as I'm concerned this ship is yours. Do with it as you like. Sink it if you are of a mind, but I am goin' ashore. I'll need six to be pullin' the oars. As soon as I am gone I suggest that no one bother followin' me because I ain't feelin' kindly toward the sea. If I even think you are on my back trail, I'll be shootin' to kill."

He stopped speaking, letting the words sink in. "Boswain, six volunteers, if you please."

He got them. The four who'd been forced to "sail the *Rake*" were already over the side.

"Ready, Buck?"

"Yes, Sir. Right behind you," he replied.

Jake Hannon descended the stairs from the quarterdeck and walked to the rope ladder that had been thrown over the side. He glanced at the sailors manning the oars below. Buck climbed over the railing as Hannon watched. Then Hannon climbed down the rope ladder, quickly finding a seat in the prow, keeping the pistols in either hand.

To the oarsmen he said, "All right, Gents take me ashore."

Shouts drifted across the waves. A line of men formed along the *Rake's* bulwarks but no one followed them. Eleven minutes later they were dockside. The original four oarsmen were up storing their oars, climbing out, and walking away, hurrying. Buck smiled at Jake, nodded, then he, too, climbed out and disappeared into the crowd that had gathered on the pier. The other two remained seated in the boat, silent, staring at Jacob Hannon.

"Gents," Jake said to them, "I thank you for mannin' the oars. If you would, take your time doin' whatever you feel you ought to. I'd like a head start. I reckon I'll be needin' one, seein' as how I shot the Captain and the First Mate. The sonstabitches." He smiled, then turned to look across the harbor at the *Rake* sitting low in the water, its cargo still aboard. Slowly he stood and climbed over the side, finding his feet on a solid wharf. The two sailors waited in silence, staring at him.

Without another word a hatless Jacob Hannon walked down the wharf, then up the street toward the buildings that were San Francisco. He disappeared into the crowd without a backwards glance. The men in the long boat waited, then waited a little longer, thinking perhaps it was safer to wait. A few minutes? What did it matter? After all, there were only two of them. Both were convinced they wanted no part of Jacob Hannon.

Hannon's legs felt odd and unsteady walking on solid ground. Feeling anxious, he hurried, his mind telling him he had little time to waste, not if he wanted to live.

First, he thought, *I'll go to my sister's house. She'll be mad, hotter than the seven pillars that braced the gates of Hell, what with me being three years late for dinner. No standin' around,* he thought. *There'll be no time to waste. A man didn't shoot the Captain and his First Mate dead without someone objecting. Wrong, though they may be. Fact is, they were irretrievably dead and I'm irreversibly on the run. Second, I'll find the Chinaman and see if I still have a horse and saddle.*

Jacob Hannon walked up the street, thinking about the two men he'd killed. *This is odd,* he thought. *Squeezing the trigger didn't make me feel any better.* He grunted in disgust. *I should feel better. Happy, even. But I don't. I do feel satisfied. I do feel that the table has been turned and the circumstances reversed. The debt sort of evened out.*

Tomorrow I'll find out if it was worth it. Jacob Hannon laughed, causing a passerby to look at him, startled. *I expect it was.*

CHAPTER TWO

Six weeks before Jacob Hannon stepped onto the wharf in San Francisco, California and walked up the street, and half a world away, a nineteen, soon to be twenty, year old girl huddled in dim light. In the thoughts of her people she was already an old maid. She sat hunched over, her arms wrapped tightly about her knees, slowly rocking back and forth, holding her breath until her lungs ached. In her world of discomfort she strained her ears, trying to hear voices.

Above her head she heard hobnailed boots scrape across the floor, the shuffle of sandals, and the quieter whisper of bare feet. In the dark crawlspace the creak and groan of the sub-flooring fell flat and died, muffled by layers of dust piled on ancient timbers. Those angry voices she sought to hear hissed like snakes and roared like tigers.

Her thigh muscles cramped. She beat the tight muscle with her fist for relief, holding her breath against the pain. Her knees ached. She struggled to breathe when the pain did not abate. A nagging tickle plagued her throat. She fought a cough, repeatedly swallowing to make it go away. For relief she shifted her weight, inadvertently striking her head on the floor joist. Footsteps slowly crossed the floor above her, moving closer and closer, stopping directly overhead.

Small dust particles settled slowly onto her nose and across the faint freckles on her cheeks, clinging to her hair, her shoulders, knees, and arms. Across the entire sub-flooring, between joist and beam, tiny shafts of candlelight leaked through cracks, striking powdered earth, cobwebs, and rat droppings.

She fought a sneeze that built up in her sinus, an itch that raged against the back of her throat, a roar that seized her chest like a whirlwind. It seemed the very elements strained to hear the beat of her heart, the growl of her stomach, the sound of dust falling in the dark.

Suddenly there was silence, then the silence was filled with her father's voice. It was interrupted by another and still another. There was a tumult of strangers' voices, voices she had never before heard. One spoke of Su Lin's marriage promise. She thought that odd. The marriage promise had been terminated; it was finished. All had agreed it was finished.

Another spoke of her Grandfather's debts, of who was to be paid, and who was not to be paid at all. She heard her Father say, "No, she is not here. No, the debt would not be paid. Not ever." *That was fairly clear*, she thought.

Something struck the flooring hard causing it to pop and creak as if it were about to be torn asunder. That bang was followed by loud cursing, then the sound of footfalls fleeing, and boots running across the floor. Thankfully the loud, angry, jumbled voices also faded. They were replaced by an eerie silence that filled the crawlspace and tightened its grip on her aching throat.

Something scurried about in the dark and brought to her mind images of black spiders with gleaming eyes, of scorpions, their menacing tails arched, of color banded snakes that slithered about the ancient timbers that supported the flooring. She hoped it was a mere field mouse searching for a kernel of rice that had fallen through the cracks.

Time passed; how much she didn't know exactly. Suddenly the floor above her gave way. She started, her heart caught in her throat. Yellow candlelight reflected off her father's grim face. Worry lines etched dark furrows in his forehead and collected in the folds of skin about his eyes. He blew out the candle and reached for her. "Come," he said. "You must hurry."

Taking his hand, she started to ask why.

"Come," he insisted.

"But Father, I don't understand. What . . . ?"

Su Lin was pulled upright. She stood, half-crouched, pain shooting up her back, her knees aching.

"What has happened? Why . . . ?" she asked.

"You must hurry," he said.

Hurry? I can't even walk. I can't stand. Look at me!

"There is little time to explain. Your mother is packing some things. Some clothing. Something to eat. You must go quickly. Su Lin," his voice changed, grew soft. He stopped speaking altogether and stood looking at her, holding her hand, patting it tenderly as if he held a week old kitten. His tenderness made her feel odd, embarrassed.

"Father . . . what has happened?"

"You heard, yes?"

"Some. But I don't understand. Where am I going? Why?"

"Your Grandfather gambled. He lost you to Kai Ming."

"He can't."

"I know he can't but he did. When he became sober, he refused to pay. Apparently, he told them you were promised to Kaieto." The older man paused. "They killed him, Su Lin."

Su Lin stared at her father, her mouth open. "Dead?"

Her father nodded. "Kaieto was also gambling with my father, and with Kai Ming. He won more than he lost. When your Grandfather lost, when he lied about the arrangement, Kaieto verified his statement. Kaieto acknowledged the marriage arrangement."

"But there is no arrangement."

"Kaieto wanted to deny Kai Ming you, so he said there was. Kai Ming became angry. This was a great embarrassment, a loss of face for him. Kai Ming vowed that my Father's head and . . . and . . . "

"My head?"

Her father nodded. ". . . will be on the pikes at Tianan . . . so that all may see. So that no one . . . " he paused. "Daughter, there is no time. Already they have sent their negotiator. Next, the assassins come. If you are to live, we must hurry."

Her father practically lifted her from the hole in the floor then drew her to him as if she were a small girl once again. This night he seemed much taller, much larger then she remembered. Before she could steady her legs, he wrapped his arm tightly around her shoulders and hurried her across the floor of the dimly lit study. He paused at the door and blew out the last candle. Half walking, half stumbling, half running, she fled with her father into the darkness beyond the doorway.

The air was hot and humid, her skin clammy. Above them fleeing figures of evening birds flitted about. Their dark shapes darted through the night, fleeting shadows with little shape and form. She heard the piercing cry of swallows, a cry so lonely, so out of kilter it caused goose bumps to run up her bare arms. She stumbled.

"Careful," her father said, his voice barely a whisper. He held her arm so tightly it hurt.

They skirted the dark windows of the main house, running through the gardens. Crowns of ancient trees were dark mushrooms against a starry sky. Her bare feet flew softly down the brick path.

Her heart raced. Her throat ached. Her breath came in short gasps, hurriedly, urgency dictated by the very air. Her father ushered her past the brick walls that separated the gardens, to the very corner of the compound, then outside. In the dark she made out the silhouettes of the barn, of a carriage, of horses, and the shadows of several people waiting, including her mother and her youngest sister.

Cold realization washed over her. She slowed, her legs suddenly heavy, but her father pulled her forward. Seconds later, he opened the door to the carriage and pushed her toward the opening. Abruptly he pulled her back, clutching her to him, holding her as he would a small child, his rigid frame shaking as a dry leaf in autumn winds.

Frantically Su Lin clutched at him. A second, then two, then the embrace shattered. His hands returned her to the open doorway, the step. Awkwardly she climbed, grasping the door frame, pulling herself up. In the thick darkness she felt her way, found the leather seat, sat down, then turned back to her father.

The carriage door shut. The lock clicked loudly. She slid across the seat to the window, her fingers fumbling with the curtains, pulling them aside. Starlight struck her face as she leaned through the opening and reached with outstretched fingers. Her father's hand touched hers. Her mother pushed him away and grabbed her hand, pressing a small box into it. "Su Lin. Su Lin. Oh, Su Lin," she cried.

She could barely see the small woman, hearing only her sobs, feeling her own welling up. Her father was staring at her. Tears ran down his cheeks. Never in her life had she seen such a thing!

The carriage lurched forward tearing her from her mother's hand. Su Lin fell against the seat, striking the back of her head against the carriage wall. In the blink of an eye they disappeared. She sat very still, conscious of the steel rimmed wheels turning, the rock of the coach, the sound of harness and horses straining in their collars. Which way would they travel? Left or right? East? West? Knowing would tell her something.

A whip snapped and the carriage turned sharply onto the road. Left. They turned left. Left was East. East? They were going east. Where to? She tried to think of someone: a relative, an old friend of Father, an associate? Someone in the government? No one came to mind. There was no one. Not in the East.

On the seat beside her she discovered a small traveling trunk. Searching further, fighting the sway of the coach, she found another satchel, a box, then a knee. Shocked, she jerked her hand back. The knee was bony. Su Lin peered into the darkness and discovered the round face of her younger brother sitting in the shadows, hidden in the far corner of the coach. She gasped. *The twit. He was going with her? Both of them? Together?*

"Kai Chung, what are you doing here? Where are we going?" she asked, then hesitated. "Do you know?"

The wheel hit a rut, lurched sideways and jarred her to the bone, causing her to bite her tongue. She tasted blood. It angered her when Kai Chung did not answer. Instead her brother sat silently, his fourteen-year-old frame swaying with the coach, barely discernable. She heard a sniffle. *He's crying? Dragons of fire! He's crying.*

The coach plunged into the night, rocking back and forth. Its wheels found each chuckhole, dropped into each rut, struck each boulder.

Finally, she persisted. "Do you know?" she asked Kai Chung. "You do. Tell me."

"Oldest Uncle," he replied.

"Oldest Uncle?"

"Yes."

"Oldest Uncle?" she repeated.

For a moment she sat lost in the silence of her own thoughts, mentally digesting those two small words. *Oldest Uncle? Unbelievable.*

"You're just saying that. Aren't you? You're just saying that," she demanded.

"No. No, I'm not."

"No?" She repeated the word to herself, not at all sure he wasn't teasing. Sometimes Kai Chung talked just to talk. But the jerking, jolting, lurching coach accented his words and made them all too real. His labored breathing, together with the choked rasp in his voice, had a cold credibility.

"But why him? He's so far away, so very far away."

"I don't know. All I know is Oldest Uncle. That's all I know."

"It's so far," Su Lin whispered. She turned and stared out the window. *Something sure wasn't right.*

On and on they traveled, bouncing to and fro, just so much popcorn in a hot skillet. Finally, she grabbed at the leather seat. That failing she scooted to the nearest corner to brace herself against the lurch and sway of the coach, her stomach queasy and nauseous. She tried not to think of her stomach. She spread her toes and pushed them against the opposite seat, suddenly realizing she was barefoot. *That won't do.*

Warm, humid night air blew through the window, wafting against her skin. Goose bumps ran up her arms. Somewhere it had rained. She could smell it. Refreshed, she filled her lungs with the rain-scrubbed air and let it out slowly. Somewhere in the passing darkness people slept quietly on their mats, safe from knocks at their doors, safe from whispers in the dark. She wished she were one of them, that she were not barefoot, that she didn't feel like throwing up a dinner that she had not eaten.

Miles and miles away streaks of lightning flashed against dark thunder heads. Catty-corner across from her the roll and pitch of the coach caused her brother's head to sway as he tried to sleep. Su Lin watched him, thinking maybe he was an illusion. Not even there. Maybe she was not there. Nor the coach. This was so ridiculous. So insanely ridiculous. *Oldest Uncle?*

For a long time they traveled east, seemingly close to forever. Sometime deep in the night they stopped. Outside she heard muffled voices, the sound of horses being led away and switched with others. Too soon they were back on the roadway. When the carriage slowed and stopped a second time Su Lin reached for the door handle.

Kai Chung grabbed her hand. "You mustn't," he whispered. "You must stay inside. No one must see you."

"See me? You gourd. It's pitch black. It's so dark I can't see my toes. I can't see the fingers on my hand." She paused and looked at the shadow that was her brother, silently thanking him for his concern, and turned the handle anyway.

"Su Lin! You must stay inside."

"Well . . . " Su Lin pushed the door open. "I also must relieve myself. I'll be careful, little brother. Besides, who could see me? Who, wherever we are, could recognize me if they saw me?"

"There are eyes."

"Yes, well you're being far too melodramatic, little brother." She shook her head. "There are eyes," she repeated, scoffing.

He said nothing.

Su Lin pushed the door open and stepped down. A fresh breeze blew through the trees carrying a sweet fragrant smell. Nearby a multiplicity of flowers bloomed. For a moment she stood still and stretched her legs and arms. Her toes felt the powdered dust of a much traveled roadway. The night did not seem so dangerous, not with a cool breeze, not with the smell of grass and flowers about her. *There are eyes,* she thought. *Yes, Kai Chung, there are.*

Gravel dug into the soles of her feet as she walked to the front of the carriage. She needed some sandals and wondered if a pair had been packed.

The hostler had unhooked the spent horses. Clicking his tongue, he led them past her, the harnesses and traces clinking. The pungent smell of salty horse sweat filled her nostrils.

Su Lin called to the driver. "I'll be back," she said. "Wait for me. Just wait."

Of course he would wait. Agitated, angry, displaced, and feeling like a tormented house cat, she picked her way through a grove of trees, walked past shadows of a building, past pens of horses. She peered into the darkness seeking some privacy. There was none. Inadvertently she stepped in something soft that clung to her foot. Grimacing, she dared not wonder what it was.

Moments later she returned. Already fresh horses stood restless in their harnesses. The driver watched her from his perch. Defiant, she stared back at him then reluctantly climbed into the carriage and seated herself beside her brother. He hadn't moved.

There was nothing to say. She could not make sense of it: running around in the dark, leaving her own bed in her own room, leaving the comfort and society of her father, her mother, her sister. She was far from the gardens, the safety of the walled compound, the village. *But why is this necessary?* she thought. *Was it because of some shadow in the dark? Some knock on the door? Because Grandfather gambled? He always gambled. He always drank. And Father is important–so important!*

"You must be careful," Kai Chung mumbled.

"I will," she snapped. "I am careful."

The carriage lurched forward.

"There are men who seek you."

"I know. I know."

Long before sunrise, when the broken hills in the east were but a dim outline and the light barely cast a yellow-red tint in a cloudless sky, they turned off the roadway. The carriage was pulled a considerable distance from the road through a stand of trees and parked in a clump of dense brush. The horses were unhitched and allowed to graze, tethered on long picket ropes.

Morning passed in silence. In the sultry, mind-baking heat of the afternoon, Su Lin slapped at blood sucking flies, swatted an occasional mosquito, and watched the green lizards bask in the sunlight. The driver and Kai Chung sought the shady side of the coach, leaning against a wheel, or stretching themselves out in the long grass. After the heat of the day had passed and the red streaked clouds of evening grew dim, they still waited.

Nothing happened. The well-rested horses continued to graze. It was long after dusk before they were again harnessed. The red orb of the sun had dropped beyond the horizon and the first stars appeared as bare glimmers in a fading sky. After the frogs came out and the crickets began to sing, the driver hitched the traces to the double-trees and the journey continued.

To the travelers the road ruts seemed deeper, the leather seats harder and far less forgiving. Though the seats' smooth exteriors were stuffed to cushion and comfort, by the second night they felt as hard as black obsidian. The air turned dry. Their lips chapped. Nothing comforted them.

Sometimes they fled before the dust clouds. Sometimes the dust rolled past them carried by racing wind. It coated their clothes, their seats, their skin, their hair, filling the air they breathed with grit. When the wind died swarms of gnats and flies rose up from the dry earth to torture and torment.

Rubbing her eyes, Su Lin tried to blink away the grit, tried to lose the heavy tightness that visited her heart and chest. Sometimes, moving back and forth on the seat, she saw herself as a bob on a fishing line that her grandfather made, weighted with a hundred weights, and cast into the swirling currents that turned her around and around and around. She awoke too frightened to sleep, the weights taking her deeper and deeper.

Hour after hour, mile after mile without a word spoken, she traveled, her thoughts tumbling. *Oldest Uncle?* She barely remembered him. He was a memory from so long ago. She'd been small and he so big.

Going to Oldest Uncle! To America! Of all places! No one asked me. No one said a thing to me. Certainly there could be no husband now. How could Father arrange for a husband half a world away? Who did he know? What about my dowry? All left behind. I don't even have shoes. Two small canvas bags. A box. That's all. Now there would be no sons to please. A husband I will not have. Nothing. My life should be here: with Father, sister, mother, GrandMaMa, my twit brother, and servants. In China. Not America. Only the poor looked east. It shouldn't be me. Father had many friends in China, people of influence and wealth. A husband could be arranged. At least here there was hope . . . a chance. But in America . . . there was nothing.

Su Lin stared at her brother. "What do you know about this?" she asked, not expecting him to answer, surprised when he did.

"I'll tell you," he said, pausing, hesitating as he thought. "Some you know."

She nodded.

"You were promised wife for Kaieto's son."

She interrupted him. "No, that was broken. The parties decided against . . . " she paused. "Old news," she said.

"Yes, well, it's sort of complicated because Grandfather gambled and lost you in a wager to Kai Ming. Grandfather said you were promised. Kaieto, he lied, said it was so. Father decided to send you to Oldest Uncle to protect you until the fighting stops."

"Fighting? What fighting?"

Kai Chung looked at her. "Su Lin, both families came for you. That's why we're here. That's why you should stay inside--so no one will see you. Word will get back. They'll come for you. They are coming for you."

"Even now?"

"Right now," he said, "this very minute."

"And how is it that Grandfather wagered me?"

"Too much rice wine, I think. He was drunk. That's what I heard. This is big trouble, Su Lin. The whole family would be dead except Father knows Tai Pei Ming."

"Fighting never stops," she added. "How long must I stay away?"

Kai Chung shrugged.

"You mean I may never go home?"

Kai Chung looked at her. "Actually. It's worse than that," he said. "There is no fighting."

"What do you mean? Is there or isn't there?"

"There isn't . . . I guess. Emissaries were sent to Tinian from Kaieto to meet with Kai Ming. It was decided that you weren't worth a war. Too many men would die for too little. It was agreed that neither family would have you. Thus, no one lost face."

"That is good. That is very good. Why am I being sent away?"

Kai Chung shook his head. "No. It's worse. It's very bad. To prevent future problems, orders were given to bring you to Tinian, to have your head placed on a pike with Grandfather's for all to see–a reminder. Last night they came for you."

"I know. I heard them. Some of it, anyway."

Youngest Brother nodded. "Father refused to give you to them. So Kai Ming and Kaieto hired warriors, swordsmen to find you and bring your head to Tinian. They were hired within hours of father's refusal. Both families did it, Su Lin."

"And Father?"

"Father does not have the power to fight both families or even one. He knows the Governor. That keeps him safe. He is sending you to Oldest Uncle, hoping they will lose interest before they find you. He takes a great risk."

He takes great risk? What about . . . me? And I didn't do anything. Su Lin touched her cheeks with both hands. "All they want is my head," she said smiling. She looked at her younger brother. "Do you have any idea how long it takes to travel to Oldest Uncle?"

He shook his head.

"Weeks. A month or more," she said. "A long time."

The second night churned slowly toward morning. The coach reached a stone road but did not stop. Buildings lined both sides of the thoroughfare. Most were several levels high, hidden in shadowed darkness. Their passing fronts appeared evil and abandoned, their dark windows blank and sinister. As she watched goose bumps crawled up and down her legs for there were no people, no signs of life, just scene after scene from the living nightmare that was becoming her life.

Kai Chung slept, half on and half off the bench seat. He hadn't moved for hours. Absentmindedly, Su Lin stared through the open window into the night. Over the roof tops she caught a glimpse of a sliver of the moon hanging low on the horizon. She imagined herself disappearing through a darkened doorway and becoming a shadow fleeing before the morning light--a ghost lost in the mist, hovering, lost in the twilight that separates night from day, never to appear again. That would be so good, so easy, so very impossible. She nodded in and out of sleep, catching herself at times to keep from falling off the bench.

Vigorously she rubbed her face, unable to concentrate. Time stood still. But the wheels did not.

They turned, iron metal grinding on cobblestone. A dog barked. She shivered as the air turned cooler, clutching herself as she felt a sudden chill. The smell of fish and saltwater stung her nose.

Daybreak was hours away. Her mind wandered. *What if they catch me?* She imagined how it would be, how it would feel to be jerked from the coach by dark, booted men, her feet bare, her knees scraped and bleeding. She saw herself forced to kneel in the gravel, her hands tied tightly behind her back, her long black hair pulled away from her neck exposing her skin. She felt a cold blade resting on her shoulder then brought down hard, fast, cutting her flesh. She resolved to hold her head high, to be very still, hoping it would be quick with no pain, hoping that the bladesman would not miss. Her brother moaned in the darkness as she imagined her head being carried away in a burlap sack tied to the saddle of a warrior bound for the gates of Tinian.

Beneath the coach a hub screamed for grease. Its metallic squeal excited first one dog, then another and another. The compartment was filled with its unceasing, mind-racking screech. Kai Chung woke and sat up, stretching his arms. Su Lin watched him. She touched the skin of her neck and thought about her head rolling away from her body. *I've got to be careful*, she thought. *I will get no second chances.*

Darkness had reigned in her world for so long. It seemed inescapably permanent. Perhaps the sun had burned itself out, disappearing to some other universe, hiding itself among the winking, blinking stars. Her head swayed with the rocking coach, back and forth, jolting, jerking, and bouncing to insane rhythms. She wished to sleep, to close her eyes, to rest. But there was no rest. There was no sleep.

Later she sensed another change. The horses no longer trotted. The carriage had slowed. It passed the fronts of shadow-shrouded buildings, wandered through stacks of wooden boxes and crates, through dark, man-made towers piled high above the top of the carriage. A breeze tugged at the curtains. Cold, damp air, laden with the smells of rotting fish, water-soaked timber, wet feathers, and the musty pungent smell of decay wafted through the coach.

Mercifully they stopped. She listened as six horses stood in their harnesses breathing heavily, blowing air through their nostrils. Their restless hooves rattled the trace chains. Su Lin didn't look outside, imagining instead that shadowy people would soon appear to change the horses as they had done so many, many times. She sat, slumped over, staring at the white knuckles on her hands. Suddenly, the coach door beside her was jerked opened. She jumped, her breath caught in her throat, knowing she'd been found by the dark men with shiny blades of steel and black boots.

"Come." It was the driver.

Neither Su Lin nor her brother moved.

"Come. Quickly. We must hurry."

Su Lin slid slowly to the open door and paused as she deliberately stepped down to the earth. But it wasn't earth. Instead she found herself standing on wood planking. The sliver of a moon had disappeared. Far off she heard a door open and close. A cool breeze picked up, tugging at her skirts: a shiver shot up her spine.

Kai Chung was so close that their clothing and bodies touched, bumping awkwardly. Not that she minded for she wanted to grab hold of him. But she did not. After all, she was almost five years older. And it would not be good if he were close to her when the dark men came, forcing her to kneel.

To their left the edge of the planking dropped away into a pitch black gulf. A seagull squawked, muttering to itself. Its irritating cry seemed to be in her very ear though she couldn't see it. A few feet down the planking an enormous hull loomed above their heads, the specter of its masts barely discernable against the night sky. She heard the pounding roar of surf close at hand. She waited for it to recede before it charged again in its eternal assault on the shore.

A sea breeze touched her legs with its icy hand. She hunched over, bracing herself against the damp. She was so hungry, so tired, so worn thin and frazzled that her mind idled, jumping from nothing to nothing and back again.

Someone grabbed her arm, startling her. In another place at some other time she would have reacted differently. Maybe it was the dark men. Maybe it wasn't. It could have been. She turned and stared up into the face of the carriage driver. She did not remember him being so big. He smelled like rotten garlic and decaying onions, something like her father's long haired billy goat.

"Come," he said. "Follow me. Be quick. Be quiet. Do not speak." He glanced past her into the blackness of the wharf.

Behind her the carriage wheels started to turn, metal on metal screeching. She started at the sound, jumped aside, and nearly fell

. *Not on my knees. Not my neck. Not yet.*

"Come," the driver urged again. "Come. Before someone sees you."

The carriage moved away. She tried to see who was driving, but the man beside her pulled her away as she turned to look. She caught only a glimpse of a figure high in the driver's seat. He seemed hunched over against the cold ocean wind. Half a minute later the coach, driver, and screeching wheels were swallowed up between two buildings.

The man's fingers tightened uncomfortably on her arm. Without resistance she followed him, too tired to argue, too tired to fight, too exhausted to care. They proceeded alongside the dark hull. At the foot of the gangplank the driver stopped, motioning for her to wait. She glanced at her brother, trying to catch his eye, but he'd turned away from her, his attention riveted on something down the wharf. A glance in that direction revealed nothing.

The driver walked stealthily up the gangplank, disappearing through the deck railing without so much as a backwards glance. Seconds later he reappeared. With the wave of his arm he motioned for them to follow him. Hesitating, Su Lin glanced at Kai Chung then down the wharf. There was nothing but crates and crates and crates. Kai Chung started walking then stopped to nudge her in the ribs when she didn't move. Reluctantly she started up the narrow walkway. Kai Chung followed.

The deck felt oddly unstable to her, as if it moved underfoot. It was probably just her--so tired, so out of sorts, a tree torn from the earth. No, maybe not that bad--but close. As she waited, their canvas bags and a small trunk were carried past her and below deck. A muffled bell rang. She heard footsteps.

In the starlight men moved about like so many mice scurrying about in a granary filled with rice. She watched as the moorings were released, the ropes pulled in. Above her head men climbed the ropes that secured the masts. Canvas sheets unfurled, filling with wind. The sailing ship slowly took on a life of its own, moving away from the wharf toward the harbor mouth and the open sea.

She imagined her father miles and days away. Perhaps he slept on his mat; perhaps he read in his study. Perhaps he was dead; his head decorating the pikes in Tinian. She imagined smoke rising from the compound, the buildings aflame. She imagined soldiers seizing her uncles, her sister. She imagined the young sold as slaves: the elderly killed, their throats slit, their bodies burned in consuming fires.

She imagined her mother gone, her father gone, GrandMaMa gone. All gone. Everything and everyone risked for her blood, for her life . . . all to keep her head off the pikes that decorated the gates at Tinian. Tears ran down her cheeks. Her brother touched her arm. She turned and followed him and the steward below deck.

CHAPTER THREE

The next morning Su Lin came up on deck, looked forward and aft, then walked toward the bow sprit. For hours she stood facing eastward, near the rusting anchor and anchor chain amid piles of coiled rope. The bow rose and fell driven by the wind. She remained there until her cheeks, her blouse, and her bare feet were cold and damp with saltwater spray, until the cold and damp forced her below.

Day after endless day followed. Time became an idle thought. Whether she sat, stood, leaned against the wall of the forecastle, or huddled in her blankets in the dark cavity in which she slept, it was the same. Water surrounded them. There were no songbirds, no green leaves, no green grass: just rolling, pitching mountains of water, wave upon wave driven by the endless wind, pulled by billowed sheets of canvas straining against spider webs of rope.

The sailors spoke English of a sort. Su Lin had learned English from the nuns and priests in the monastery. The language she learned was of mathematics and science and was not the same as that spoken by the sailors trimming the sails overhead. Father had told her to learn this language and had sent her to the monastery for that purpose. She discovered many words that she had not heard before.

During the night Su Lin laid awake in thick darkness and listened to the creaking deck, the craft groaning as it fled before the wind, chased by the hounds of hell. Sometimes she'd lay with her hands around her neck, feeling the skin of her throat with her fingers, imagining her fate.

The weather changed rapidly and often, like pages of an old book flipping furiously in the wind. It turned warm, cold, and blustery, but never in any specific order. At times icy winds ruled the deck. Sometimes the sun reigned. Sometimes rain stung her face, matting her long black hair. Sometimes the ship pitched up and down and sideways, wind screaming wildly through the rigging. During those times no one stood on deck who was not tied to a rope. Sometimes waves roared, crested, and tumbled, crashing across the bow like a blacksmith's hammer on an iron anvil.

In sleep she envisioned the tormented tear-streaked face of her father. Though she tried to avoid these dreams, they refused to release their hold on her. At times she wished to turn back, to stand in the square of Tinian, her long hair pulled from her neck, waiting for the song of the executioner's blade. She imagined the raven's squawk, muttering to itself as it waited impatiently for her head to rest on the bloodied pike next to Grandfather's. Then she'd awake and try not to remember.

Pushing herself she tried to look forward, tried to find hope. Yet always she saw her father's face, and smelled smoke from the burning compound. In her dreams she heard the rattle of swords, imagined the mockery of ten thousand faces turning away from Father. She saw them sneering at the rotting face of her grandfather, maggots falling from his eye sockets, the ravens picking at the ragged strands of his grey hair, an example for all. Impatiently they waited, and always for her.

She told herself that her imaginings were false; that they never happened, that they never would happen. Ever. Yet she did not know and thought they could, even that they may have already taken place. Surely her Father could be disgraced before the Governor, turned out before the tribunal, never to be spoken to, banned from library and school and monasteries, even from polite conversations with the priests: no how are you this afternoon?: no nods of the head: no curtsy in passing. It could have happened.

In her fantasies the tongues in the courts would wag back and forth. Their heads would nod as they spoke to one another. "Such a small debt, so easy to pay," they'd say. "What is one scrawny daughter?" "Has he lost his mind?" "Surely he sacrificed too much for too little. Surely."

The dreaded day, the expected day, that hoped for day finally arrived. It stole upon her as a thief in the night. In the darkness of her cabin she awoke and sensed a difference. Puzzled, she lay in that haze between one world and another and tried to figure out the oddity. It was so quiet, so still: no pitch, no roll, no heave of the deck, nor resounding crash of waves. Everything had stopped and was suspended in time.

Su Lin dressed in a rush, ran out the narrow door and down the passage way. She climbed the all-too-familiar stairs and stumbled out onto the deck. Green land rose above her. Seagulls cried. Pelicans flew by in their tight, floating formations. In the distance the surf roared as it flung itself against a rocky beach.

Morning sunlight struck the tall masts and bathed the vessel in a warm glow. The canvas sheets had been taken in, wrapped tightly and tied about the spars. Wind no longer whistled and whined through the rigging. The anchor chain was taut, the anchor no longer visible. The two long boats were gone. Around her the sailors bantered, laughed, and teased one another. More importantly, the hillsides gleamed green in the sun. Green. What a beautiful color. And there were birds, everywhere, birds. She saw and heard songbirds, terns, pelicans, seagulls by the hundreds, blackbirds and others she had never before seen, voices she'd never before heard.

It was nearly a quarter of a mile to shore; not far, but far enough that no one was going to swim. That seemed certain. Farther up the coast ship after ship was lined up against the green background. Wood piers stretched out into the sea. Miniature men walked the decks, loading and unloading. As she waited, the longboats traveled between her ship and the docks again and again.

Word needed to be sent to Oldest Uncle informing him of her arrival. *He'll be surprised*, she thought. She went looking for her younger brother but did not find him. He'd disappeared.

Midmorning fog engulfed the ship, hiding the sun, and, to her disappointment, the bright green hills and the birds. A cold, damp, icy breeze picked up, twisting the red, white, and blue flag that flew atop the mizzenmast. It flapped noisily, barely visible in the mist. Several sailors went below deck and returned with coats but Su Lin, her arms wrapped tightly around herself, didn't move. No one noticed her leaning against the base of the mast, hidden amidst the ropes, sealed barrels, and crates of silk. There was no sign of Kai Chung.

Where was he? In the evening Su Lin went below, worried. It was long after dark when youngest Brother reappeared without a word of explanation. He sat across from her on the edge of his bunk bed and worried his hands about his face. She waited, angrily resolving not to speak first. *Disappearing without a word! Now sitting wordless! With nothing to say for himself! At least tell me where you've been*, she thought. Soon she found herself tiring of this game and became agitated, her fingers drumming against the blankets on the bunk.

Finally he said, "No one must see you leave this ship. Oldest Uncle thinks it best."

"You spoke to him?" She thought he had. *Where else could he have been? Yet why all the secrecy? Why act like some idiot!*

"Yes."

"He was surprised? Yes?"

"No. He knew we were coming."

"He knew?" Su Lin's jaw dropped in amazement. "How could he? How could he know? You're just saying that. Why are you treating me like a child? It is you that is the child." Su Lin was furious.

Kai Chung did not answer.

Su Lin swallowed hard thoughts, well-rehearsed conclusions that leaped through her mind with incredible speed. *If Oldest Uncle knew, others knew. But how?* "How will I leave then?" Su Lin stared at her brother. Without giving him a chance to answer she said, "How could he know we were coming?"

"In a trunk. It will be here soon. You must get ready."

"What? What did you say? In a trunk? I'm leaving in a . . . trunk? What's wrong with walking right through the door?"

They heard a noise outside in the galley way. She stopped talking and listened. She started to speak, staring at her brother.

"Shh . . . " he whispered, motioning for her to sit on his bunk behind the door. Hesitating briefly, she did as he asked, thinking it would do no harm to go along with the charade until she knew what was going on.

Besides, how am I going to fit in a trunk? How am I to breathe? Who would lift a trunk with me in it? Su Lin grew belligerent. *Just who did he think he was . . . ordering me around?*

Kai Chung glanced at her, then opened the door and stepped out, closing it quickly behind him. She heard him thank someone and say he'd call for help in a few minutes--after the trunk was packed. The sound of footsteps receded. A long moment later the door reopened. Kai Chung pulled a trunk inside and locked the door behind him.

She gazed at it and then at her brother. It wasn't a very big trunk. She couldn't fit inside. Not unless she folded herself up tight, and she wasn't going to do that. Kai Chung unbuckled and slipped the leather belts from the trunk, pulled the latches back, and then opened it. Inside, shifted to one end, were several blankets tied in a bundle. Several holes had been bored into one side. It was so small.

I couldn't fit even if I wanted to--and I don't. No, this wouldn't work. I'm not doing it.

Kai Chung spread the blankets out inside the trunk and then looked at her. "Get in," he said. "We must hurry."

"Did Oldest Uncle arrange this?" she asked.

"Yes. Get in. You must hurry. Already men come to carry the trunks. We must be ready. Lay your head and nose near the holes . . . so you can breathe."

"No. I'm not doing this. If for no other reason, I don't fit."

"Try."

"No."

"Just try."

But Su Lin did not move from the bunk.

"Su Lin . . . come. We must hurry."

Reluctantly, Su Lin stood, shaking her head. "Listen," she said. "I will show you that I do not fit. But even if I did, I wouldn't get in this trunk for Oldest Uncle or you or anybody. Do you understand? Is it clear in your thick head?"

"Yes." Kai Chung had begun to look worried.

"For one thing those air holes are not big enough to give me air." She stepped inside the walls of the trunk. "For another, I just don't fit. You wouldn't fit either." Grabbing the sides, she lowered herself, pulled her knees up to her chest then worked herself into the box until she lay on her side.

"See," she said, "I just don't fit. I would suffocate. These blankets are worthless, certainly uncomfortable. What are they for anyway?"

With her knees drawn to her chest, the bottoms of her feet and the top of her head touched opposite ends of the trunk. "Do you see? This will never do. This is much too small. So no, I'm not going to be carried ashore in this trunk. I will walk."

With considerable effort, she slid her hand and arm beneath her so she could push herself up to a sitting position. Just as she was starting to push up, Kai Chung slammed the lid closed, striking her head hard. All light was extinguished except for what filtered through the five tiny air holes in front of her face.

"Kai Chung! Kai Chung!" she screamed, waiting for the lid to open, certain he'd realize the danger. She'd told him "no" but the lid remained shut. "Kai Chung! Kai Chung! Let me out. Now!"

"Kai Chung! Kai Chung, open . . . " Her voice was reduced to a whisper; she could barely speak. There was no air to breathe. Fear gripped her heart. "Kai Chung," her lips moved. "Kai Chung," she prayed. "Let me out. Kai Chung, this isn't working. I told you it's too small. Let me out. Please hurry. I'm dying. There's not enough air."

Suddenly it was hot. A loud bang shook the trunk, knocking Su Lin's head against the side, ringing her ears. *What . . . ?* Frantic, she pushed against the lid but she had no leverage. She had no room to move. Her arm was wedged under her body. A scream built up in her lungs but there was no air to give it life.

A click reverberated loudly inside her head. *Kai Chung has locked the trunk!* The sounds of belts being cinched down, latches secured, buckled, and tested were amplified inside the trunk. Her mouth was dry. *"I am going to kill you."* She tried to swallow. She forced herself to take a deep breath, tried to let the air out slowly. Hysteria clutched at her. Every fiber of her body knew she was dead, dying, buried in a trunk. In another minute . . .

A muffled knock. She heard her brother's voice and someone else's. Laughter followed a string of obscenities. A kick was delivered to the side of the trunk. Su Lin held her breath and choked back a scream that took a long time dying. One side of the trunk came up. Her feet were suddenly above her head; then she was slammed back onto the deck.

"What you got in here?"

"Books," she heard her brother say.

"Damn heavy them books." The voice was not Chinese. There was no accent or rhythm to it.

White men? Not White men!

The end of the trunk came up abruptly and again forced the weight of her body onto her head and neck. The other end was picked up. The trunk was moving.

Please don't drop me. Please, God.

The side of the trunk struck something solid, the force of the blow banging her skull so hard that lights went off in her head. Nausea swept over her. The trunk swayed back and forth. Suddenly she was turned upside left, the back of her neck pressing against the trunk wall. Pain shot up her neck. To take the pressure from her neck, she tried to push against the side of the trunk with her knees, pressing her back against the wall. Her efforts yielded little success.

It was sweaty-hot. Fuzzy thoughts blurred her thinking. *Had they crossed the gangway? What if they dropped her in the water? What if they stood the trunk up on end?*

Sweat trickled down her face into her eyes. Panic seized her again, washing over her in waves. Her chest felt as if it was about to explode. There was not enough air. She closed her eyes, clenching her teeth. *How much longer?* She ached to unfold her knees. Her head roared, filled with a noise she'd never heard before. The voices and laughter that seemed so close began to recede. She forced herself to listen.

For a long time the trunk remained still. She thought she must be in a long boat. She had no ability to gauge time. After what seemed like forever the trunk was picked up, set down, then picked up again.

"Hold it. Hold it. Losin' my grip here."

"You got it?"

"Got it. Get goin' before my hand slips again. This son of a bitch is heavy."

"You got that right."

"Where's that buckboard?"

"Over there. To the side."

"All right. Ready? Steady."

Abruptly the trunk was flung upwards. It slammed down. The landing knocked the air from her lungs, sending a pain shooting up her shoulder and arm.

"There. There. Got one. Let's get the rest. Why these Chinese bastards gotta move in the middle of the night is beyond me."

"Who knows? They're payin,' ain't they? Ya ungrateful son of a bitch."

"Take it easy. I was just talkin'. What's ailin' you?"

"ah, nuts. Nothin', just shut up."

The voices faded. Silence followed. The trunk remained still as her heart ticked off seconds. She forced herself to relax. Folded awkwardly under her body her arm ached and burned until it grew numb. Sweat dripped off her cheeks and her nose. It ran between her breasts and across the small of her back. Her nose itched and itched until she cried tears of frustration just to touch it. She wanted to sneeze but couldn't. There was no light coming through the holes in front of her face. *It's night*, she reminded herself. There was no light yet small specks of light gathered at the edge of her eyes. *I'm going to kill him*, she thought. *I'm going to kill him.*

Finally she felt a bump, heard a bang that rang her ears, jolting the trunk. *I'm hiding from eyes that see in the night*, she told herself. *Eyes? What eyes? No one even knows I'm here. That was the second trunk? There should be one more. I'm not going to make it. There is nothing I can do.* She found herself wishing for oblivion, for quiet death to come and snatch her from the confines of the trunk, to free her.

Small specks of light continued to circle the edge of her vision. They merged, faded. They came quicker now. Fascinated, she watched them. The small sparkles of light grew and diminished, hazy fireflies riding the evening breeze. A pleasant, milky darkness enveloped her, washing over her sweetly.

Su Lin blinked her eyes and looked. Her father held her tiny fingers in the vastness of his hand. They stood together on the walkway of the biggest city she had ever seen. He told her of the great deeds that had taken place there, of the wise men who had lived out their lives in the temples.

Intrigued, she looked across the street and beheld a man in dark armor. He leaned against a long bloodstained battle sword. His black, piercing eyes stared right at her, cutting her soul asunder, slicing through her. There was no place to hide--not even behind her father's pants--nowhere.

Su Lin's eyelids flipped open on ink-black darkness. In the quiet her heartbeat sounded like thunder in her ears. Nothing stirred. There was no sound. Had she died? Her fingers traced the fibers of the blanket she lay on. Was she dreaming? The air smelled like her sleeping quarters, like her very own room. The mat felt like her mat. Cautiously, she stretched a leg. *oh, Gods and dragons, my knee . . . it hurts so badly. What have I done?*

Suddenly two eyes peered down at her. A thought, a brilliant ray of shimmering sunlight, burst upon her mind telling her this was no dream. She was hungry beyond belief. And thirsty.

"Ah, you are awake."

Su Lin froze. She blinked several times, trying to focus. In the dark the face above her appeared as wrinkled as a dark prune, wind-dried, baked too long in the hot summer sun. Past the face she could see a shadowed ceiling, a window, and through it, a handful of twinkling sparkles: stars.

"You are not so dead after all."

"Am I dreaming? I thought I was dreaming."

"I do not know. I do not think so."

"Where's my brother? Where's Kai Chung?" She remembered how badly she wanted her fingers around his throat, how she wanted to slap him silly.

"Sleeping."

Sleeping? she thought. *Who? Who?* "Are . . . are you Oldest Uncle?"

"I am. And you must be hungry. Come with me. You must eat."

The old man waited, gripped her arm, and helped her to her feet. She swayed, holding on to his hand.

"Too long in that trunk, I think."

Oldest Uncle's grip did not wane. Her knees hurt. It felt as though someone had stomped on each with the heels of large boots! She gasped, wanting to scream. Oldest Uncle hesitated then led her slowly into another room, leaving her side to light an oil lamp. Exhausted, she collapsed into a chair and leaned heavily on a table with her elbows, something she had never done before. She did not care.

Oldest Uncle brought cold rice and fish, setting the dishes before her. Without hesitation Su Lin ate hungrily, dipping into the bowls with her fingers. Oldest Uncle watched. She was too hungry to mind. The cold rice and dried fish tasted so good. Bony fingers handed her a glass of water. Even in the lamplight the man looked incredibly ancient, his eyes sunken deep into his head, half hidden under bushy eyebrows. *Perhaps it is just the light*, she thought.

She glanced at him, suddenly remembering her manners. "Oldest Uncle . . . "

He stared at her. At the sound of her voice she could see his eyes sparkle with life, soft glowing fires burning in the hearth.

"Oldest Uncle . . . I am so sorry. I have inconvenienced you."

"Yes, you have. You are a very beautiful grandniece."

"I . . . thank you. I . . ."

"Your father, he has great feelings for you."

Su Lin did not know what to say to that. She wanted to tell him that she was in trouble; instead he told her.

"You have enormous troubles." It was a statement more than a question.

"Yes. How do you know this?"

"I read your father's letter. Tomorrow I will consider what it is you should do. Finish eating. I will show you where to sleep. We will talk tomorrow. Perhaps you can work in the kitchen."

"Oldest Uncle, I . . ." Su Lin started and stopped. "Thank you. Thank you for your kindness and hospitality."

"You speak well. My Nephew has an educated daughter?"

"Yes, I suppose, but . . ."

"That is good. You will need every advantage. Come. Finish eating and I will take you to your room. We will speak later."

Su Lin was speechless. She chewed. She swallowed. *It wasn't that--it was just that no man had ever said that an education was good. Not for a girl. No one except Father, and now, Oldest Uncle.* Su Lin hesitated then finished eating. Afterwards she followed the old man and his oil lamp from the kitchen up a set of stairs and into a room at the very top. He left her standing in the darkness, surprised, relieved, tired, bewildered, and worried. She stood thinking she was doomed crazy: a misfit, dependent on a tiny, wrinkled, aged man to defend her from the glaring blade of men in dark boots. *Not likely.*

She lay on her mat staring into the dark. Not for the first time and not for the last, she thought maybe she should return home. Perhaps it was best. Instead of Father saving her she should save him, end the intrigue, solve the unsolvable, and save everyone a lot of bother. All she had to do was walk down to the wharf. *If I could find it. Not too long hence I'd be standing in Tinian Square listening to the ravens. It'd be over. Father would be saved.*

She blinked her eyes. Oldest Uncle surely had better be a magician, a wizard of uncommon powers--for I have none.

"Later," he said. Later he will tell me. Later he would explain what was to happen to a Chinese girl in America, in San Francisco, without any dowry, without the hope of a husband. In spite of herself, Su Lin wept, too tired to control her tears.

She slept fitfully and was awake long before anyone else. She just lay on her mat. Finally the downstairs noise pulled her upright and she wandered down and into the kitchen to see what was going on. Around her cooks moved about carrying pots, bowls, plates, cooked rice, baked fish.

As of yet there were no patrons. In the confusion she saw her brother sitting at a table speaking with someone, a thin man with a black beard. Anger flooded her soul. Angrily she walked up behind him. He looked up at her from his chair and smiled. She hit him in the nose and bloodied his mouth. Down he went. He tried to get up. She slapped him. When he tripped and fell she kicked at him and missed and kicked at him again, striking him in the ribs. He tried to roll away from her but she wouldn't have it. She kicked at him again and again. Then she jumped on him, slamming his head into the floor. In the midst of this activity she looked up to find Oldest Uncle staring down at her. His face was immovable.

"I will not be placed in a trunk against my will," she said. "Never."

"I see," the old man replied. "Never against your will."

"No, sir, Oldest Uncle. Never against my will."

"Are you going to kill him?" The old man asked. "Your brother? Are you going to kill him?"

"I want to."

The old man nodded. "Perhaps not, then?"

"I . . . perhaps . . . perhaps not." She stood up. Tears were running down her cheeks. "But never again," she said.

The old man smiled, nodded his understanding. "Never again," he said. "I think your brother will remember that without difficulty. Perhaps you will also remember he is your brother."

"Perhaps," she said. "But never again."

CHAPTER FOUR

Hot steam, the rice dragon's fiery breath, rose up in her face from the rice kettle she carried. It burned her nose, her cheeks, her fingers. Su Lin grimaced, squinting against the pain, barely able to see through the rising mist. Stubbornly she gripped the kettle, willing herself to move faster. Her feet flew quickly across the floor.

She turned her head to avert the searing heat, desperately searching for the table. She did not remember it being so far away. It was just fifteen steps yet it seemed a journey of ten thousand miles. Her mind screamed "drop it." She refused. She ran, dodging a chair and skirting several dirty pots stacked on the floor. The heat drove all thought of etiquette from her mind. What anyone thought was the least of her concerns. Her final step to the table was a lunge. In one hurried motion she dropped the rice kettle, released the handles, and turned away from the searing steam. Breathless, she leaned against a chair and tried to blink away the hurt, rubbing her fingers to quiet the pain.

Amidst her mental confusion she struggled for composure, conscious that the room was too quiet. Gone were the sounds of pots banging against each other, the scraping of plates, the rattling of cups, the chatter between the dishwashers and servers. Even the patrons were silent. The only sounds she could measure were the rhythmic pounding of her heart and her own ragged gasps for air. *My mistake. But what have I done so wrong? Hasn't anyone ever picked up hot rice before?* Su Lin hesitated. She was reluctant to glance around, not daring to look, fearing that everyone's eyes would be on her. Warm blood rose to her face. She glanced about. No one's eyes were upon her. No one stared. No one smacked their lips in disgust.

Instead she found herself alone in a crowded room. Su Lin breathed a sigh of relief. The impending embarrassment evaporated. It was a reprieve. It was as if she never had picked up the hot rice kettle and never had taken the first step toward the serving table. *No one is looking at me. I am all right. But what, then?*

The cooks, the servers, the dishwashers, even Kai Chung who had come from his study cubicle: all looked past her. Chagrined, overcome with gratitude and amazed at her good fortune, she turned, looking for what had everyone's attention. She glanced across the counter--nothing. Above the stacks of dirty dishes, toward the front door--nothing. There were so many people eating this morning. Then through the haze of steam and smoke she saw a White man standing just inside the doorway. *A White man? A White man here?*

Not believing her eyes, she looked again. From where she stood, he appeared neither big nor small. Except for being white he wasn't particularly different from any other man she had seen except for his hat; it appeared to be new. That was her first impression. Being white was difference enough. Su Lin moved away from the table to get a better look. *Such an oddity--a*

White man. He certainly wasn't welcome: not here, not in this café, not in all of Chinatown. Oldest Uncle would surely kill him the way he crushed the head of a rat or a dozen rats. Just as he'd killed whites before. She was sure of it.

Where was Oldest Uncle? Somebody ought to get him.

She watched the White man look at the back of the café. There was nothing there: no tables, just a wall supporting a broken clock. *Was he looking at the clock?* In the silence she could actually hear the clock's steady tick. *Could he be listening to the clock?* Su Lin shook her head in disbelief. *No,* she told herself. *Who would do that?*

The old clock was an oddity. It hung on a bent nail on the back wall, its minute hand pointing limply to the floor. Only the hour hand moved. That morning she had wound its mainspring because Oldest Uncle had told her to. Even as she wound it, she questioned its use. *What good is a White man's broken clock?* Su Lin had not asked Oldest Uncle about it. Asking may be considered rude, even unforgivable. Father did not mind questions but she wasn't sure about Oldest Uncle. He had not yet spoken to her about her situation. It had been ten days. Each day she expected to be summoned. Perhaps he had forgotten. He was old. It was just as well. Already she'd forgiven him his forgetfulness.

Su Lin's attention returned to the White man as his eyes searched the room. Apparently not finding what he was looking for, he turned toward the door and the open street. A commotion from among the patrons caused him to hesitate. A slightly built man had risen to his feet. He turned to his three seated companions and bid them remain seated. He spoke to them in Cantonese. The sarcasm in his words was not lost on Su Lin.

The White man stared at him briefly then glanced to his left.

"Students," the Chinese man said, drawing out his words, speaking a little too loudly. "Pay close attention. I am going to demonstrate an ancient art form on this almond-eyed piglet. Be grateful for this entertainment. It is free."

The man seated to his left laughed. "Be careful that he doesn't demonstrate on you," he said.

The White man stood quietly eyeing the lone man who had spoken so arrogantly to the seated patrons.

Jung. Yes, Jung. That was the man's name. Su Lin nodded knowingly. *This one, he would be the first to cause trouble. He would kill the White man for Jung was a bad man. He had no conscience. That was the talk. But a killing in the café? Even worse . . . a White man.*

Oldest Uncle! What was she thinking? Su Lin ran to find him. Oldest Uncle would be in the alcove, or perhaps upstairs, or he could be anywhere. She decided in mid-stride to check the alcove first, then if she couldn't find him, she'd check upstairs.

A burst of laughter rose from Jung's table, his companions eager to watch the sport. The entire café joined them. Su Lin skirted the black iron stove and hurried toward the back door. Inadvertently, she glanced at the White man's clock. The hour hand pointed at the number six. It hadn't moved.

Reaching the doorway, she glanced back. The wiry Jung was moving toward the White man. Though she knew that she'd better hurry, Su Lin hesitated, fascinated by the scene unfolding before her. There was something about death--even if it was only a White man's–something fascinating. It was so final, so permanent. And this was trouble, bad trouble for Oldest Uncle. No one wanted the hoodlums to come with badges and night sticks. Though she needed to move quickly she stood transfixed, rooted to the floor.

Jung was walking toward the front door. But he wasn't leaving. Su Lin knew that. Everyone did, except the stupid White man. He wasn't even watching! Instead of looking at Jung who was almost in front of him, he, again, methodically searched the room, his right hand rubbing his chin.

This was going to be too simple for Jung; much too easy, not even sporting. Certainly, it was no contest. The distance between the two men closed quickly. Jung bowed slightly and moved as if to go around the White man. But Jung's hand, barely a blur, shot out at the unsuspecting man's chin. Jung's fist committed to a ghost; the White man wasn't there to receive it. To Su Lin's amazement, it was the White man who hit Jung, not once, but twice, managing to look more startled than anything else.

Jung dropped like a sack of wet rice to the hardwood floor. He was down flat on his back without a moan or groan, not even a whimper. The White man towered above him, then shifted his weight to leave, shouldering the canvas bag he carried, and glancing down at Jung.

Su Lin blinked. Not as simple as she had thought. One had to admire this tragic figure. Without meaning to he had just insulted Jung's entire Tong. To die may have been easier, maybe even preferable to what would happen next. Life for him had just become complicated. The thought brought a smile to her lips. It was certainly something with which she could identify.

Su Lin glanced across the room at Jung's companions. They sat like rocks in their chairs, their thoughts and emotions hidden behind expressionless faces. *Would they let him leave? Was it over?* Every eye turned to see. She thought it was kind of funny. Jung hadn't seen that one coming. *Indeed this White man was tricky. Every dog has its hour in the sun, to bask in its warmth--but the night cometh. Who had said that--her father? Yes, probably.*

Jung's companions rose as one. They shoved their chairs back as if to say they really meant business, their eyes fixed on the White man who neither moved nor offered to move. He seemed frozen, too frightened to know what was good for him--a dog lying in the sun, not mindful of the wheels of an approaching wagon.

The people seated at the tables nearest the White man scrambled to their feet, hurriedly moving away, leaving behind steaming bowls of rice and broiled fish. Su Lin did not think their moving cowardice exactly. Jung and the fat one in the middle were backed by others not present: protectors, influence peddlers, gangs, powerful families similar to the two families that sought her.

She had worked in Oldest Uncle's café only ten days and already she knew that avoiding any Tong was a very good, intelligent idea. The White man had simply walked into bad fortune. Like her, what choice did he have? Jung would have killed him. But he hadn't. Now Jung's companions would. If not them, Oldest Uncle. Surprisingly, it saddened her. The White man was dead as soon as he walked into the room. There wasn't anything anyone could do, which was exactly her predicament.

Su Lin shuddered. Like her, misfortune followed this one. She hadn't chosen it. Neither had he. His fate was what it was. There was no choice. Her fate was also grim. She had slept and worked the last ten days, a target, the living dead waiting for the inevitable.

Several wary individuals hurried past the White man and disappeared out the front door. He took no notice, looking straight ahead, staring at the three walking toward him.

The code was old. For as long as she remembered it had not changed. Jung was down on the floor felled by an infidel, a greasy-faced White man. That insulted the family's reputation. It usually didn't take much. Maintaining face was critically important. She should know. He must die just as she must die, to save face, to prevent embarrassment. Jung, with a single blow, had become an embarrassment, a liability. It would have been easy to feel sorry for Jung's companions, except they deserved their predicament. She did not. The infidel did not. But Jung was down and his companions would have to explain it. Su Lin imagined the scene they would face--the scene Jung would face--if he was alive.

"Yes, employer, we were sitting, eating our rice and fish and Jung was slugged in the face by a White man. It was an unavoidable accident. No one saw it coming. No one could-- the treacherous White man."

Certainly that conversation would not play well. Su Lin smiled to herself. The Tong wharf rats would appear most understanding, except they'd know the truth. They'd know the lie before it was told.

One way or the other, dead or alive, Su Lin wouldn't miss those four in this café. After all, they shouldn't be here. Oldest Uncle had warned them. "Stay away," he'd said. Perhaps the starving snake would now swallow itself to satisfy its hunger.

Su Lin's hand flew to her mouth. *What am I doing? I can't just stand here. I must find Oldest Uncle.* She took a step then stopped to watch the three advancing on the White man. *This should be good. Three against one.* They all deserved one another, even the White man. After all he was White; he had no business being here.

The middle man, the fat one, waved his two companions behind him. The size of the room, the arrangement of tables, chairs, kitchen and counter, made it impossible for the three to attack as one. They were caught like rice wine and forced through the narrow neck of a bottle.

Yes, the infidel would die. He had no chance, not three against one. But the White man did not move. She thought he must be very crazy . . . or very brave, not that it mattered.

The White man dropped his canvas bag, slipping the leather straps from his shoulder, and shoved it to the side with his foot, a quiet look of resignation on his face. *No small wonder. What had he expected? Surely not to eat, not in Chinatown, not in Oldest Uncle's café. At least death would be quick for him, though probably not as quick as he would like.*

Now the largest of the three men was alone, advancing confidently toward the white intruder. Suddenly, he rushed forward on the attack. The White man stepped backwards away from Jung's body. Su Lin shook her head. Things were never as they appeared. Fat man leaped Jung's body, punching, no doubt wishing it was not there. But the White man eluded his attacker, caught the man's arm as it lanced out, and jerked him off balance, pulling the aggressor into him.

Su Lin stood on tiptoe and peered above the onlookers, unable to see exactly what was happening. Clearly, the forward progress of the Chinese man had stopped. Both men were standing but neither seemed to move. Several teeth flew across the floor, so many white marbles tumbling from a ripped bag. But whose? She couldn't see either man's face. *Surely it must be the White man's teeth.*

The Chinese thug rose slightly on his toes, his hands flopping to his sides. He crumpled in a heap on the floor. Only the White man remained standing, a pistol in his right hand.

Tigers, gods, and dragons. How . . .? Su Lin jumped as a shout rang from the back of the room, originating right next to her--almost in her ear. It was Oldest Uncle's voice. The shout was not one of anger but of extreme controlled displeasure. Everyone was in trouble . . . even her, especially her. Why had she waited?

Moving past her, through the tobacco smoke and hush, flowed the small, slightly built man, no more than five feet three inches tall without an ounce of fat on his frame, old beyond dreams. He was older than Father for he was Father's uncle. Behind him walked Kai Chung. Youngest brother looked so serious. The thought that her brother had informed Oldest Uncle made her uneasy. A tinge of embarrassment darkened her face. She should have found Oldest Uncle. She should have told him first. It was her duty.

Oldest Uncle and Kai Chung's faces reflected a great insult for which there could be no apology, no repair. Kai Chung was always serious. Well, mostly. But what harm could he do? He could do little more than look serious. He was good at serious. She thought of the small knife he carried. If he were to use it he'd only cut himself.

Jung's two remaining companions turned at the shout, looking quickly from the white intruder to Oldest Uncle. The two separated, not out of design but fear. One ran past the White man clearly intent on escape, taking his life and his tomorrows with him. The second was not so fortunate.

Much of what happened Su Lin could not see. There were too many people blocking her view, standing between her and Oldest Uncle. She did see the thug suddenly bending over, trying furtively to move away, to escape. Bones cracked loudly in the room and the unfortunate man crumpled to the floor.

Silence gripped the morning crowd. In the center of the floor towering over two of the Tong's best, the White man stood alone still holding the Colt. Oldest Uncle didn't seem bothered by it. He absolutely did not like the Tongs. Yet they seemed to give him respect, allowing him to exist in his small restaurant. They did not sent enforcers for payment, and once in a while they ate in the small café, present yet not obtrusive. Oldest Uncle paid them no mind, never spoke to them, never gave them any regard or recognition. His warning had been the exception.

Oldest Uncle moved across the floor towards the White man, stepping around a fallen chair, broken plates, and spilled cups of tea. He stood in front of him. Between the two lay the bodies of the two Tong men. The tension in the room increased immeasurably, every eye upon Oldest Uncle, a White man, and a pistol.

Su Lin held her breath, stretching on her tiptoes to see. The other spectators stood backed up against the wall. To her amazement the pistol was holstered. Oldest Uncle stared at the White man. Instead of killing the infidel he spoke to him, in English. A murmur surged through the crowd like a cold wind. One head turned, then another as the diners looked at each other in wonderment.

Oldest Uncle . . . What are you doing? Why wait? He has made himself defenseless. Kill him. Kill him.

"Jacob Hannon. My friend. You live. It is good." Oldest Uncle bowed slightly, using English, clipping the words, slurring some. Interrupting himself, he instructed Kai Chung to "remove the garbage" from the premises, and then turned again to the White man, speaking to him.

Garbage? It is the White garbage that should be removed, Oldest Uncle. What are you doing?

"Please . . . accept hospitality. Most welcome. Please come," her Oldest Uncle said.

Su Lin stared in disbelief. *Oldest Uncle, what are you doing? What are you saying? What hospitality could you possibly have for a White man?* Glancing about, Su Lin saw heads nod, tongues wag. She was not the only one amazed.

CHAPTER FIVE

Bowing ever so slightly, Jacob Hannon smiled at the old man, picked up his bag, stepped around the two bodies, and followed Oldest Uncle. Both men passed Su Lin without a glance. She noticed the smell of the open sea about him, in his clothes. She knew that smell and thought that the White man must be a sailor: the kind that ran up and down the ropes, that unfurled the sails, that scrubbed and mopped the decks on their knees.

He certainly didn't look like one. He didn't have the walk. Those men ran barefoot at the slightest growl from the captain; they lurked about, like rats in the dark, slaves, grudgingly obedient to the tyrant master. She'd spent days, weeks watching and listening to them. This man wasn't like that at all.

Oldest Uncle and the White man disappeared into the hallway through a curtain of jade and topaz beads. Su Lin hesitated. She waited in the doorway thinking that Oldest Uncle would want her soon. A moment passed before she entered the hallway behind them. Mere steps from Oldest Uncle's alcove she heard his hands clap together as he summoned her.

She found Oldest Uncle sitting on his bamboo mat, nodding approval. She entered, interrupting his conversation. Both men turned to her.

"Oldest Uncle . . .?" Su Lin bowed, first to Oldest Uncle and then to his guest. Already Oldest Uncle had made him comfortable. *A White man? Unbelievable. And so soon? Why see to his needs at all? What was he thinking?*

"Yes," the old man replied to her, speaking Cantonese. "Please bring us our meal and something to drink. My friend has traveled a long distance. He is weary. He is hungry. He has many stories to tell me. I have much to learn of his experiences."

Your friend? Startled by Oldest Uncle's use of the familiar tone, Su Lin glanced at the White man, wondering who he was. Endearing words were used in the house of one's family, among the closest of friends, not with the "demon white, the almond-eyed," not with the enemy, a killer of women and children. Oldest Uncle often surprised and amazed her but this was shocking.

She bowed and vanished from their presence wondering if it was even possible to have a White man for a friend. After all, dogs could be trained. With work they could be taught to come when called, to bark and growl at one's enemies. Maybe a White man could . . . *No. Not so, not possible.*

Su Lin walked to the kitchen to look for the cook. She found him at the counter removing fish heads and cutting the remainder into portions. The blade in his hand never stopped, not even when she spoke to him. "Oldest Uncle wants his meal," she said. "He wants to entertain the White man. I'll need bowls for two: rice wine, rice, fish, and gravy."

Kai Chung came from his cubicle behind the pantry door, a towel in hand. "What's Oldest Uncle doing?" he asked.

"Who knows?" she shrugged. "Come with me. I need help. You can see for yourself. He calls that white devil 'friend.' Can you believe that? I am surprised he didn't kill him when he had the chance. But he waits. Why do you think?" She looked inquisitively at her brother, "What did you do with those other two . . . the bodies? Were they dead?"

"One was dead, the other wishing for death."

"And?"

Youngest Brother smiled. "I had them thrown into the garbage as Oldest Uncle wished. They don't smell so good. I think Oldest Uncle will have trouble as soon as `you know who' discovers what has happened."

Su Lin nodded. "They probably know already. What will they do?"

"I don't know."

"It isn't going to be good."

Her brother agreed, following Su Lin, disappearing behind her into the darkened hall. Between them they carried two bottles of rice wine, tea cups, a teapot, a platter of fish, and bowls of steaming rice. The White man looked up from speaking with Oldest Uncle when Su Lin entered the alcove. Both men were laughing. His eyes watched her as she and Kai Chung set the bowls down, arranging the tea cups, pouring tea and setting aside the rice wine for later. Oldest Uncle sat silently. Neither man spoke.

As they finished, Oldest Uncle broke the silence. "Beautiful . . . My niece is beautiful to look upon," the old man stated.

Blood surged to her cheeks. Kai Chung grinned at her. Instantly she wanted to wring the twit's neck. From outside the alcove she heard him chuckle. *I'll get you*, she thought, glancing at the White man only to see him wink at her, laugh, and nod. She was infuriated.

"That she is," the White man said. "Makes me wish I was a young buck. The more years I stack on this here frame of mine, the more beautiful the ladies get and the less they're lookin' at me. How's your kin folk? Got them under the same roof?"

"Not yet . . . in time. Your sister?"

"Spent yesterday with her."

"You have woman?" The old man inquired. Su Lin finished serving the rice and baked fish.

The White man laughed. "No . . . no woman. Been doin' a little forced travelin'. No time to look after a woman, let alone find one. Anyway, I'm a little old for that sort of thing. Besides I done danced that dance. Long before I met you, my good friend."

Su Lin left the room, rolling her eyes and shaking her head in disbelief.

Beautiful . . . My niece is beautiful to look upon. I cannot believe it. Her brother's mischievous grin met her as she re-entered the kitchen.

"My niece is . . ."

"Don't say it. Just don't you say it. I'll scramble your brains. And you know I can do it."

"Beautiful," he mimicked the word, rolling it off his tongue like sugar. Su Lin glanced at him as she collected the last bowl of sauce, holding the last dish in her hands. Kai Chung stood with folded arms, leaning against the doorway of his cubicle and watched her, laughing. He was still smiling when she left the kitchen.

Su Lin re-entered the alcove, carrying soup and sauce bowls. Oldest Uncle sat quietly, listening to the White man as she placed the final serving plates before them. Finished, she surveyed the dishes of food and drink, looking to see if she had forgotten anything.

The old man had been silent, listening. Finally he cleared his throat. "You need woman," Oldest Uncle stated solemnly. "A young woman make you young. You need. A young woman give you energy, make you whole, complete. You not old. Making excuse."

Su Lin stifled a laugh. Abruptly she turned to leave. *That's right, Oldest Uncle*, she thought. *Find this White man a nice fat, young wife to give him energy. She could kill him and then you wouldn't have to.* Reaching the doorway she turned to see if Oldest Uncle wanted anything else.

"Naw," the White man replied. He swallowed a mouthful of rice and fish. "What I'm needin' is my horse and my gear . . . not a wife. Most certainly not a wife." He laughed. "That I know I don't need."

"I ate horse."

The White man choked and gagged, barely able to breathe. Teary-eyed and he stared at his host, fighting to clear his throat. Su Lin watched his distress in amusement and smothered a laugh, wondering if she should do something for him, not sure what it would be. *Maybe he won't need a fat wife to kill him after all. Maybe the rice and fish will do it.*

"You what? You ate my horse?" he stammered.

"Yes," the old man replied. He took a mouth full of rice and slowly chewed. After he swallowed, he looked up at his dinner guest. "I ate horse. He old. I ate him. Good horse. Customers liked him very much."

The White man paused, studied his chopsticks and stared at the fish, a smile on his face. "Well," he said, "at least he served his purpose."

She hesitated outside the doorway, not knowing whether she should stay or go. She started to leave but stopped at the sound of Oldest Uncle's voice.

"I have new horse for Jacob. Jacob will be happy with new horse. Jacob need woman to go with new horse."

"Thanks anyway, my friend," the White man said. "I'll settle for the horse. I certainly appreciate the concern, mind you, but no woman. That I don't need."

The White man laughed nervously, digging into the rice and gravy with renewed interest. He ate as though it had been a long time since he had tasted good food. And he ate like he might never eat again. "He broke?" the White man asked.

"What broke?"

"The horse? Can I ride him without gettin' myself thrown to the ground and stomped on, without gettin' my brains kicked out?"

"Ah. Yes. Can be ridden. Very much. Good horse. Jacob will be most happy. Now eat. Rest. We talk. You rest. Morning, go see horse."

Smiling, Su Lin left the two men. *Oldest Uncle had eaten the man's horse. That was very funny. What was Oldest Uncle doing with his horse anyway? It served the White man right. He should be more careful where he left his horse.* Su Lin hurried to the kitchen. She stopped at Kai Chung's cubicle still amused at Oldest Uncle having eaten the White man's horse.

Kai Chung glanced up. "Well, beautiful sister, what is Oldest Uncle doing with his guest?" he asked.

Su Lin laughed. "He's trying to talk him into a nice, fat wife to make him feel young. Unbelievable."

"And?"

"And what? The White man said he wanted his horse instead, that he was too old for a wife."

"A horse?"

"Yes. Oldest Uncle told him he ate his horse. The White man choked. It was all very funny."

Su Lin heard the distant clap of hands. *Oldest Uncle summoning me already? So soon?* She had barely left his presence. Could she have forgotten something? She reviewed what she had served. Nothing was missing. She glanced at Kai Chung, and shrugged her shoulders as if to say "What now?" then quickly retraced her steps. *Perhaps Oldest Uncle wanted more rice wine. Men liked a lot of rice wine. More than they needed. More than was good for them . . . and anyone else.*

Oldest Uncle turned to her as she entered the alcove. For a moment he simply looked at her, squinting through old eyes as if he were seeing her from far off, lost in some ancient thought in another place, in another time. A tangible discomfort arose inside her. She thought that Oldest Uncle had lost himself in the manner of old people. She felt embarrassed for him. Clearly Oldest Uncle had forgotten why he had summoned her. She stood waiting, unsure of what she should do. Across from the old man the White man continued eating, oblivious to Oldest Uncle's silence, to her discomfort.

She hoped he choked.

Finally, Oldest Uncle spoke, breaking his self-imposed silence. He talked to her in Cantonese as if they were alone. "My niece," Oldest Uncle said. "This man will be your husband."

Su Lin blinked, her mouth dropped open, her eyes grew wide. She choked, her fingers touching her lips. "What?" she stammered.

The White man glanced at her, holding some rice to his lips.

"You will go with this man. You will leave with him when he leaves. You will be his wife."

"What?" That was all she could say. She'd been in America a week. One week. No, ten days, it was ten days. And Oldest Uncle was giving her as wife to a White man? What had she done to deserve this? "What?" was all that she could say. Su Lin opened her mouth again but nothing came out--not even breath. She tried again. "But Oldest Uncle, he's . . ." She couldn't find words. Her thoughts collided with each other; her mind raced blindly in dark confusion.

"You will need to pack your things. As of yet I do not know how long he will visit with me. He may leave tomorrow. Possibly sooner. You must prepare yourself to leave with him. Go. You have much to do."

"But Oldest Uncle, he's White. He's, he's . . .White. He doesn't want a wife." Her voice trailed off. "He's a White man, Oldest Uncle. He's White!"

The old man nodded in agreement, smiling knowingly. "He doesn't know he wants a wife. He will. He will in time. Be patient."

"But Oldest Uncle, I don't want . . ."

Oldest Uncle interrupted her before she could finish her sentence. "You will," he said. "In time you will. You have many things to do to prepare yourself."

Oldest Uncle turned his attention from her, dismissing her.

Su Lin nodded and bowed slightly. She glanced at the White man who, oblivious to the change in her countenance, continued eating, lifting more rice to his mouth.

Tigers, Gods, Dragons, Ancestors of the dead! This wasn't the way my marriage was supposed to happen. To be arranged, yes. Not to a White man. Not ever to a White man. Her mind was a tangle of overcooked noodles. *This just wasn't supposed to happen. Not to me.*

It would do no good to argue just yet. Later we will speak. Oldest Uncle will change his mind. I'll persuade him. He will see reason. This absolutely is not going to happen. Of all things. Marriage--to a White man. Impossible. Ridiculous. Unthinkable. Me, Su Lin, of the House of Kou, mate with a White man? Such a disgrace. So embarrassing. This was punishment. But for what? No. This was a joke. It had to be.

She took a few steps down the hallway and paused at the foot of the stairs.

Dragons of fire! Tigers in the dark forest! This was not right. Not right at all. Oldest Uncle is supposed to protect me--not humiliate me. I've never even spoken to a White man. Not once. I've got to think this over. I must consider my life. Can I possibly go on? Now? How could I? Could anyone . . . with any concern for themselves . . . with any self-dignity? Surely this was one step too many on a road too long. Now it would be far better for my head to be stuck on a pike at Tinian. Anything would be better. Not this. Never this.

The quiet solitude of the room upstairs beckoned her, calling her, drawing her into the sheltering safety of darkness. She did not return to the kitchen. Instead she went directly to her room filled with an unspeakable dread. *Oldest Uncle had to be joking*, she thought for the umpteenth time. A wave of sheer horror washed over her. Tears leaked from her eyes. Oldest Uncle never joked. Never. Dragons of Fire, what was she to do?

The sounds of Oldest Uncle and the White man laughing, their tongues loosened by rice wine and full stomachs, floated up the stairwell. *Friends? How can this happen?*

Su Lin began to cry in earnest. What had she done? She certainly wasn't a package to be given away. Surely there was no sign taped to her back saying, "Give this girl to the next White man walking through the door," or "This is Su Lin, kick her hard, she's an idiot." Anger bubbled up inside her. *Maybe I should get a rope and tie it around my waist and hand it to the White man. That's what I should do. Here you are . . . your personal slave. Go ahead, beat me.*

She clutched her sides and collapsed in a heap on the mat, sobbing uncontrollably, her mind in total disarray, her head throbbing. Each beat of her heart resonated with waves of pain. *Oldest Uncle, why are you doing this to me?*

Darkness gathered about her. How long had she been in her room? Su Lin was vaguely aware that the conversation downstairs had ceased. The men had gone. How long before they would return? Silence hung heavy, a damp blanket draped around her shoulders, her body, her mind. She lay clinging to the floor, her thoughts squeezing her heart in its grip. *Pack? No. No. No. How can I? It's just a joke. Just a joke. Just a joke.*

Holding herself still, she breathed quietly, slowly, deeply. Soon Father would come. Soon he would wake her. Soon his hand would touch her shoulder and she would awake. "It's just a dream," he'd say. "Just a bad, bad dream. Come, come with me. Forget this thing. It is only a dream."

CHAPTER SIX

She slept, drifting in and out of consciousness until she heard Oldest Uncle's voice; he spoke to someone, his words muffled, distant, and feeble. She thought he must be downstairs. Then she asked herself again, "How could this be?" Her grandfather, his head on a pike: her father with no respect in his own village nor among his own people: herself without the proper dowry, without the proper arrangements? And marriage to a White man? To someone who didn't want her?

The stairway creaked. *Oldest Uncle is coming,* she thought, imagining the little man ascending the stairs, pausing at the landing, standing before the doorway to her room. For a moment it was very still. She could hear no sound, not even the ticking of the White man's clock. But he was there. She could feel him.

Out of respect she stood, wrapped herself in her blanket, and waited. Through the small window she watched a distant star twinkle across the bay, beyond the green hills. The moonlit fog hung over the bay, drifting low on the tide, smothering the island, held there by an invisible hand. It was so late.

Oldest Uncle must not find her crying. In a moment he would walk into her room. He'd laugh. "Good joke," he'd say. "I was only teasing." She'd feel like killing him but she wouldn't. Killing Oldest Uncle would not be a good thing. He'd been so kind. She decided that she would not speak first. She would show respect; she would choose her words carefully, thoughtfully.

The floor creaked as Oldest Uncle entered. He held a candle. Immediately her resolve melted. She started to speak. Well-chosen words fled her mind, evaporating like drops of water in the noonday sun.

"Oldest Uncle . . . "

Abruptly Oldest Uncle raised his hand. She stopped speaking. He motioned for her to sit. She sat and watched Oldest Uncle slowly kneel, setting the candle on the floor beside him, arranging his robes about himself. His careful preparations, his attention to detail, made her self-conscious. Surely she was a sight: tear-stained cheeks, red eyes, wrinkled clothes, uncombed hair.

Yet, Su Lin sat ramrod straight, her black hair flowing down her back, the tapered ends nearly touching the mat. She looked directly into the eyes of Oldest Uncle. Only the small candle lit the room but she could see his dark eyes clearly. Everything about him was distinct. *Be calm*, she told herself. *Think clearly.* But she wasn't calm. She felt anything but calm.

"Oldest Uncle, my marriage . . . this is not appropriate," she said. "This man . . . he is the demon white. Please Uncle, you cannot give me as wife to this man. He's heathen, Oldest Uncle. Most debased of men. He will not want me as wife. If he has a chance, he will sell me, Uncle. He will treat me like he would a horse, like a cow. He will use me. He will beat me. I do not deserve this, not at your hands, Oldest Uncle. Please!"

"Niece," he said, "you are so headstrong, so untamed. Sometimes you have the manners of a goat. You speak when no one speaks to you. You think, perhaps too much. You are impetuous." Oldest Uncle paused. "I find you refreshing. Of all my nieces, my nephews, my sons, my daughters, you are my favorite. For ten days I have agonized more over you than any other. You are all I have thought about. My thoughts are of how best to protect you. I must act or you will be lost. There is no time for the niceties of the customary marriage arrangements."

The old man was silent, staring at her. "An army follows you, Su Lin. Each day you are here endangers not only you but everyone. So far you are just another face hidden behind a bowl of rice. This will change soon." The old man paused. "Su Lin, you do not know this man as I do."

Su Lin wasn't listening. She was too busy thinking. "I've only been here a few days, Oldest Uncle. Could you not find someone else, a Chinese man?" Su Lin started to say more but Oldest Uncle interrupted.

"Old ways will not work. It will not do for you to remain here. Listen carefully. Hear my words. I am old. I am experienced. You are young. You are inexperienced. You cannot know what is best for you. I have chosen for you a man, a man who thinks his own thoughts, stands for his own deeds, walks his own paths. He will take you away from here. Perhaps you will be good for each other. Perhaps you will have a good life. No one knows, not in the beginning."

She began again, rushing her words, hopelessness leaking into her thoughts like sand through crushed glass. "But Oldest Uncle, he's white," she said. "You can't be serious . . . Would it not be better to die?" Su Lin's emotions boiled over, her words full of anguish and resentment. "What have I done that you would curse me? Curse my children? Oldest Uncle, what have I done?" Her voice broke. "Surely there is a man among our people that would have me to wife? Could you not seek him out? Please, Oldest Uncle. If not, truly it is better that I not marry. I could go away. Please . . . ? Perhaps it is even better to return to my father's home. End this misery. In death I could not degrade myself."

Oldest Uncle rose to his feet. Taking her hands in his, he assisted her in standing and let his gaze hold her eyes. "My niece. My niece." The old man paused, his eyes looking up at her from bushy eyebrows. "Talk no more of death. Talk of life. Many have sacrificed much for you. There is no other like you. In ten days, there is no one so close to my heart, so close to my thoughts. Soon, maybe tomorrow, you will no longer live in my house. The sun will rise and set many days before I see you again. Perhaps, we will never see each other again. Only the Gods know the end of the paths we choose to walk. For your leaving I have great sorrow, a sorrow that burdens my heart."

"Oldest Uncle . . . please," she murmured. "You must not . . . you can't . . ."

"Soon I bid you farewell. Prepare yourself. You have much to do. My grandnephew will help you pack the things you wish to take. You will not have much space in which to carry your belongings. Choose well."

His words fell upon her ears, a heavy rain on her soul. She wanted to reach out and stop his lips from speaking, to stop her ears from hearing. But he turned and walked from the room, hesitating at the door.

"Grandniece, behind you rides death. I have seen him. Swiftly he rides the dark horse, coming for you. If you are to live, that life is before you. Now be quick. Gather your things. No longer think of going back. There is no back. Your father has given all that he has for you . . . for your possibilities. Live well. Do not shame his good deeds by ungrateful thoughts."

With those heavy words Oldest Uncle left the room. His steps whispered in the night, followed by the creak of the wooden stairs, and then silence. A vast emptiness welled up in her heart, choking her. Unable to think, she cried until she could cry no more. She stood quietly in the middle of her room, her arms wrapped around herself shaking, the condemned awaiting the axe blade. She stood thus until her brother walked into the room carrying two canvas bags.

Embarrassed, she turned away, heard him drop them on the floor and did not move until he touched her arm, his face full of pity. They hugged each other. Unable to stop the tears, she clung to her younger brother, afraid to be alone, afraid that he'd leave.

Her brother would have stayed. She could see that he wanted to. But his staying was just too much--far too difficult. Each time she looked at him she started to cry. Finally she sent him off. Afterwards she spent the night fumbling through her possessions, picking, choosing, and casting away. She'd brought very little with her. Now she had even less. When she ran out of space she repacked, rearranged, and discarded more.

It was so degrading, so useless. Surely her life was just a dream--a very bad dream, one of many very bad dreams. The candle that Oldest Uncle had brought with him had burned down to the floor. Sitting in the midst of her belongings, Su Lin fingered the small wooden box given to her by her mother. Removing the wooden lid, she looked inside at a stone. It was the size of the first two joints of her little finger. It was worn smooth from handling. In the flickering candlelight it glowed green. It seemed alive.

She leaned back against the wall and closed her eyes. "There is no difference between you and me, Mother." Angrily, Su Lin threw the box with the stone across the room and burst into tears. *No difference. No difference. None at all.*

CHAPTER SEVEN

Su Lin dozed, waking with a start, surprised to find Oldest Uncle shaking her shoulder. Blinking her eyes, she suddenly remembered the horrors of the night before. Frantic, she grabbed Oldest Uncle's hands. Maybe he'd changed his mind.

He lifted her to her feet. "It is time," he said. "It is time for you to go. My friend leaves this morning. He is urgent in his leaving. Like you, there are men that come after him. Your things have already been taken to the place where the horses are kept. You must hurry."

"Oldest Uncle, please reconsider. Please, Oldest Uncle," she begged. "Please do not do this to me."

The old man put his arm around her waist and hugged her. "I have thought long on this matter. This is best for you. Your life is before you. I am the past. Remember, death rides behind you. You must go quickly." He handed her Kai Chung's hat and the small wooden box she had thrown across the room.

She felt the stone move within it, rattling against the wooden sides. Without a word he turned toward the door. "But Oldest Uncle . . . " she mumbled.

"Come," he said, "we must go."

Oldest Uncle passed through the doorway, not pausing at the top of the stairs. Obediently, Su Lin followed. Why wouldn't he let her finish? Surely it would be better to be dead–better to be a slave than to be a wife to a White man. Which was worse? Which could possibly be worse? Shouldn't Oldest Uncle just kill her? Wouldn't that be better?

At the bottom of the stairs they were met by Kai Chung. Together the three walked outside into the predawn darkness. A rickshaw waited. Youngest brother climbed in. Su Lin followed and seated herself, her back to the cabbie, wondering why everyone was in such a hurry.

Oldest Uncle had disappeared. She looked for him. The cabby moved off, pulling the rickshaw through the dim shadows of buildings. Neither Su Lin nor her brother spoke, finding nothing to say. She stared at the buildings disappearing in the darkness as they moved past them.

The night sky was a little lighter by the time they arrived at the livery stable. The two-story barn loomed large above the rickshaw. A pole corral extended from its corners in both directions. Inside the corrals horses chewed hay, flipping their tails back and forth. They'd already been fed. Their heads turned as the rickshaw stopped and Su Lin stepped out.

The canvas satchels Su Lin had packed lay outside the door of the barn. Two horses, both tied to the fence, stood by the satchels. One was saddled and bridled, the other bareback. Su Lin looked at the two animals in disbelief, realizing that she was going to travel on one of them. She'd never ridden a horse herself.

As she waited for Kai Chung a man emerged from the barn, untied the bareback from the fence, and led it to the canvas bags. Wasting no movement, he swiftly arranged a small blanket on the horse's back followed by a pack saddle. After he cinched it around the horse's girth, he hung and tied the canvas bags to the pack saddle.

Su Lin watched, conscious of her brother beside her. Slowly, she shook her head, tears leaking from the corners of her eyes. She turned to him. "Why am I here, Kai Chung?" she asked. "Why am I here? What have I done?"

Kai Chung did not answer.

"Listen, little brother," she sobbed. "I hardly know what to say to you. Already I miss you and I haven't even left." She stopped talking, interrupted by the hostler tapping her on the shoulder and handing her the reins to the two horses. The beasts were so big and so close she stepped back. Without a backwards glance the man walked away with a slow shuffling walk, disappearing through the barn door. She did not see him again.

Horses. What should she do with them? They were so . . . huge! Su Lin glanced at her brother and saw that his cheeks were wet with tears. Without a thought she dropped the useless reins, grabbing him, wrapping him in her arms, hugging him to her. She ran her fingers through his thick black hair and clutched his thin body to hers. There was so much she wanted to tell him. Their parting wasn't supposed to happen this way.

"Be careful, little Brother," she murmured. "Don't let anybody scramble your brains."

"I won't, Su Lin. I won't. You're the only one." Finally, he pulled away a little embarrassed. Wordlessly, she shook her head.

"I know," Kai Chung agreed. "I know. Nothing makes sense to me either."

"Kai Chung, why the White man?"

"I don't know," he replied. "I have no idea. Oldest Uncle . . .I don't know," he paused. Behind Kai Chung the cabby noisily spat onto the dusty earth, shuffling his feet, impatient, agitated. "I must go," Kai Chung mumbled. Both stared momentarily at the little, dried up cabby. Abruptly Kai Chung kissed her on the cheek then backed away until he reached the rickshaw. She watched him climb onto the worn seat. He waved. The cabby immediately set off.

For a few steps, Su Lin ran after him, reaching for her brother's outstretched hand, touching his fingers before the rickshaw took him away from her forever. Kai Chung leaned out of the seat to see her. Seconds later he was lost from sight. *I'll never see him again. Never again. Never. Never again.*

Tears welled up in her eyes. She wanted to scream. The two horses stood and stared at her as if she was supposed to do something. "What? What?" Angrily she took up the reins and returned to the shelter of the barn wall, vaguely aware that the horses actually followed her.

What is happening to me? Tired, perplexed, feeling abandoned, she slouched down on her behind, leaning against the barn wall; the two horses towered above her, their ears pointed at her, waiting. *What did they want?* The bay sniffed at her knee. A little leery she pulled away thinking he'd bite her, wondering what to do to prevent it. Su Lin dabbed at her eyes with her shirt sleeve, wiping wet tears from her cheeks.

It was no use. A new flood of tears replaced those. She shook her head, her lower lip trembling. Her nose ran. Sobs erupted from deep inside. Her body shuddered. She buried her face in her hands and unabashedly wept. Her life was over. She was nothing but the living dead waiting to feel the executioner's blade on her neck, waiting to be served up as so much table meat to the horrid White man. Everything she had ever had or ever been was gone. All hope ended.

A little hysterical, she suddenly laughed. *This is my wedding day. Oh, yes. This was it: no dress, no maid to comb my hair, to dress me. No herbs, no incense burning, no wedding feast, no dowry, no promise of children. Only fear. Only death.*

The lump in her throat grew in immensity, aching so badly.

Minutes later Oldest Uncle appeared in a rickshaw, followed by another. The White man rode with him. She stared at the two men from between the horses' legs. They laughed together. *How could they do that? How could they laugh?* Oldest Uncle got out first. Su Lin sat a little straighter, half expecting Oldest Uncle to see her, to call to her. He did neither.

Men walked in and out of the stable conducting their business. They led harnessed horses. Off to the side they hitched teams to wagons, saddled horses. Others stood smoking long black cigars and freshly rolled cigarettes. Someone inside the corral shouted. Another cursed and spat, said, "Ah, shit."

The golden yellow rays of a morning sun struck the roof of the barn, ran down the wall, and warmed the backs of the horses. Across from her the White man had climbed out of the other side of the rickshaw and strolled to where Oldest Uncle was standing. The White man was taller than she remembered and looked vastly different in the morning sunlight. He was older--maybe forty years, maybe less, but old and big. It was hard for her to tell. A well-oiled cartridge belt hung from his shoulder sporting round after round of cartridges. A pistol belt was girded around his waist. Another pistol was tucked inside his trousers under his belt buckle. Leather saddle bags had replaced the canvas seabag.

Nothing about him seemed out of place. His manner was casual, yet aware. She thought that impossible. It was just that his eyes were busy. Part of him listened to Oldest Uncle; part of him was a snake poised, waiting. Part of him saw the stable and another part the men that saddled horses and hitched teams to wagons. Oddly, he didn't see her.

He wore faded, loose fitting, grey-blue trousers and an equally faded blue shirt. On his feet were tall, well-worn boots. Once they may have been black but no longer. The bottoms of his pant legs were tucked inside them. A faded red bandanna hung loosely around his neck and a huge, dingy grey hat sat on his head. Whenever he moved his feet the spurs on his boots jingled like harness bells. He was hardly the same White man.

Oldest Uncle had the man's attention, pointing at two striking horses standing down the fence line from Su Lin. She followed the direction of the pointing finger. The animals were very large and very beautiful, their coats gleaming in the sunshine. One was light brown, the other bluish with spots on its hind quarters

. . . a horse of many colors and patterns. Oldest Uncle's servant-bodyguard held the lead ropes. He was the same man who drove his carriage, who stood by him in times of trouble, always around but seldom seen. There were stories about that one. She stared at him wondering if they were true.

The White man looked at Oldest Uncle incredulously, but said nothing.

"You like horses?" Oldest Uncle's face was impassive; his voice held no emotion. The question was probably rhetorical.

The White man could hardly contain himself. "Hell's fire," he said. "A man can't steal this sort of horse flesh . . . " His voice trailed off. He examined first one animal, then the other. He looked up and was about to speak when Oldest Uncle interrupted him.

"I give gift to Jacob." Oldest Uncle touched himself lightly on the chest. "Jacob gave life to beggar who had no life. No gift is too great for one's life. For life, all gifts are small. I am pleased."

The White man stared at Oldest Uncle. "Well sir," he said, "you owe me nothin'. I ain't takin' no gift for savin' your life. It's not like you didn't save mine. I can't do that. Don't let that be botherin' you. I just happened along. It could just as easily have been someone one else. You owe me nothin', nothin' at all."

"Perhaps. Perhaps, no one else happened. You happened. I live."

"I suppose. Don't get me wrong. These horses? I'm eternally grateful. I appreciate what you're doin' here. More than you'll ever know. But I need to pay you for these horses. They'll be worth a lot of money. How much will I be owin'? How much will you take?"

"It is good that you are grateful. I, too, am grateful," the old man said. "For you they are gift."

"Naw. I can't be doin' that. Really."

Oldest Uncle glided across the cobblestones, taking the White man by both arms, and looked up into the man's face. He started to speak in Cantonese but stopped then started in English. "Horses are gift. It is customary to give gift at wedding feast."

"Pardon?"

"I did not say it all right. I try again."

The White man nodded his head ever so slightly.

"It is custom in my country to give gift to friend. Example: One, out of respect, gives gift at feast for marriage. One does this. It is appropriate. We have customs. It is acceptable to give gifts. You agree?"

"I reckon it sounds right. But I don't want no charity. I can't be takin' no charity. That ain't right. That ain't my custom."

"No charity. Gift. Marriage gift. It is proper, I believe. I am grateful. You are grateful. You have been of great service to me. Important. You my friend. You care for priceless gifts by me to you. This is all I ask. You care for gift. Take good care. You understand this?"

"I reckon I'm catchin' the drift here. You want me to take care of these here critters."

"Yes. Yes. It is not good that you are alone. Must take care of gift. Must protect gift. Must take good care of it, her. Very important to me, my family, these horses, this gift. You understand this? These you need. Like marriage gift. This is good for you right now."

The White man nodded. He reached out and shook Oldest Uncle's hand. "All right, I'll take care of yours, like they were mine. I'll be makin' it right with you. I think I got the drift, what you're tryin' to say. Anyways, I can sure use the help right now. I surely can."

Su Lin stood and dusted the seat of her pants expecting to be summoned, listening to her Oldest Uncle stumble through the English language.

"My gift keep you warm in long night," he said. "Not good for Jacob to be without gift. Gift need Jacob. Jacob take care of gift. This makes for good time, good life. You helped me like I now help you. This is good."

"You got that right. I'm not sure 'bout the 'warm' part but walkin' sure as hell ain't good. And there's nothin' like an ornery horse to make things hot right quick. Bein' without one, . . . well that'd be worse. It'll get a man dead quicker than anythin' I know."

"Good. Good. I agree. Jacob need gift."

In speaking, Oldest Uncle had pointed directly toward Su Lin but the White man did not look in her direction, he was watching the horses. Oldest Uncle looked at Su Lin from across the expanse that separated them, then back to the White man. He said to him, "Now have good journey. Take gift. Protect gift. Please."

"Reckon I will."

Several men leading horses blocked her view as they passed between her and the two men. By the time she saw them again the conversation was over. Oldest Uncle took the lead ropes from his employee and placed them in the White man's hands. Abruptly, without another word, he returned to the rickshaw, climbed in and seated himself, his servant by his side. He did not even glance in her direction. Minutes later Oldest Uncle was lost from view, obscured by the foot and wagon traffic. Oldest Uncle was gone. Su Lin was truly alone with the White man, her new husband.

That new husband turned to his horses, not to her. His fascination with these beasts of burden was intense, almost comical. He inspected their legs, their mouth, their teeth, their hooves. He walked around them, slapped them on the rump, picked up each of their hooves, and examined one after another. From time to time during this process he'd stop and rub the horse's nose and scratch between his ears.

Even worse, he spoke to them. Finally, having done all of those things, he stepped ten or fifteen feet back and just looked at them. Seconds passed. He then grunted like a pig, grabbed the blanket that lay on the ground next to the pole fence and arranged it across the back of the blue spotted horse, smoothing out the wrinkles. Amused at something, he laughed, then walked around to the other side of the horse. Never did he look in her direction. So she waited. It was just as well. With one hand, he picked up a saddle and effortlessly threw it upon the horse's back. The horse shied away, then stood still as he spoke to it, its ears pointed at him as if to say "What do you think you're doing?"

She smiled, thinking Oldest Uncle had pointed right at her. But the White man still might not know. He might not have understood. Maybe she could take her two horses and leave. The White man would never know. *What a thought!* She grimaced. *Oldest Uncle would know.*

The spotted blue horse was saddled. The White man knelt on the ground next to the pole fence, his back to her, and examined the pack saddle and the packs Oldest Uncle had provided him. One after another, he pulled sacks out of the canvas containers, hefting and handling each. Sometimes he'd whistle or chuckle.

Closing her eyes, she imagined herself riding away, escaping. She could. There was no one to stop her. Her fingers worried the reins as she thought about riding a horse. Could she? When she looked again, the White man was methodically loading the traveling provisions onto the back of the brown horse. He called him "sorry" or "sorrel" or something. A lot of his time was spent packing and balancing the load on the horse's back, far too much time for the "hurry" Oldest Uncle had said he was in.

Finally he tied a canvas tarp over the pack saddle, the lead rope secured to the back of the saddle of the spotted blue horse. The gear was rechecked on both horses. He seemed about to leave. Anxiety climbed into her throat like the rush of many waters, choking her. Her fingers nervously gripped the reins, worrying them back and forth. Slowly she stepped away from the security of the barn wall into the sunlight, instantly regretting it. Driven by necessity, she walked up behind him leading two horses. When she was within ten feet, her feet dragged her to a standstill. *I hope he likes surprises*, she thought. A frantic desire to run washed over her. Mentally she bid her feet to move. They would not.

With a grin hanging on his face, he turned to the bluish horse, the one with the spotted rump. Then he saw her. She dared not move. His dark eyes pierced her like daggers. Every fiber of her body wanted to flee. A startled, puzzled look crossed his face.

Picture a young girl who all her life was dressed for the evening meal by servants in courtly, elegant fashion. Imagine the care given to each article of clothing-- from the soft, black, leather sandals to the sparkling jewels that appropriately adorned her long, black hair. Picture her hair washed and curled, rolled up on her head in a bun--tasks all performed for her by another.

Picture ivory combs in her hair, necklaces of jade hanging casually from her neck, rings of gold and silver on her fingers. Picture a girl growing up in brocaded silk gowns adorned in lace, not a thread out of place, not a button undone, not a hem without borders.

Picture servants scurrying about, burdened with exotic dishes, carrying the finest of wines, the most delicate of Champagnes; servants serving men of state, soldiers of fortune, merchants whose tentacles reached around the world and back.

Picture silk bed sheets being turned down by slave girls long before she even thought of sleep, sweet mint laid on goose down pillows, the smell of lilac perfumed water, someone to dry her hands, to read to her from a book, from ancient parchments rolled and beaded in red and green jade stones.

Picture her father, an educated man, a teacher who lived in the house of his father, and he, his father's: generations of men who had fought and died under mighty war lords: fighting men who brought home gold, silver, and riches from the conquered: stealing it from peoples who no longer needed it, hoarding it against times of peace. Her father, a teacher--a man given to academia--a philosopher who because of his father's fathers could afford philosophy and education, himself schooled in the arts of war and politics.

Picture the life of Su Lin, a tall, slender girl raised in the house of her father where she was taught to read and write, to cipher numbers at a time no woman learned these things, a house where such activities were as commonplace as used chopsticks and callouses on bare feet.

And now picture the girl Jacob Hannon sees standing in front of him, wearing her brother's worn out shoes, the toes covered in livery stable dust, standing in a countryside that most recently belonged to Mexico, and before that Spain, and before that to whoever wielded the biggest gun, the longest spear, the sharpest blade. The girl he sees stands unconsciously wiping her cheek with the back of her free hand, nervously moving her fingers back and forth across her lips. He sees tracks left by tears that have run down her cheeks, and red puffy eyes. The girl he sees is tall, five foot eight inches, with regal high-boned cheeks and clear olive skin. He knows nothing of her.

Her long black hair is wrapped tightly in a bun hidden under her brother's beat-up felt hat. Long baggy pants and a loose-fitting shirt hide her slender frame. Nothing she is wearing fits. Certainly she does not wear the silk-laced wedding dress she'd imagined, not the one that lay in her dowry trunks half a world away.

What Jacob Hannon sees is the face of a Chinese girl standing in front of him, her feet lost in her brother's oversized shoes, staring at him, a man she knows nothing about.

Nodding in recognition, Jacob Hannon touched the brim of his hat with his gloved fingers. A man did that. For an instant his eyes focused on the saddle horse and pack horse behind her. A dark thought crossed his face. He grimaced, then he stared at her as the realization swept over him. Conscious of his bad manners, he averted his eyes to the ground at his feet. Again he looked at her, his piercing eyes holding hers.

"Horseshit," he said, shaking his head slowly. "Damn my luck. Damn my everlastin', rotten luck."

Every nerve fiber in Su Lin's body stood on end. She had expectations, bad ones, really bad ones. *Horse shit? What was this horse shit? Was she to do something?* Urgently, she tried to remember what these English words meant. The nuns had never spoken those words, not together, not like that. They'd never mentioned them.

He appeared angry, especially nervous to her. *Horse shit . . . ?* She glanced at her brother's worn shoes, holding her breath. This was going to be terrible. Slowly she raised her eyes to meet his. Truly this was one ugly man, probably insane. Two days of dark stubble grew on his face. When she looked at him, he again averted his eyes looking past her, looking over her head as if she weren't there. He laughed to himself, smiled as if he enjoyed some cruel joke.

I am the joke, she thought.

After what seemed a long time, he turned his gaze back to her, smiled, started to speak, stopped, and started again. Nothing came out of his mouth.

How strange, she thought. *He's angry, he laughs. He has something to say, he says nothing. Except "horseshit."*

"Look, Miss." He pinched the end of his nose with his thumb and forefinger. "Reckon there's been some sorta mistake. Your uncle . . . he's a damned good man. He means well, bless his soul. I love and admire him. He helped me when no one else would." His voice sounded deep, sort of gravelly. "Look, I'm travelin' light. Do you understand?"

Traveling light? She thought about the words and found no meaning. *There was divine light, moonlight, sunlight, but traveling light? What was that? Carrying a lantern? A candle?*

Abruptly, he stopped speaking. He shook his head, took a deep breath, exhaled and mumbled to no one, "I surely don't need this. I surely don't need this at all. So help me, I don't." He looked quizzically at Su Lin. "Do you hear what I'm sayin', girl? Understand?" he said.

Again she didn't. *Yes, I hear but . . .*

Quietly, Su Lin stared at him, seeing him from under the brim of the old hat, not daring to speak. Waiting.

"Look, you're a fine, fine lookin' young woman. Really you are. It ain't that I'm blind, mind ya. I'd be damn proud to . . . you know, ride the river with you. But I can't, girl. Lord knows, I got saddles older than you. It's not in the cards. The bones just don't roll that away. Not for me they don't."

From behind her passive face, Su Lin was trying to understand the references to old saddles, cards, and bones. There was "proud to ride the river." She remembered the nuns didn't like pride. They said so. *Did this mean he didn't like her? Was a "fine looking young woman" good?* She thought it might be.

Squinting, the White man scratched his head and looked intently at her, coming closer. This time his words came slow and easy.

"Well, puttin' it straight," he said, "I can't be marryin'. Don't mean to disrespect your uncle. I just can't be part of all that. Some pretty nasty folks are gunnin' for me. Seems I killed their Captain, his First Mate. Good Lord," the White man said. Obviously frustrated, he looked down the pole fence. "If this ain't one hell of a note."

Su Lin mentally repeated the words, "hell of a note" and "Good Lord" and tried to imagine a meaning from words she hadn't heard in that order. The nuns had talked "Good Lord" a lot.

"Now, listen . . . " He stopped mid-sentence, looked at the ground, smiled to himself and shook his head. "Well, I'll be damned. I sure as hell will be. That uncle of yours does the damnedest things . . . Eatin' my horse. Saddlin' me with a woman, a fine lookin' one at that. That poor bastard sure knows how to cut a man deep." He laughed and shook his head. "Eatin' that crow-bait. Ain't that somethin'? A gift? Givin' me a gift! That's you, ain't it? You're the gift to keep me warm on a cold night. Not a damn horse. And me not listenin'. Him a sayin' it right here. Tell me, girl, what'd I ever do to him? I should've let those bastards hang him. Course I did that and there would be no one to set my leg and feed me for six months. You know, I really like him." He chuckled.

Casting a sideways glance at Su Lin, he scowled and shook his head, then slapped the reins hard against his thigh. Su Lin jumped back, frightened of what the gibberish-talking demon, the almond-eyed, White man was going to do. Beat her, surely. It was certainly to be expected. She thought of her sister and that wasn't that long ago. She swallowed the fear that suddenly choked her.

"Easy, girl," he said. "Easy." He spoke softly in the same voice he had used when he talked to the light brown horse. "I ain't gonna wallop you none. Ain't never hit no woman. I sure as hell ain't gonna start. You just need to understand that I can't keep you. I just can't. Besides, I'm old enough to be your father. Feel as old as your grandfather. Wouldn't be right. Now you go back to that uncle of yours. Tell him thanks. Tell him I'm grateful as all billy hell. Tell him that. I'd be much obliged." Abruptly, the White man turned his back to her and mounted his horse. A certain urgency seemed to compel him. He saluted her, touching the brim of his hat again with his gloved fingers.

He's leaving. Good. He wants no woman. That's what he said. He doesn't want me. This was good! Wasn't it? Wasn't that what he said among all of the things he said? Didn't he say that? Now what?

Oldest Uncle didn't want to see her. She had no home. And . . . and death came after her. Already the blade to take her head had been tempered in fire, sharpened, honed. The weight of Oldest Uncle's expectations, his instructions and orders pummeled her mind, weighed on her heart. The path before her split. She bit her tongue. She had to decide. She had to do something.

With a wave of his hand, the White man reined his saddle horse around, tightening the lead rope on the light brown horse. The spurred heels of his boots poked at the underbelly of the bluish horse. Instantly the horse was in motion, trotting along the edge of the livery stable corrals. Once, for a brief second, he glanced over his shoulder at her, the sun shining brightly on horse and rider, then disappeared from her sight.

Su Lin hesitated. Beneath the slouch hat her eyes were hidden and sheltered from the brilliance of the morning sun. It seemed so quiet, as if the earth was standing still, waiting, holding itself back. She remembered that moment.

Thinking of her Youngest Brother, of Oldest Uncle, she glanced back toward San Francisco. Clouds had drifted out over the bay. She felt the cold sea breeze on her forearms. *I can't go back.* From the direction of the barn she heard someone swear. A door closed. Out on the bay she watched a clipper ship shed its canvas. *I can't go home.* In her mind she saw the black boots of the assassin, his hand on the hilt of his sword; behind him stood the earthen jar meant to carry her head to the battlements of Tinian.

She resigned herself to death. Later that is what she remembered the most, resignation. Turning her attention to the saddle horse, she stared at the dangling stirrup. It seemed too high for her foot to reach. *I must try.* Holding onto the horse's mane, she stuck her foot in the stirrup and awkwardly, and with great effort, pulled herself into the saddle.

Perched high above the ground she felt unnerved, anxious. She tried to settle herself on the hard leather seat, seeking the other stirrup with her right foot, but it was too far away. Her leg was too short; her toes barely touched it. The bay saddle horse eyed her suspiciously.

"How do I make you go?" she asked him. With some effort, she pulled the pack horse closer and tied the lead rope to the back of her saddle just as she'd watched the White man do. And there she was.

I'm alone. I no longer have a home. I have no place to sleep, nowhere to stay, nothing to eat. She glanced at her pack horses and the canvas covered pack saddle.

My only possessions. This is all I have. Now what? Oldest Uncle, in his madness has given me to a White man. White men! A race of mongrels, worse than carrion birds, worse than the cur-dogs that wallowed in dung heaps and gathered rancid scraps from the gutters. How despicable! Me to mate with such a gutter dog! What's worse, he doesn't want me! She found her voice. "Don't let that bother you, sister," she said aloud to no one. "I don't want him to want me. I don't want him even more than he doesn't want me. Is that possible?"

"You no longer live here," Oldest Uncle had said. "You are now wife for Jacob. What is done is done. There is no more talk."

How could he have possibly said that? And he's my uncle. My very own uncle.

Su Lin nudged the saddle horse forward. He didn't move.

Oldest Uncle has that right . . . the right, the prerogative to arrange my marriage. I know that. Everyone knows that. I have no choice, not in marriage.

Resignation. Her life and her new husband rode before her.

"No. No. No. No." She brought her hand down hard on the saddle's shoulder; so hard it hurt. Taking the reins in hand, she glanced down the fence line. *I have to ride after him. It is my place.*

No, it isn't.

It was her duty to obey Oldest Uncle.

Yes, but . . .but no. Just no. No. No. No.

Obedience. That was something MaMa would do, and GrandMaMa and sister. Father would expect it. He would demand it; he would depend on it. The thought made her more angry. *There are always alternatives. Always. But why doesn't it feel like it?*

"Dragons of fire," she finally said. "Dragons of fire! What now?"

CHAPTER EIGHT

In disgust, Su Lin kicked the bay horse in the sides. He didn't move. She kicked the horse again. Turning his head, the horse eyed her. She clucked her tongue as the Old Gardener had done. She tried kicking again. This time he took a step, then another and soon both horses were walking down the fence line.

Elation washed over her. In this sudden euphoria Su Lin breathed, trying to calm herself. It did not work. The horses were moving but she had no control and she knew it. At first the bay seemed willing but the farther he traveled from the barn the less willing he became. A mile down the road he began to fight the bridle, turning right or left every chance he got. Resolutely, Su Lin tried to keep him walking forward, a rein held loosely in each hand.

The horse kept turning back. Behind him was a bucket of grain, a manger of hay, someone to curry his back, and pump cool water from a shallow well. Behind him was a wall that kept him out of the wind. The bay was a knowing horse and he knew he wanted to go back to the comfort of the barn.

Stretching his neck as far as he could, he shook himself violently, effortlessly pulling the reins through

Su Lin's fingers. Suddenly he had so much slack, the reins were so loose, that the rider didn't matter. One good shake and he was free. He was a very knowing horse. With this new found freedom he turned himself about and headed toward San Francisco, back to the stable. Once redirected he perked up. His step quickened. He walked faster and faster until he broke into a trot, dragging the pack horse behind him. The old "homer" was on his way home.

Frantic, Su Lin pulled and yanked at both reins, collecting more rein in the process but getting no favorable response. The horse just kept moving faster, his trot turning into a canter. Su Lin bounced in the saddle, her butt pounding hard leather. She grabbed more rein, took up more slack, kept pulling until there was no slack. But that didn't make any difference either. The canter turned into a gallop. Frantically, she pulled with all of her strength and cinched the horse's nose down until it was buried in his chest.

He increased his speed until he ran belly to the ground, galloping across desert sod. He raced through sagebrush as tall as the horse's back, across the wagon road, and onto the flat beyond. The pack horse ran beside him, then behind him. She lost a rein. Bouncing in and out of the saddle, she pulled the remaining rein hard to the left and sucked the horse's nose around until it practically touched her toes. The bay horse stopped short, throwing dirt and gravel, creating a cloud of dust. The pack horse rear-ended him, nearly knocking him down. It was a miracle to Su Lin that she remained in the saddle.

Both horses milled around and around until finally they stood still, sucking in great gulps of air, wheezing and snorting. Foam dripped from their mouths. Sweat glistened on their hides. Su Lin retrieved the loose rein, nearly falling out of the saddle. Sitting pale and exhausted in the sunlight, she forced the fat barn horse around by kicking him repeatedly in the sides. Reluctantly, he started south, taking a few steps before stopping. He glared at her wall-eyed, his ears laid back, blowing air as if to say, "Do you have any idea where you're going?"

She didn't.

Not to be undone, she pummeled his sleek, fat sides with the heels of her brother's shoes. The horse took a step, stopped, got kicked, took another step. The punishment hardly seemed to bother him for a hundred yards later he had his head again, hell bent and forever determined to return to barn, stable, and hostler.

But Su Lin learned. She pulled one rein taut, bringing his nose around to her shoe and the prairie dance repeated itself. Eventually, she wore him out, and herself as well. An hour later she had two horses walking, ever so slowly, if not reluctantly, southward along the stage road, away from San Francisco. By then the rider she followed was a distant figure made more indistinct by heat waves that danced and shimmered off the roadway. He was a figure so small that Su Lin could barely make him out. One second she turned in the saddle to check the pack horse and the next the rider had disappeared all together.

In that instant there was nothing but empty road: no one in front, no one behind, nobody anywhere. She was utterly alone. "Alone" was a harsh, devastating, empty word for Su Lin. Someone had always been in the next room or across the street, or down the hall; close enough for her to hear their chattering, their breathing, a cough, a laugh. Suddenly there was no one, no human sound, no one at all. Su Lin was completely and absolutely alone. An overpowering, illogical, disconcerting urgency washed over her. *Catch the White man. Do it now.* She bit her lip just to feel pain and tried unsuccessfully to refocus. The dreaded White man had simply disappeared.

Fortunately for Su Lin the bay kept walking, one step after another. Fortunately it had rained earlier that morning. The hooves of the White man's horses had sunk through a three-inch layer of wet crust and released the dust underneath. A school boy could follow the trail on the darkest of days and not miss a track.

Su Lin urged the bay to move faster. He reacted no differently to her efforts. Whether or not she clucked, or kicked, or yelled, he just kept walking. Minutes stretched into hours. Morning transformed itself into afternoon and evening. She hadn't seen the White man since he left the road. His horses' tracks were the only proof that he existed. Even that proof seemed inconsequential. All she saw were miles and miles of miles and miles. Her reality became pain. The saddle hurt her butt. Flesh, bone, and hard leather jarred together, again and again until her skin chafed raw. The wide expanse of saddle spread over a fat horse pulled her legs apart until they grew numb and felt detached from her body.

The tracks she followed were steps repeated so often that Su Lin stopped studying them. Her horses followed the trail on their own. Morning turned into midday. Midday turned into evening. Evening disappeared into night. Then darkness hid the remnants of the trail. Su Lin couldn't have seen it even if she had tried. Slumped over, she no longer held the reins taut. Saddle-high sage brush and juniper moved by her like ghostly dragons.

Something rattled in the brush. The horse jumped aside, snapping Su Lin's neck back. She gripped the saddle horn to keep herself from falling. The horse shook itself and noisily blew air through his nose, then kept walking as if nothing had occurred. Su Lin blinked her eyes against the dead weight of sleep, inhaled deeply, and looked around. The smell of the sweating horse choked her. She was lost.

CHAPTER NINE

Quiet reigned. Nothing moved anywhere. The only sounds breaking the stillness were the creak of saddle leather, the rhythmic plodding of tired horses, and the piercing cry of night birds. Su Lin sat, half expecting, perhaps hoping, a giant Bengal tiger would spring out of the darkness and end her miserable, frightened existence.

The sky was alive with twinkling stars, a splattering of sparkling dust thrown across the heavens by a fiery dragon.

A warm wind picked up, rustling the sage, bending the branches of sporadic cottonwood trees. It was so late. She was so tired. It seemed like days and weeks since she had slept on her mat above the kitchen with the smells of steamed rice, smoked salmon, and broiled chicken breast wafting up the stairway.

As she rode, her mind drifted through images of giant sails billowed tight and filled with the ceaseless westerlies, and the smells and aromas from a warm, lamplit kitchen. Riding amid dense barranca she caught a glimpse of fire light, a dim flickering glow that burned shades of yellow and orange. In what seemed a great distance she could see its shadowy, winsome light reflecting off leaves and tree branches overhead.

Occasionally she heard a sound so like a baby crying, a babe with no mother, a child with no nurse to wrap it in blankets and protect it from the cold damp of evening. Sometimes the sound hung in the air, a tortured suffering that grabbed her heart and squeezed the blood from her face and hands, leaving them tingling.

Her horses stopped. She waited for the bay to take another step. It did only after she kicked it in the side. An hour, five minutes--it was the same. The fire seemed no closer. Her mind remembered the clock hanging on the wall of the cafe . . . no minutes, only hours, ticking slowly away. She wondered if anyone had wound it that morning; it had been her job to do so.

The horses plodded on until it occurred to her that she could actually see packs, a saddle, a pot by the fire, and wood stacked to the side. The bay stopped. The pack horse did as well. Su Lin saw no one. There was no demon White man, no baby crying its heart out. Just a fire burning, its flames flickering under a coffee pot. She felt like bawling but she was too exhausted to muster the effort.

She heard the crying sound again, this time distant and faraway. Su Lin dismounted, sliding slowly off the horse, absently smoothing her oversized pants. She stood on wobbly legs. Her feet and legs were numb from saddle fatigue; she was barely able to remain erect. The firelight called to her. She just wanted to lie down, to forget everything, to crawl under a rock and die. But she stood still, waiting. A moment passed. Her feet began to tingle, prickled by a thousand tiny, itching needles. The insides of her legs burned, a forest fire of pain, a hive of tiny bees crawling up her skin, stinging.

The firelight played off her clothing, her face. She could feel its warmth but she didn't move. She stood, waiting for permission, for an invitation.

Please. Just let me sit down.

In the shadows beyond the fire, in the darkness cast by cottonwood and sage, her eyes detected a movement. Her heart stopped. Her breath failed her. Her thoughts raced. *There he is . . . the same man. No one different.* She had hoped. What had she hoped? *But, he is white. What? Of course he is white.*

The man had stood. He was staring at her, a rifle in his hand, his eyes and most of his face hidden under the brim of his hat. He would beat her. She knew it. Or shoot her. She tried to step backwards but her legs refused to co-operate. *I'm losing my mind.*

Slowly he walked into the edge of the firelight, the rifle barrel relaxed, no longer directed at her chest. For an instant she thought she saw a smile; wrinkles gathered around the corners of his mouth. She glimpsed white teeth. She watched him lean the rifle across a saddle, then kneel by the fire. He magically produced a cup, wiping the inside with his bandanna. He filled it with black, steaming liquid, then set the container in the campfire, working the base down into hot coals. He pinched some white granules into the cup and stirred it with a small stick.

What are you doing? she thought.

Su Lin still hadn't moved. She felt dizzy, as though her body was disconnected and disjointed, as if she wasn't there at all. The campfire smoke got into her lungs. She wanted to cough but couldn't. Rising to his feet, the White man wiped his free hand on his shirt, then walked to where she stood and held the cup out to her. She looked from the man to the cup.

"Do you want this?" he asked.

She nodded, dropped the reins and took the cup in her hands, holding it. It was so warm. It felt so good on her fingers. It smelled so . . . she was so hungry. Tears leaked from her eyes. She didn't want them to but they came anyway.

He said, "You probably ought to drink it." Her lips trembled. He watched her take a sip. Nodding in approval, he picked up her horse's reins and walked off, disappearing behind her. Still she didn't move, nor did she look to see what he was doing. She was just too tired to care. She heard a twig snap, a horse shake itself, the rattle of tack, saddle and harness. She heard him talking to her horses. Moments later he reappeared with her bedroll, walked past her and spread it out close to the fire. When he finished, he motioned for her to sit on it.

She did as she was told, waiting like a beaten dog for the evil that she knew was coming. After all he was her husband. She was his wife. And this was her very first time at having a husband and being a wife. He knelt by the fire again and fed it sticks of dry wood, then glanced over at her. There came that cry again. A shiver went up her spine. Abruptly, the White man rose and moved into the darkness. She could hear him rummaging around. Seconds later he came back carrying another blanket. He walked toward her, directly at her. This was it.

No . . . not yet. Please . . . I'm not ready.

Quivering uncontrollably, she stared up at him through wide, brown eyes. This time she jumped at the crying sound. Without a word, he wrapped the blanket around her shoulders, motioning to her to lie down. Before she could comply, he pulled a saddle up close, motioning for her to use it as a rest for her head. Hesitating, obedient, she laid her head on its flat leather surface, staring at him. She forced herself to breathe slowly, waiting.

From his saddle bags, the White man dug out a strip of jerked meat, broke it in half, and handed half to her. Warily she accepted it, then hungrily chewed at it. The baby sound echoed through the trees. Nervously, she glanced in the direction of the cry. He saw her.

"Cat," he said. "Probably won't bother us. Don't like man much. Just curious, I reckon."

A cat? What was a cat doing prowling in the dark? Would it . . . ? She'd never heard a cat that sounded like that. A tiger, maybe. The question remained unasked. Again the White man had disappeared into the shadows cast by trees and was lost from her sight. She watched the spot where he had vanished, expecting his return, waiting and waiting, but he did not reappear.

Yellow firelight played on her face as she lay by the fire--his fire--in his blankets. She imagined him out in the cold darkness, alone somewhere with a cat that cried like a baby. It was too much. Absurd. Ridiculous. Staring at the dying fire, she closed her eyes and held them shut against the night, her ears reaching out against the dangers of the dark. She'd stay awake. Yes, she would. But she could not.

Several times cold seeped through her blankets, leaking in around her knees and onto her back. Sometimes the cold disappeared and she found herself running with her sister. Holding her hand, laughing, her father chased them through green grass, through the trees that grew by the brook and down the garden path. They stopped and watched the white kid goats browsing in the brush, bleating for their mothers. Puffy clouds gathered across the river.

Su Lin's eyes flashed open. She found herself huddled in the chill, her body warm under blankets. To her disappointment there was no sister, no father. There was just dark, hard, unforgiving earth. Every tiny little rock seemed a mountain. And movement. Her breath caught. It was him. She dared not breathe. She wanted to crawl under the saddle for safety. He was so close she could have touched him. He knelt by the ashes of the evening fire and minutes later it was burning. Sticks of wood popped and snapped as the fire caught hold. Old coffee was heating, the smell tantalizing.

Su Lin pulled the blankets tighter about her shoulders. Beyond the fire it was still pitch dark. It seemed only a few minutes since she had closed her eyes waiting for his return. The blankets were so warm. *Blankets?* Where there had been one, then two, now there were three. No, this was an illusion. Nothing was as it should be, nothing except the hard, unforgiving ground. That was real. The cold outside her blankets was real. The rocks underneath her hip were real. But three blankets?

She closed her eyes and willed her muscles to relax, concentrating on a small breeze that pulled strands of black hair across her cheeks, softly caressing her skin, lightly tickling it. Thankfully the White man disappeared from her thoughts. She dozed. Vividly she recalled herself as a small knobby kneed girl; she saw her sister. Then she saw the seven heads of White men stuck on pikes, rotting. She saw the circling of crows, heard the clucking of chickens picking at maggots as they fell to earth. Yet one head lived, blinking his eyes, staring at her.

The man shook her shoulder. Su Lin screamed. Her eyes flipped open, her vision filled with the image of a huge grey hat, a whiskered face. She heard a grunt. For a second the beast just looked at her.

"Dreamin'?" the beast said. "Better rise and shine, girl. Bacon's burnin', coffee's boilin' and the beans . . . well we ain't got any. But there's bread. And it's harder than fire bricks in hell." A steaming cup in his hands was extended toward her. She stared at him. "Here, have some coffee. Careful. That stuff will grow hair–you get it on you."

Hurriedly, she managed to sit up and take the cup and the proffered bread and meat.

"I'd soak that hard tack in that coffee some . . . loosen it up a bit. Otherwise, it's likely to bust the teeth right outta your head." The White man returned to the fire, added sticks, moved the coffee pot around in the coals, then reached for a skillet. Turning briefly, he watched her sip at her cup.

What was he looking at her for?

He smiled. "It's not what you're used to havin' but it's the best this hotel's got," he said. From the coffee pot he poured himself a cup, then hunched down on the ground beside her, sitting on the saddle she'd used as a pillow.

Anxiously, Su Lin gnawed on the corner of the dried bread, pausing to drink some coffee and wash down the crumbs. It was hard. She watched him as she ate, readying herself.

"Suspect we ought to be movin'," he said, "soon as you finish eatin', drinkin' your coffee."

Moving? She swallowed, gulping the remaining coffee, then held the empty cup, not sure what to do with it. Oh, she was stiff. Every muscle in her body ached. What had she done to herself? She blinked her eyes to force the sleep out, trying to clear her head. Beyond the edge of the fire she made out the shapes of the horses. Two were saddled and two bore packs; all waited.

This man was ready. He'd been working and she'd been sleeping. She glanced at him only to discover he was looking at her. She cringed under his appraisement, trying to shrink away into nothing. She felt as if he were undressing her button by button, thread by thread.

"Easy girl . . . we got time for you to drink your coffee . . . for hell's sake. Want some more?" He paused, his eyes watching her. "Do you understand English?"

Su Lin slowly nodded.

"Not a hell of a lot?"

"A little," she replied.

"At least you talk. As I recall those are the first words I've heard you say." He laughed again. "Well–girl, I don't understand Chinese worth a damn. Guess we'll just struggle with English. Reckon I don't know it, either. But we'll make do." He nodded as if responding to some silent conversation.

"Got ourselves a predicament," he said. "We sure do. Can't take you back to Frisco. I got some trouble on my back trail." The White man looked at her apologetically. "I reckon some folks want my hide. The way I figure it, I got to take you with me. Sure can't leave you here. Got no choice. Understand, girl? Do you hear what I'm sayin'?"

Su Lin nodded. "I can hear," she said.

"Me, too. I just don't listen too good." He looked at her doubtfully, the wrinkles on his forehead bunched together in lines. "This here ain't no church picnic, girl. I got to tell you. Things can and will get rough, real fast. Can't be helped." He reseated his hat, tugging on the brim. "You gotta stay on your toes. You hear? You got to be a watchin' all the time."

Su Lin stared at the White man, wondering why he was bothering to explain anything to her, a woman, his woman--a slave girl, his slave girl. She recoiled at the thought. *No I'm not. I'll die first.* Anger welled up inside her. She could hardly think. It puzzled her. He actually wanted her to understand him. And she did not. Not very well. But why? Why bother? What did he mean by this "stay on your toes?" Was she to stand all day? How was this?

Where he goes I go. I do what he wants. No. No. No. Oh, who am I fooling. I'm here, aren't I? Yes, she was there. Yes, she would follow. And she didn't understand. But she said she did. Didn't she have options? Yes, there were always alternatives. But what? He spoke of going back when there was only going forward. Finally she said evenly, "I will go where you go." And, "I am not telling the truth."

A smile crept across his face. He had a habit of rubbing his whiskered jaw and was doing it. "Which? You'll go with me or you're lyin'?"

She was slow to respond. "I will go with you. I must. I have . . . no choice. But I do not understand you. When I said I did, this is not true."

"All right, sister. I can live with that."

"You said someone is looking for you that wants hide. What is 'hide'?"

"Hide?"

"You said someone wants your hide."

He smiled. "I guess I gotta watch what I say and how I say it. I meant to say that someone wants me dead. That's what I meant."

There was silence as Su Lin mulled over his words. "You mean," she was staring at him her hand over her lips, "you mean someone wants to kill you?"

"That about ties a knot in it. That is exactly what I mean."

"What knot?"

"I meant you got it right. Damn, ladies, you're hard to talk to."

"I am sorry."

"Don't be sorry. It ain't your fault."

"Me also. Men in black boots with long swords, they come for me."

"What?"

"Men in black boots come for me, to take my head with the long knife. Soon I will be dead, on the long journey running to the land of ancestors. Oldest Uncle thinks you can stop that which will be. He sends me with you for wife . . . for protection of my life. He thinks only you can do this thing."

"Jesus."

"I do not understand this Jesus. This is not church. How do you say it? Killer comes. Not church.

If I am in San Francisco I be dead now. They come for my head, to take to China."

"I'll be damned."

"You are a sinner?"

"If you do not mind me askin', how many of these black booted fellows are trailin' you?"

"I do not know. Two families want my head. They hire many soldiers. How many I do not know. But they come. Already paid, I believe."

Jacob Hannon peered at her from beneath the brim of his hat. He nodded as if thinking. "More than one?"

She nodded watching him.

"You're sure?"

Did he think she was lying? "They never come alone," she said.

He grunted, no longer looking at her.

She questioned what a grunt meant. Acceptance? She didn't want to go with him any more than he wanted to take her. But what was she to do?

"You got a name?"

Su Lin nodded.

"Well?"

"I am Su Lin."

"Su Lin?" He said looking at her, pausing as he rose to his feet. "Well, Su Lin it is. I'm Jake Hannon. John Jacob Hannon accordin' to my Mother. Yes, I have a mother."

"John Jacob Hannon," she repeated. "It is big name."

"Big?" he laughed. "There's bigger. Ma liked Bible. Prophets, preachers and such . . . so I got Bible. Call me Jake. I'll answer to it."

"John Jacob Hannon?"

He nodded. "Irish. Must be ten million of us. Those that didn't starve to death caught the boat and here we are. Leastwise, that's what my folks did."

"There are so many?"

"Naw. Stretched it some. But there's Irish 'til hell won't have it."

"What is it that you would have me look for?"

The White man stared at her puzzled.

"You said I must be watching. For what am I watching?"

Jacob Hannon smiled. "Now that's a new one. A greenhorn that wants to know what to look for. Well, Susie . . . I tell you, you look for what ain't right. For a sudden movement . . . knowin' that if there's one, somethin's a runnin' for its life and you best beware or you'll be runnin' for yours. You listen for noises that ain't normal. You look for silence when there should be birds singin', squawkin', and carryin' on. You watch for movement in the grass or brush and such where all around it is dead still. Those sorts of things tell you that there's hell to pay and you best be on your toes or you'll be dead."

Su Lin watched the White man's eyes. It was puzzling; his eyes never stopped moving. They were grey-blue in color, an oddity that she'd seen one time. In the village of her Father there was a man who sat near the gate, a man with one leg who never cut his hair. Some said he'd been a soldier, some an assassin. Who knew? But he had eyes like this one. Eyes full of pain. Eyes full of death. Even the little children, those that did not know better, stayed away. There was no mercy in that one. No tolerance. She had asked her father about the old man. Father had looked at her, then he'd said, "Remember Su Lin, often what appears to be, isn't." *What did that mean?* A strand of long black hair dangled down into her face, touching her nose, tickling her chapped lips. She pulled it out of the way, tucking it behind her ear.

"You'll come to understand, Su Lin," he said. "It takes a while. Those that don't learn quick, they're soon dead. So pay attention. You'll get the hang of it. It'll come. You'll be all right," he assured her. "You'll stay alive. I'll see to it. I promised the old man and didn't even know what I was promisin'."

Jacob Hannon stood up. Just like that and he was going. Su Lin stood, took a step and bent over in incredible pain. Her thigh muscles seized; her back muscles cramped. She thought she was literally going to die right there, right then. Searing pain shot up the insides of her legs. Dizziness washed over her in waves. Furtively, she looked across the campfire at the horses. They seemed a million miles away and she had to get to them. If only she could, she'd be all right. But what if she couldn't? She bit her lip to keep from crying.

He'll leave me! I'll die.

Su Lin started to move again but the muscles in her legs knotted up and she fell over, hitting the ground with her shoulder, clutching madly at the pain. When she opened her eyes, Hannon was standing over her, hands on his knees. Frantically she tried to crawl away from him but she couldn't move.

He said, "What's ailin' you, girl?"

She spoke in gasps. "Nothing. I do not . . . nothing. I am well. I am well."

"Nothin'? I sure as hell don't want nothin' ailin' me. You ride a horse before?"

"No. Not ever," she gasped and released her breath through her teeth. "Yesterday," she said.

Jacob Hannon shook his head. "If it ain't one thing it'd just be another," he said.

"What?"

"Nothin,'" he replied.

Turning his back he walked to his horse, worked open the buckle on his saddle bag, and peered inside. He rummaged around and pulled out a dark brown, glass bottle. Su Lin watched him apprehensively, willing the pain to subside. It did not. Dawn was creeping up, dimly lighting the rim of the distant mountains.

When he returned, she was still lying on the ground. He shook his head. "Drop your britches, girl, let's have a look at those legs." Startled Su Lin sucked her breath in, amazed at how quickly the White man changed directions. She'd heard they were all like that. A moment before he was anxious to go. Now he was anxious to make babies. She wondered what the bottle was for and if being a woman for a man would cause her pain, knowing that it would. *Beatings will come*, she thought. *Stripes of a tiger never change. Never.*

Su Lin remembered the screams of her sister, the horror living in her vacant eyes. Suddenly she wanted to run but she couldn't stand; she couldn't move. She started to shake uncontrollably, her mind on the verge of hysteria. She tried to wave him away with her hand, shaking her head no, no, a thousand times no. Her mind screamed, *Oh God in heaven, please. Please let me die. Please don't . . .*

Jacob Hannon pulled the cork out of the bottle. He stared at her again. "Take it easy, girl," he said. "I gotta put this here stuff on your legs. It's just medicine. You'll be all right." He paused, "Well, it is goin' to hurt. Ain't no doubt about that."

Not understanding, she tried to crawl away. Just as quickly he was kneeling beside her, his hand on her shoulder.

"I know it hurts. I know it hurts like hell." It was the horse voice he used. "Tell you what I'm gonna do, Susie. I'm gonna lift you up . . . set you on that log over there. That way you won't have to move them legs. You won't have to move at all."

Su Lin stared at the White man's face and in that instant gave up. Her life was over. It had come to this. Just as she had told Oldest Uncle it would. Soon she'd take the long journey running. Taking a deep breath, she resigned herself to death.

Jacob Hannon set the dark bottle down and turned to her, his jaw set.

This is it, she thought. Would he break her neck like a chicken? Choke her? Would it be quick? She hoped it would. Would he rape her first? A scream formed in her lungs. She closed her eyes tightly and held her breath. Without warning he picked her up, lifting her like she was a feather. Pain raced up her legs. She sobbed, clutching his neck, grinding her teeth. A shriek leaked out her lips, melting into a groan. *Please kill me now. Please do it. Please get it over.*

As quickly as he picked her up, he eased her down and Su Lin found herself standing by the log, bent over herself like she had to pee and there was nowhere to pee. And she did have to pee. His voice caressed her shattered sensibilities.

"Easy, girl. Take it easy. Stand still. I'm gonna work your pants down. Got to get a look at those legs." The horse voice came gentle, soothing.

She held her breath while the White man worked the buckle on her belt. *Not this. Please, no. Please just break my neck. Not this.*

He loosened the belt. "Hold still, girl. Hold still."

Su Lin thought again of her sister, thought of the sun coming up over the mountains behind her home, of Oldest Uncle, of her father's hand on her head, of MaMa's smile. MaMa smiled so seldom.

The air was cold on her legs. He had her pants down to the ground. *Please. Please not this.* He whistled. Su Lin's mind froze. She no longer had the ability to agree, to disagree, or understand. The worst was happening, the very worst. Life had gone beyond her control.

The White man looked up at her. "Can you sit on that log?" he asked.

Su Lin didn't move. She didn't even hear him.

"Here, I'll help you." The White man was behind her and pulling her backwards, practically lifting her by the elbows. "Now lean back. Steady, steady . . . I won't drop you. Go slow. It'll sure as hell hurt."

Before she realized what had happened, Su Lin was sitting on the log, dry bark jabbing the bare skin on her legs.

Now what? What was he going to do? When was he . . . When . . . ?

Kneeling in front of her, Jacob Hannon stared at the insides of her legs but Su Lin didn't see what he was looking at. Su Lin held herself rigid, her eyes clamped shut. She waited. And waited. She heard the White man grunt. When she peeked he was gone. He'd left her to retrieve the dark bottle. When he returned he drew a faded, red rag from his back pocket. He shook his head and smiled at her. *How can he do that? How can he smile with what he was about to do to her. How?*

"When you ain't used to it, a saddle will sure raise hell with a pair of legs. Make your muscles so sore you'd rather die than ride. Don't I know it. You done wore a hole in your hide. That's what you did. Take a look there."

She looked where he pointed, her hands shaking, her mouth dry as old bones. The insides of her legs were raw, a bright pink. *So?* A sore had scabbed over and was leaking pink pus. Traces of dried blood streaked angry, red skin. The inside of the right leg was worse than the left. When she looked up again, Jacob Hannon was directly in front of her on his knees. *What is he doing?*

He held the dark bottle up for her to see. "Su Lin, this is horse liniment," he said. "I'm gonna put it on your leg and it's gonna hurt like seven hells standin' in a hand basket. But I gotta doctor you up or you're gonna be one sorry girl. I surely don't mean to pain you none but I gotta get this medicine on your legs. You understand?"

Medicine? Just medicine?

Rag in hand, Jacob Hannon poured liniment on it and hesitated. It smelled. He glanced at her, then began to gingerly apply the liquid to the raw skin. The pain was immediate, incredible, and totally intolerable. Involuntarily she jerked away but he seized her knee and continued, not looking up, not stopping. His fingers were incredibly strong. She couldn't move. Tears came to her eyes, running down her cheeks. Her lips quivered; her fists were knots of white bones, sucked blood dry.

But she held still, stayed by his grip on her knee, stayed by pain clutching at her heart. She couldn't move. She couldn't run. She couldn't speak. She couldn't breathe. Her mind screamed to stop him, but she sat immobilized, afraid to move, afraid to touch him. Certain it wasn't her place, certain it wasn't permitted, certain she preferred death, she grabbed the hand that held her knee. It was like holding onto a rock. The other hand moved steadily until he finished one leg and started on the other.

Minutes, hours, years, eternities later, he stood, releasing his grip on her leg. Never had she been more relieved. She shook all over, a leaf in the wind. A dizzy, lightheaded nausea swept over her. Darkness spun about her head.

His voice said, "Hurts like hell . . . don't it? Drive a fellow right up a wall and across the ceilin' . . . hurts so damn bad. You got grit, girl. I like that. You sure as hell got grit. When you can, work those pants of yours up and I'll get your horse squared away."

Get my horse? Dragons of fire! Please kill me. The girl couldn't even talk; her mouth didn't work.

Jacob Hannon popped the cork back in the liniment bottle and turned to the horses.

With his back turned she would have run if only she could. Nothing and no one would catch her.

But Su Lin remained on the log, her face full of tears, biting her lip from the agony and struggling to keep herself from passing out. The pain slowly diminished. Never had she been so glad to see anyone walk away--not in all her young life--and never so surprised, never so bewildered when he did.

My horse! Oh please. This cannot happen.

She watched him remove the saddle. *Oh good.* She watched him looking for something. He found a saddle blanket, folded it over in thirds, and draped it over her horse's back. He attached her saddle to a pack saddle on the other horse. *What is he doing?*

Su Lin had not moved from the log. Her pants were still down around her ankles, her torso still bent over her legs, the ends of her hair dragging in the dirt.

She watched him finish and walk toward her. The closer he got the more she wanted to run, to hide under a rock. She began to sob, tears wetting her bare knees, her heart pounding like a blacksmith's hammer. "*Oh God, . . .*" she prayed. *Oh please, God. Please.*

He sat down beside her and rolled himself a cigarette. She struggled mightily to contain her emotions. But it was useless. Her chest heaved. Her nose leaked. She sobbed.

"Ah, girl," he said smiling, "I do that to all the women. They see me comin' an' they just naturally start to bawlin'. It's the damnedest thing ever." He put his arm around her shoulders, holding her close, patting her back gently, comforting her as if she were a little hurt child lost and alone with nowhere to go, nowhere to be. His kindness made it worse for it was all wrong. From the depths of her feelings, gut wrenching, heaving sobs boiled up inside her and spilled over.

"I know it hurts like hell," he said. For awhile he was quiet, letting the storm blow over. "I wish we didn't . . . but we got to be movin'. Sorry. Really I am." Still he waited, smoking 'til his cigarette was gone and he'd built himself another. He waited until a cloud passed over the morning sun. He talked about everything and nothing, until the sobs stopped and Su Lin sat immobile, numbly listening. The words came soft and easy, water tumbling over a waterfall, a gentle wind tossing waves of grass.

How did he do that? How?

Finally, he stood. "Here, let me help you up." A hand loomed in front of her face. Reluctantly she took it, clutching his fingers, gritting her teeth as he pulled her to her feet. She wanted to scream, her inner thighs once again alive with fire. It hurt so badly she couldn't reach down and grab her pants. He did it for her, working them slowly over her hips, notching her belt. Momentarily he watched her, then without warning he scooped her up in his arms, took several steps, and set her on her horse's back atop the blanket. She looked down at him, her mind a fog, vaguely aware that she wasn't dead, vaguely aware that he hadn't forced sex on her, that he hadn't beat her, that he hadn't yelled or even cursed at her.

"Bareback'll do you," he said, "'til those legs of yours heal up. Keep that blanket smooth now . . . we don't want no sore-back horse."

Jacob Hannon mounted his horse and walked the Sorrel up close to hers. He smiled at her. Reaching over, he brushed the hair from her eyes. "You're gonna make it, girl. You got grit."

She just stared at him. *Who was this man?*

Without another word he nudged his horse into motion, followed by the Appaloosa, then Su Lin's pack horse. She watched as they moved in front of her, walking through the cottonwood trees, riding south by southeast toward the far blue mountains. Without any motivation from her, Su Lin's horse followed.

The sun had barely climbed above the distant peaks, its rays striking the tops of the trees. A breeze rattled the leaves and tugged at the long stands of her black hair. Her lower lip trembled. Gingerly she bit it. She felt like she'd already spent a lifetime with this Jacob Hannon and the day had hardly begun. Amazingly she was still alive. She wondered if she should be grateful or if, maybe, she was just lucky.

CHAPTER TEN

Their steady pace ate up distance. The country changed slowly, imperceptibly. It all looked the same; to look back was to look forward. Each step became a yard, each yard a mile, hour after hour, day after day. At first she held herself very rigid on the horse's back, but soon the warmth of his body soaked into her legs and she felt better. The blanket did not rub against her already raw skin like rock hard saddle leather. Su Lin began to relax.

They were up and moving before false dawn, before the eastern sky held even the slightest promise of a new day. Each morning for five mornings, Jacob Hannon grained the horses, feeding them extra oats. At noon he did so again: graining them, loosening their cinches, letting them stand in the shade of a tree swatting flies with their tails, cropping grass. After dark when he stopped, it was Su Lin who watered the horses while Jacob Hannon fed them extra oats and rubbed them down. As he worked she made a small fire for coffee.

After having done all of that, Su Lin ate the White man's meal of hardtack, dried venison, and drank a cup of hot coffee. Already half asleep she fell into her blankets, collapsing gratefully on hard ground. She was asleep immediately, thankful for any reprieve from dust, sun, wind, horse flies, deer flies, mosquitoes, gnats, and those "damn" horses. Each night she was thankful to be lying on the hard earth, hidden between her blankets, oblivious to an intolerant, unforgiving world.

In the beginning Su Lin watched Jacob Hannon very closely, her dire expectations running wild, unfettered by restraints, fueled by her imagination. But he surprised her. He didn't grab her in the night. He didn't force her into his blankets; he didn't make her perform unspeakable, depraved acts like some trained animal in a circus. Nothing like that. If she was a wife, he didn't recognize it; nor did he act like her master. If she were excess baggage or unimportant he never treated her so.

Instead he was solicitous of her needs, her thoughts, her comfort. He helped her from her horse, made her comfortable in her pain, handed her a cup of coffee before he sipped his. He apologized for not having tea, got her a damp rag to wipe the dust from her face, a drink of cool water to soothe her dry throat. He did for her what a wife should have done for him. There was absolutely no sense to it. What living man ever acted as he acted toward her?

Each morning they switched their riding horses with the pack horses of the previous day. Each morning, midday, and night Jacob Hannon doctored Su Lin's legs with horse liniment. The pain wasn't as intense the second time. Liniment and time toughened her skin. By the fifth day she was able to sit a saddle again. No more medicine.

For five days Jacob Hannon pushed himself, Su Lin, and the horses. By the fifth day the horses' plodding steps were slowed; their hooves were not lifted as high; their heads drooped ever lower. Evenings were more inviting. Stopping was easier. Sleep came quickly. Soon the oats were gone.

In the early evening of the fifth day shortly after dusk, when the first stars showed themselves as sparkling lights across a darkening sky, he discovered a firelight. With that distant light in mind there was no stop in him. For encouragement he pointed out the light each time they crested a rise. Once he had it in mind, he steadily pursued it, ignoring time, tired horses, and her.

Despite Jacob Hannon's obsession, Su Lin dozed to the rhythm of the plodding saddle horse. Twice she nearly fell off. Each time she managed to catch herself. Moments later she nodded off again, a mere dead weight on a tired horse's back, kept in the saddle by some unseen magical force. Finally, the bay stopped. Su Lin's eyes popped open. She grabbed the saddle horn to keep herself upright. Stopping unnerved her. She shook her head, trying to clear the fuzzy thoughts from her mind, trying to focus her eyes.

A hundred yards in front of her two wagons stood in the silent glow of a dying camp fire. They had made it. Thank . . . something was wrong. There was something different, odd. Or was she just tired? There were no people, no voices. On her right Jacob Hannon sat his saddle stone still, his back ramrod straight, focused, alert, attentive. Unconsciously he removed the leather loop from the hammer of his holstered pistol.

Su Lin saw nothing to alarm her. There were just two wagons standing at ninety degree angles of each other. It looked peaceful enough. Inviting. Why wait? They could be warming themselves by the fire, drinking hot coffee, eating something . . . anything. A rash of goose bumps sprinkled her arms. It was far too quiet. Absent also was the piercing cry of the night birds, the aching sound of crickets, and the croaking of a host of frogs.

Jacob Hannon nudged his horse forward. Su Lin followed, wary now, mostly awake. Well within shouting distance he stopped again, keeping his horse still while he studied the camp, a voiceless rider on the extreme edge of dancing firelight.

An explosion walloped the warm night air, echoing up and down the creek bottom, followed by another. Jacob Hannon's horse jumped, prancing sideways. A woman screamed. Suddenly from between the wagons she sprang, the firelight illuminating her face and clothing. She ran with a quick backwards glance over her shoulder. Abruptly, as if she ran into a wall, she stopped and was jerked backwards, held captive by her long skirts. Turning frantically, twisting herself, she tugged violently at her dress. Once loosened, she tried to run again.

A man's laugh punctuated the stillness. Su Lin found the source of the laughter on the edge of the firelight standing between the wagons, just behind the woman. The man had the end of the woman's long skirts tightly in his grasp. The fabric ripped as she struggled to free herself. Leaping forward he seized her arm and slapped her viciously across the face. Once, twice. Her head jerked sharply with each blow; her cries echoed across the chaparral.

Su Lin sat her saddle, stunned. The woman's hysterical screams slashed at her, chasing the drowsiness from her body as if she had fallen naked into a barrel of ice water, her very soul pierced by the sound of flesh striking flesh, the screams of pain. Beside her Jacob Hannon slipped out of the saddle and began walking toward the firelight.

Unaware of Jacob Hannon, the man flung the embattled woman to the ground. She rolled away trying to escape but he jumped on her, cat-like, pinning her down, losing his hat in the process.

In this sound and fury Jacob Hannon stepped into the edge of the firelight, a tall thin man made taller and thinner by long shadows cast by dwindling firelight. A movement caught Su Lin's eye. Across the camp another man staggered drunkenly from the shadows beyond the wagon tongue, his eyes fixed on his companion. There were two! The second steadied himself, his jaw working as if he were trying to say something but the words refused to fall from his lips. She should do something. But . . . what? Instinctively, she threw her leg over the saddle horn and slid to the ground.

Next to the fire the bareheaded White man had straddled the fallen woman, his knees pressing her arms against the hard earth. Frantically she turned under his weight shifting, twisting her torso one way then another, straining, kicking at him, trying to strike him in the back with her knee.

Dragons and Gods! They'll kill themselves. Wasn't it just like White people, beating, killing, drinking the rice wine? They were such animals!

The bareheaded one hammered the woman, smashing her face with a closed fist, placing the full weight of his shoulders and arms behind the blows.

The woman's resistance collapsed, her screams abruptly reduced to a whimper, then silence.

Su Lin swallowed hard and looked for Jacob Hannon. His strides had carried him into the yellow light of the campfire. Neither man seemed aware of him. Like carrion birds of prey they had eyes only for the subdued woman.

What a tragic figure the Jacob Hannon made, she thought, *his arms hanging loosely at his side. He looked as though he had stopped in for dinner, without a care in the world: no weapon drawn, no intimidating stance. He looked completely unprepared for a life fight.* Then she remembered thinking that before.

"Evenin'. You folks burnin' any coffee?"

What kind of idiot talk was that?

The effect of Jacob Hannon's voice on the man sitting in the middle of the woman's stomach was electrifying. Like lightning, he leaped to his feet. Crouching dog-low to the ground, he stepped forward, his hand and fingers a blur streaking for a pistol butt. Su Lin had never seen anything so incredibly quick. The hand moved like a snake's tongue. What was worse she realized that Jacob Hannon seemed paralyzed by the swiftness of the man's reaction. He stood, an icicle frozen in time, a witness to his own death. Su Lin shouted a warning that caught and died in her throat for already the evil one's hand was wrapped around the butt of his pistol. He yanked it free from the holster. She heard the metallic, clicking sound of a cylinder rotating though she didn't know what it was.

In one smooth, instantaneous motion, Jacob Hannon responded. It was like magic, like Oldest Uncle wielding the battle sword of the House of Kou, his fists full of folded steel. Jacob Hannon's fist was a pistol, its barrel pointing like a long finger, flame leaping out, his hand bucking with the discharge. Once. Twice. The percussions tore at the silence like claps of thunder. Lead bullets slammed into the man's chest, knocking him backwards, twisting his body, and rolling him past the fire in a disheveled heap.

Su Lin gasped. It was so unexpected. Everything Jacob Hannon did was so unexpected. Near the wagon on the right, hidden in the shadows, the second man had pulled his pistol. On wobbling legs, he aimed and discharged it. In the flickering and dying firelight, Su Lin saw life compressed into a heart beat, saw Jacob Hannon shifting his weight, heard the lead bullet whistling past her head into the dark night. She saw his hand coming around in one fluid motion, the pistol thundering, discharging again and again in one sustained volley, until there were no live cartridges left and the clicking sound was all that remained, the hammer falling on spent cartridges and empty chambers.

The percussions rang loud across the dark stillness of the countryside, followed by deafening silence. The second man was knocked backwards across the wagon tongue, his body sprawling between the double tree, rolling awkwardly on the ground. His pistol dropped useless in the dust. Jacob Hannon shoved the empty pistol into his holster and pulled another from his waistband. Half running, he reached the body that lay across the wagon tongue and double tree, then glanced about.

Something rattled in the brush behind her. Su Lin turned to the noise. But it was not repeated. All was quiet. *Maybe a rabbit, maybe nothing.* When she looked back, Jacob Hannon was nowhere to be seen. Yet death walked the camp. Su Lin could feel it, a feather brushing her skin, the smell of burnt gun powder, the coppery smell of blood.

In the confused silence she vividly remembered the bodies of the six men lying in the village square, their hands bound behind their backs, their heads separated from their torsos by the whisper of Oldest Uncle's sword. Blood had sprayed everywhere . . . a burnt copper smell. Her empty stomach twisted and churned at the thought.

Jacob Hannon came out of the shadows between the wagons. She watched him again switch pistols. He tapped the body with his foot, making sure the man was dead. Casually, almost too casually, he reloaded his pistol, spent cartridges dropping into the dust, his eyes elsewhere, searching. Su Lin glanced about, listened, and tried to see what he saw. But there was nothing to alarm her. Already the crickets had returned to their song. She heard the yap of coyotes. Across the camp by the fire the woman moaned.

Dragons! I should do something. She glanced at Jacob Hannon, heard the clicking spin of the cylinder of his pistol.

The woman dies and you play with a gun! How was this important? She thought it odd and glanced toward the woman, one of his own kind lying, a heap on the ground, moaning, perhaps injured, while he stood dropping spent cartridges from a pistol. *What could he be thinking? Had he a soul?* She turned to look but he was gone.

CHAPTER ELEVEN

Su Lin sprang forward thinking that she, herself, was an idiot. A woman lay suffering, dying. And she watched! Reaching her side, she took up her limp hand. It was cold and clammy. *What should she do? Think, think.*

Truly, this was an ugly, ugly deed, and to such a small woman. Her eyes were already swollen shut. A trickle of blood oozed from a split lip. It ran from the corner of her mouth down her cheek and into the dust. There was no rise and fall in her chest, no breath of life. Perhaps she had already begun the long journey toward the land of her ancestors.

Su Lin closed her eyes and took a breath. She tried to think but her head felt as useless as a swollen melon. She had to do something! Anything. Ten seconds later she opened her eyes and found Jacob Hannon bending over her studying the woman also. She looked at him in surprise.

In one motion, he bent down, gathered the small woman in his arms, and hoisted her from the dust. The woman's head lolled back across his arm and bobbed as he turned, her mouth wide open. She seemed a child: small wrists, thin waist, long straggly brown hair that dragged in the dirt.

Effortlessly Jacob Hannon carried the woman's body to the nearest wagon, laying her on some blankets. He stood up. Su Lin brushed past him, bending over the woman. What a mess! Her disheveled body lay half turned, one leg stuck under the other, her head turned to one side, her blank eyes partially open. Pushing and pulling, Su Lin straightened the leg out, propping the woman's head with a blanket. She looked dead, lifeless. *What else? Do something.*

Under the wagon box, Su Lin found another blanket and tucked it around her body. She laid her head on the woman's chest, listening. She thought she could make out the slow, rhythmic thumping of life. It wasn't much. There was no discernable breath. *Perhaps her neck was broken. Such a shame.* Beneath the bruises and blood, the girl had been pretty, with delicate features.

Darkness gathered under the edge of the wagon box as the flames diminished to glowing coals. Stars provided some light but not nearly enough. Jacob Hannon brought Su Lin rags and a kettle of water, spilling some of it on her arm. It was surprisingly cold. She looked up to say something but he'd disappeared again. Su Lin turned to the young woman too annoyed and too exhausted to wonder any more about this Jacob Hannon.

She dipped the rag into the kettle of cold water, wrung it out, paused, trying to decide where to start. The girl could have been asleep, she was so still. Except for the bruises, the bleeding nose, the puffy face, she could have been a princess in a tale of beauty and love, living happily in the storied mountains of Tibet.

Yes, but this isn't Tibet.

Shaking the damp rag loose, Su Lin bathed the woman's face, dabbing the fresh blood that dripped from the cut on her lip, catching more as it ran down her cheek from her nose. Water ran in little streamlets across the woman's skin into her scalp and hair.

Jacob Hannon returned; he stood bent over, his hands braced on his knees, watching. Behind her the fire burned brighter, snapping and popping as the flames began to drive the shadows away. He'd added wood. *That was good.*

A whiff of cool evening air blew through the trees, catching and rattling the leaves overhead. Whirling about, it picked up dust, playing with the flames and ashes, then disappeared into the night. Goose bumps rose on the unconscious woman's arms. At least her skin lived.

"Get away from her, mister. Get away! Get away!"

Su Lin started, lost her balance, and fell sideways, turning to a new voice. She rolled on her side and glimpsed a boy with a large pistol held in both hands, his arms shaking from the weight. He wasn't big. Indeed the pistol seemed larger than he.

Jake Hannon swung around and launched himself, his arms stretched out, grabbing for child and pistol. The pistol exploded, a result of either the boy's hasty finger or Jacob Hannon knocking the boy rolling. In one continuous motion Jacob Hannon was on his feet, the boy dangling in his grip.

"Damn you, boy, what the hell do you think you're doin'? I have half a mind to . . ."

The boy screamed. Jacob Hannon's nose was mere inches from the boy's face, his left fist instinctively cocked back. Su Lin scrambled to her feet and grabbed Jacob Hannon's arm. Jacob Hannon stared at her, then at the boy writhing in his grip.

"Please," she said, "let the boy down."

Jacob Hannon released the boy's shirt and he fell to the ground.

Oh . . . what have I done? What have I done? A half smile crowded Jacob Hannon's face. Su Lin's eyes grew large as she realized her hand was on his arm. *Gods and Dragons. What am I thinking!* She jerked her hand away as if her fingers were afire.

Jacob Hannon turned to the child, picked him up by the shoulders, and started to brush dirt from the boy's shirt and pants. Su Lin exhaled. "You scared the hell out of me, boy," Jacob Hannon said.

The child cried hysterically, his lip quivering.

"You all right?" Jacob Hannon said. "I ain't gonna hurt you none. Susie, here, would pop me a good one if I did."

The child choked on sobs; his whole body shuddered.

"Now get hold of yourself, boy. A man that holds a hog leg like you can't be scared. Not for long. Certainly you're not bothered by a crippled old man and a Chinese gal."

It was the same patting, soothing voice, that Jacob Hannon used on horses, the same tone, the same inflections. Su Lin began to shake her head in disbelief. *What did he mean "crippled old man" and "hog leg"? What did that mean?*

"Where's your Pa? You got kin folk hangin' around here, boy? Somebody else gonna start shootin'?"

The child did not answer, his face partially hidden in shadows, his legs unsteady, looking grim as if he expected to be caned. His chest heaved. Tears ran down his cheeks but Jacob Hannon's voice--the easy drawl, the no hurry, "we got the rest of our lives to talk about nothin'," voice--had an effect. The sobs subsided.

"Where's your Pa, boy?" Jacob Hannon asked again. "Can you take me to him? Where is he?"

The boy said nothing; he was far too preoccupied with trying not to cry, his body trembling in an uncertain wind. Jacob Hannon did not ask again.

CHAPTER TWELVE

Su Lin sat down on a saddle. She stared at the dust on her shoes, then watched the orange flames lick at the sticks she had fed the fire. She waited, her body crying for sleep, her stomach crying for food, her mouth dry, her tongue sore, crying for water. She closed her eyes and once again wished she were dead. A hand touched her shoulder. Without moving her head from her knees, she struggled to open her eyes, to focus. She dimly made out a blur of hat, face, and nose.

"Better lay'er down, girl, before you fall in the fire. If I were you, I'd use one of those bed rolls under the wagon. Ain't no one usin' them."

That's all he said. He might have said more but that's all she heard. In the grit and grind of barely breathing, she longed for her father to pick her up and carry her to her bed, to tickle her as they walked along the garden path. Perhaps some rice would be good, perhaps a song, a simple tune, a nursery rhyme of golden geese, gentle giants and fiery dragons. *I like dragons,* she thought, *big fiery, red ones.* Somehow she got to the wagon; somehow she laid down and slept.

The smell of salt pork and coffee was the stick that poked her in the belly and woke her. Her eyes flipped open and focused on the underside of a well-used wagon box. *Where am I?* she thought. Asleep, her dreams had her safe in her bed, thousands of miles away, in another land, in another country, in another time. But the smell of hot bacon found her in a different bed, one that defied all reason.

She crawled from under the wagon box a little confused. She stared at the two wagons and a fire, at someone frying pork, a kettle boiling coffee. Momentarily her mind refused to release her from the safety of her own blankets, from her own room, from her mother's touch, from her sister sitting, rocking slowly back and forth on her mat playing with a blue lace doll.

What she saw brought instant tears. Her breath caught. She couldn't move her legs. The face of a man appeared in front of her. He said something. Half-a second later, he picked her up, carried her to the fire, set her on a log, wrapped a blanket around her shoulders, and shoved a hot cup of coffee into her hands. It was so warm on her fingers. It was then that Su Lin remembered where she was. She didn't want to think about it so she quietly watched yellow-orange flames licking at ash-covered sticks, the edges turning white and dropping away, ash flakes carried away on the same cool breeze that brushed the hair against her cheeks.

Hannon glanced at her, then back at the salt pork bubbling in its own grease. He grabbed a slice of bread, dunked it in the pork grease, and held it out in the air to cool. He ate it, sucking it down like a piece of hard rock candy. The expression on his face made her mouth water. It said that nothing could be better than bread dipped in pork grease, not in the morning, not with coffee coming to a boil. She glanced about. Already, he'd taken care of his dead. Both bodies were gone. And she was glad. Seeing another dead body wasn't what she wanted.

Hannon pulled a tin plate from a stack of plates, stabbed a chunk of pork and pushed it onto the plate, followed by a piece of bread he'd torn from a loaf. He handed the plate to Su Lin and then watched her slowly chew bread and pork steak.

"Figured your belly was beginnn' to think your throat was cut," he said, smiling.

Su Lin stopped chewing. *Throat cut? What? My throat is not cut. My belly cannot think. English: such a filthy, rotten, no good, useless language. Words were much too difficult to understand, either meaningless or with too many meanings. Clearly, too much trouble. Only an idiot would use this language.*

The side pork was stringy, its taste strong. Some of the muscle caught between her teeth. *Must have been a boar*, she thought, *an old one. But it was a very good, old one.*

The boy came to the fire in the middle of her thoughts. He appeared at her side while she was chewing bread, wondering where it came from, and thanking God for it. The boy had on homemade cotton pants that did not fit, a shirt without buttons, sleeves, or pockets. It had no collar. He wore a pair of well-oiled leather, lace-up shoes in need of laces. He stood, his hands jammed in his pants pockets and looked from Su Lin to Jacob Hannon without saying a word.

"How you doin', boy?" Hannon asked.

"Who are you?" the boy asked.

"Name's Hannon. This here is Su Lin. Sit and I'll fill you a plate. Get some of these fixin's inside you before you fall over."

The boy hesitated, then sat on the log beside her, his eyes following Hannon, watching him fill a tin plate, loading it with several pieces of side pork and a slice of bread soaked in hot grease. The plate was offered but the urchin just looked at it, distrusting it. Then resting his eyes on Hannon, he asked, "What are you doing here?"

"Passin' through, boy. You want this plate?" Hannon extended it to him. "Take it," he said. "Get yourself around that hog meat. Appears you folks ran into some hard times, but that ain't no need to quit eatin'."

The boy took the plate, holding it with two hands. He looked at it as if he didn't know what it was, as though it offended him. "Yeah," he replied. "We sure gots ourselves a passel of trouble."

Hannon eyed the lad. "Those your horses standin' yonder?"

Both Su Lin and the boy turned to look in the direction Hannon pointed. Su Lin didn't see anything except trees. The boy took his time, looking at the trees as if he saw something out there. Su Lin couldn't see what.

Finally, he said, "I don't reckon they'd be ours. Ours are picketed on the other side of the creek on grass."

Su Lin looked at the cottonwoods again.

"You reckon they belonged to the gents that brought you grief?"

The boy answered Hannon, still gripping his plate, "Yeah. They belong to that Jocund fellow. That's whose they are. There his'n. Got to be. They ain't ours. That's sure." Having had his say, the boy picked up a piece of side pork with his fingers, took a bite, then chewed slowly, some grease dribbling down his chin. His eyes wandered about the camp, searching. "Where you got those two?" he asked.

"They're layin' beyond those cottonwoods. Supposin' you tell me why they were makin' trouble? You know'd those gents?"

"Yes sir . . . We know'd them. One anyway. Jocund, he's big. Well, his Pa, he's right big. Gots lots of stuff. And he's real mean and he's real old. He done run us off, you know. That's what he did. You know that dead one out there . . ." There was a hesitation before he looked at Hannon. He asked, "He's dead, ain't he, mister? He's real dead . . . ain't it so?"

"About as dead as he can get."

The boy stopped chewing, letting his breath out slowly. "That's good, mister. That's real good." Then his jaw began to work faster. "You know he got Judith in the old man's barn. Weren't none too pretty. Papa caught him. Worked him over something awful. Then his old man done run us off. Said we best be leaving . . . so we left. That's what we did."

"Who's Judith?"

"My sis. She's over there." The boy looked toward the wagons.

"Thought she might be your ma."

"Naw, mister, she's my sister. My ma, she's dead. Ain't got no ma. Not no more. Apache got her. Kilt her plum dead."

"And that fellow, layin' yonder, the other side of those wagons? That be your Pa?"

For the second time, Su Lin and the boy turned to look where Hannon pointed. A body lay in the shadow side of the wagon, a hat rested on his face; his arm was lying at his side like he was sleeping. He could have been sleeping except it looked uncomfortable lying on that hard pack ground.

The boy turned back toward Hannon. He said nothing, solemnly staring down at his plate. He held himself still as though the pork on his plate might wake up. "He's dead, ain't he, mister? Took one dead center. Ain't it so?"

"I reckon."

"That sure ain't good."

"Naw, it ain't. How old you, boy?"

"I'd be nine last April. What's gonna happen now, mister?"

"Well, boy, I'll be buryin' your Pa and you better get some of that side pork in you. The rest we'll figure out when the time comes and we get to it."

The boy stared at Hannon. "All right, mister," he said, "I'll give it a try."

Jacob Hannon turned to Su Lin.

\ "Girl," he said. "You look after this boy for me. Soon as you got him settled see to bringin' in those horses. I'll go have a look at his sis."

Su Lin looked at the child, thinking. *Settle a nine-year-old boy? Settle a boy who sat, holding a plate of uneaten pork and a piece of bread. How does one do that?*

"You better eat," she whispered. These three words caused tears to cascade down his cheeks like his poor heart was shattered, broken into ten thousand pieces. *Now what?* She put her arm around his shoulders and did not dare to say anything more. His body shuddered against her. He looked as if he was going to drop the plate in the dirt. Before he did, she took it from him. Sobs followed tears. He buried his head in her lap. She held him, patting him on the back, rubbing the muscles in his shoulders. *What a pair we are*, she thought. Several minutes passed before he stopped crying. At the end of it he sat up, rubbing his red eyes with both fists.

"Sorry," he said to her.

"There is no need to have regret," she replied.

"Got your pants all wet crying, I did."

"It is all right. I cry when I hurt."

"Yeah, but you're a girl and I ain't hurt none."

"Inside you are. Inside you are bleeding with sorrow."

The boy looked at her, blinking his eyes. "You think so? You think I'm gonna croak?"

She shook her head, no. "Want to eat more?" she asked.

"Naw, I ain't so hungry."

"Then come with me, please. We will get those horses."

By the time they returned, Jacob Hannon had the woman perched on the edge of the log, facing the fire. She stared into the flames, shivering, her yellow hair disheveled, full of dirt and grit, and more rats and tangles than a long-haired goat. A once pretty face was a dark cloud of black and blue stains. One eye was swollen completely shut, the other a mere slit. The white of her eye had disappeared behind a curtain of bright red blood.

Jacob Hannon found a clean coffee cup and filled it almost to overflowing, spilling some on his fingers. He didn't seem to mind, his thoughts elsewhere. "You ought to get some of this in your belly," he said, handing it to the woman. Pausing, he stared at her. "I knew him, you know. Your pa. He was a good man. Damn good man. One to ride the river with. Someone you could trust in a poker game, though, come to think of it, never saw him waste his time at cards. Good shot, too. I saw him hit an antelope at three hundred yards, runnin' away. Hit him in the head, bouncin' all over like they do. Told him he was damn lucky, that critter jumpin' in front of his shot."

The woman listened to Hannon, then quickly set the cup down, rubbing her fingers vigorously.

Hannon glanced at the boy standing beside Su Lin. "What's your name, boy?" he said.

"Teddy. She's Judith," he answered.

Hannon turned to Judith, "So, you're brother, sister." The woman looked silently at Hannon through one blood-shot eye. He said, "Can't say that I remember you, Judith. Can't say that I remember this boy. Course it's been a long time. Six years, eight, maybe. You'd have been pretty young. The boy, just a baby. About three, I'd guess, last time I seen him."

"Who are you?" she asked, her words slurred through painfully swollen lips.

"Name's Hannon. You'd better drink that coffee and get somethin' in your belly, lady. You'll be needin' strength."

"You hunted with my father? How come I don't remember it?"

"Young and dumb, I reckon. More than likely it was before you were born. First time was in Nebraska. That was sure somethin'. Second time was in the Cooley. Your pa, he stopped in sellin' knifes and tall tales. Had to buy them all to get him to stay. That fellow could throw a rope. Him and me tied into a bear once. Took us all day to figure how to turn him loose. Damn bear wasn't havin' any of it." Hannon smiled.

"You're that Hannon? The Jacob Hannon?"

He looked at her without answering.

"Folks told Papa you were dead," she said. "That you'd been killed."

Teddy had found himself a place to sit on the log. He said, "Yeah, and after folks said that, he told us that he didn't think you know'd it if you were and that if ever he got in bad trouble and maybe killed, we were to find you no matter what. That's what he said."

Hannon listened and nodded. "Well, I reckon you found me."

The woman stared past him at the two horses and spoke slowly with some difficulty. "They'll be coming," she said.

"Who?" Hannon asked.

"Jocund."

"Think so?"

"Yes." Painfully sore, already uncomfortable, she tried to find another way to sit. "You shot his son," she said. "He'll be coming soon as he hears he's dead. Count on it. When he don't return, his pa will come looking for him."

"How long's he been gone you think?"

"Don't know. He and that other fellow had been here two days troublin' us."

Hannon knelt beside the log Teddy was sitting on and added more sticks to the fire.

"Mr. Hannon," Teddy interjected, "we're lucky we didn't have to go looking for you. We didn't know where you were to go looking."

"I see that, boy."

"We're in trouble, Mister Hannon. Bad trouble." Judith continued. "That first one you killed was his son. You don't just kill a Jocund and live. What's worse, we're Gypsies."

"He deserved killin'."

Judith nodded in agreement and fell silent.

Hannon fed another stick to the flame, then rose to his feet, his hands resting on his hips, "Well, Ted . . . " he said, "get your horses up. Help your sis pack what you'll need. I'll see to diggin' Henry a grave. We'll leave soon as we can."

"What are you going to do? Where . . . ?" Judith stood. The coffee cup fell from the log, the contents spilling onto the ground, a steam geyser erupting into the morning air. Guiltily she stared at Jacob Hannon as if to say she was sorry. If he cared, it didn't register.

"Well, lady," he said, "I sure as hell ain't goin' to stand around here and explain to a man and sixty riders how come I shot that worthless boy of his. You're welcome to come with me if you're of a mind. You stay . . . I figure they'll be hangin' you. Probably shoot the boy. So I'm offerin' you my help not just because I know'd your pa. Fact is, I owed him, but I'd like to think I'd help folks in need either way. Suit yourself."

She turned to the boy. "Teddy, do as he says. Get up the horses."

"Where are we going?" she asked Jacob Hannon.

"I'm goin' home."

"Where is that?"

"East of here. It's called the Coulee. Down on the Nevada-Arizona border. It'll be quite a ways. You best be packin' what you'll need."

"Mr. Hannon," Judith took a step toward him. "We ain't got nobody."

"You got me, girl."

"Is that enough?"

Hannon smiled. "Maybe not. But it's what you got."

Su Lin listened to the exchange feeling exhausted. There were men after her also. She was sure of that. And some after Jacob Hannon; at least he thought so. Now, others were after the woman and the boy. Was there no end?

CHAPTER THIRTEEN

The sun climbed high in the blue sky as Jacob Hannon dug a grave. Its rays beat down heavily in waves of dancing heat. Beyond the cottonwood grove the buttons popped on the chests of the dead as their flesh swelled, their bodies bloated. Mere yards away the water in the creek bubbled and gurgled, growing warm as it moved aimlessly through rocks, large and small.

In the bright sunlight Su Lin watched Hannon shovel then take a break, scratching his head, looking all too mortal. Vulnerability swept over her and sent her into some serious "what if" thinking. It wasn't just her vulnerability. It was Jacob Hannon's as well.

What if the wily Jung had punched him first? What if the White man had fallen before the charge of Jung's friends? What if the younger Jocund had been a split second faster or his companion a little less drunk? Jacob Hannon could be dead. It would be his body swelling and his buttons popping in the noonday heat and I would be saddling the horse, hanging packs, planning what to do next. I wouldn't know what to do. I would be waiting for an assassin to arrive with a sharp sword and an evil disposition.

A shiver ran up her spine. She felt so vulnerable, so incapable, so without knowledge and learning.

After he finished digging, after the body was wrapped in a blanket and carefully placed in the ground, after the words were said with bowed heads after the manner of the nuns, after the cross was pounded into the ground and rocks were brought from the creek to cover the hiding place of the dead--after all of these things she went to him holding the saddle blanket and pack saddle. She said to him, "I want to learn this. I want to learn this, please."

"What?" Hannon said and looked at her.

She swallowed.

Holding the saddle blanket out she said, "I want to learn this. Teach me this, please."

He nodded, looking at her, puzzled. "A little learnin' can take you a long way. But why the pack saddle? Why all of a sudden?"

"I want to go a long way."

"And where might that be?" A smile grew on his face.

"I do not know," she said.

"Hard as hell to go someplace not knowin' where you're goin'. I ain't never seen it done."

"I have no choice. I . . . I think you could be dead."

"What?"

"I have no choice."

"There's always choices, girl. Maybe they ain't good. But there's always choices."

"No. No choice. I have no choices. If you are dead I must go on living, if I can."

Hannon looked at her, giving her his full attention. His eyes seemed to look right through her.

She wished for him to turn his head elsewhere. "What are you sayin'?"

Su Lin stared at the White man. "Oldest Uncle sent me away. I cannot go back. I am saying that. I am saying that if you are not here, if you are dead, I am in trouble. In trouble like those two." She pointed at Teddy and Judith.

Jake looked at Su Lin, reacting to her distress. "That uncle of yours, he ain't that hard a fellow. He's not a mean man. Time comes, I'll be explainin' the whole thing to him. He'll not turn you out."

"Turn me out? What is this?"

"You know, throw you out the damn door. Tell you adios, and don't come back." He paused. "Don't worry, Susie. Soon as I can I'll talk to him. Your uncle, he's a good man. A real good man. He ain't gonna cause you no harm."

"It is not Oldest Uncle, Jacob Hannon. I told you. He . . . he gave me to you to save my life. Not to send me away or throw me out. It was not to be rid of me. It is to protect me from death. To save my life."

"Save your life from the boys who want your head?"

"You do not understand . . ."

"I sure don't. Maybe you could just set me straight."

"What?"

"Give it to me again. What's the story? Tell me again who would lift a hand against you? Your uncle cuts a fairly big swath himself. He's right handy. That man can take care of himself."

"There are many."

"Suppose you name a few?"

"I do not think you understand my words."

"I'm listenin'."

"It is a story . . . a long story. I thought I told you . . ." He waited, gazing at her. For an instant she was quiet, not knowing where to start. "The soldiers, many. They come . . . " she stammered. "From my home. It is agreed. They come for my head. It is a very long story. I . . ."

"Perhaps I'll just sit down right here on this log and you just tell me this very long story. I'd like to know what sorta wind is blowin' up my back trail and just who thinks so highly of that pretty little head of yours."

"What?"

"Nothin'. Just tell me everythn' I oughta know. Don't be leavin' nothin' out. Take your time. I want to hear it all."

Hannon sat on the log next to a dead fire, amid packs and saddles. He looked up at her, waiting as if he had nowhere to go and nothing to do.

Su Lin knew differently but she stood there, holding a saddle blanket in one hand and a pack saddle in the other. Her lips moved without speaking. There were no words. Su Lin closed her eyes and took a deep breath wondering if it was worth it; such great effort was needed. She started speaking slowly, mentally searching for the proper English words.

He listened, nodded from time to time, his eyes a well of attention. Once he said, "I'll be damned." Once he scratched his head, running his hand through his dark hair before replacing his hat. Finally she stopped talking and waited until he broke the silence.

"Well, hell," he finally said, "I guess we'll pick those apples soon as they take on a little color."

"What?"

"I ain't got a clue, girl. We got some Chinese toughs sharpenin' their razors lookin' for you. We got this Jocund fellow fixin' to stretch a couple of necks. And there's Virginia. Not to mention those boys I suppose wish to hang me for shootin' and killin' that damn Captain and his First Mate."

"Virginia? Who is Virginia?"

"Yes, Virginia. She's my girl."

"You have a girl?"

"Yes." Hannon looked at her and chuckled. "No. I ain't got no girl. Not a woman type girl. But I do have a daughter. She's definitely a girl. That's trouble enough. Her mother died when she was young. Her mom was twenty-six then. So I raised Virginia without no mother. Had Henry though. Lucky for me he was married. That sure helped."

"But what should I do, Jacob Hannon? I must learn before you are killed, before you die."

"Die? Me? I ain't fixin' to be dyin'." He laughed. "What made you say that?"

"You take chances. Big chances. Gamble like my grandfather."

"So you figure there's a bullet out there lookin' for me?"

"How is a bullet looking? I do not know the meaning of this."

"Just as well. But you are right about one thing. I ought to be teachin' you about stayin' alive. It's right important for you to be learnin' that skill. That'd be a good thing for you to be doin'. Thankfully those China boys ain't here and we ain't gonna be."

"I should do what?"

"Well . . . you could shake a leg and help me get this outfit on the road. Considerin' the folks crowdin' our back trail, we'd better be movin'. Soon enough there'll be hell to pay. And we might as well get to your education . . . such as it is."

"What?"

"What part don't you get?"

"I do not understand anything. Why shake my leg? Why pay hell? I . . ."

Hannon started to laugh. He stopped abruptly, reached out with his calloused fingers and caressed her cheek. He smiled, and shook his head. "You're priceless, girl. You're priceless."

"I am without price?"

"You surely are," he said. "And we'd better get to movin'."

Abruptly, he took the pack saddle and saddle blanket.

"Come with me, girl," he said. "I'll show you what you need to know about saddlin' a horse." He started walking toward the horses.

She followed. *What did he mean? Priceless? Without price? I have no value?* She glanced at the man in front of her, trying to understand what had just happened.

Their four horses had grain bags on their heads. She wondered where he got the oats. They'd run out two days ago. His hands moved quickly, oblivious of her, concerned instead with halter strap, saddle blanket, and pack saddle.

"Now watch closely, girl," he said. "Next time you'll be doin' this. Do not hesitate to ask questions. It ain't bein' ignorant to ask a question. It is bein' ignorant not to."

"Please. I want to understand. Just one thing. Please."

"What's that?"

"Why am I without value? I should have value. I am not priceless. I am somebody."

Jacob Hannon dropped the pack saddle and blanket. In one step he was standing in front of her, his hand cupped behind her head, pulling her to him. She was closer than she'd ever been, his eyes locked on to hers. "Girl," he said, "there's no sorry son of a bitch in this entire world who has enough money to purchase you. Not to mention, you're simply not for sale. Understand? You're so valuable that no one has the money."

"Not for sale," she stammered, "is 'priceless?'"

"No. But you are not for sale either. 'Priceless' is you bein' one of a kind. So valuable a price cannot be set. All right? Got it?" He released his grip on her head, smiling.

"Now, girl, pick up that blanket and I'll show you how to saddle this damn pack horse. I want you to remember that the blanket on his back must have no wrinkles. Wrinkles mean sores." He hesitated, smiled, and kissed her on the forehead as though she were a small child.

"All right, girl. Got it? If you do, let's get after it. We're burnin' daylight. And Lord knows we can use all we can get."

Su Lin was astonished. *Dragons of fire,* she thought. *What just happened?*

CHAPTER FOURTEEN

The White man did not run away fast. He did not seem to run at all. And he did not seem to hide unless hiding could be accomplished in plain sight. He was a mystery, too strange to fathom. Judith was running. That was obvious. Often, she'd turn in the saddle and stare at the receding back trail as if she expected visitors for dinner and the dinner party was late--very late. Like the waiting cook, she worried herself, bothering each passing moment as though her rice were cooling and her wine growing flat. Perhaps Judith already thought of throwing dinner to the chickens, to the ducks, and dogs.

Not so, Jacob Hannon. Keeping a southeasterly direction, he moved, studying the land as if he were lost and seeing it for the first time. Creeks were not forded. Instead, they were used to cool the hooves of seven horses and a mule. Which was odd to her. Whenever he could, he followed the stream bed for miles, leaving the water on hard rock, staying away from soft dirt or sand. They stopped but never for very long. They kept moving, changing directions often. If he was hurrying, it was difficult for Su Lin to tell. For some reason he seemed serious about keeping the horses' hooves wet. Why? Su Lin did not know and could not fathom a reason.

A week became ten days with each day merging into the next. For Su Lin, baked by ceaseless dry heat and endless wind, time no longer existed. They'd crossed a desert and found yet another and beyond that still another. Jacob Hannon kept moving.

Somewhere in the midst of the hot, baking sun, and dry, gusting winds, they stopped. Su Lin hoped it would be to rest, though none of Jacob Hannon's stops lasted long enough to do anything more than get down and stretch her legs. His rests were like his eating. Eating was not predictable. They ate late at night or in the predawn dark, so early that Su Lin would have to say it was yet night. They ate in the saddle; they ate walking. Rarely did they sit in the shade of a juniper or under the wide canopy of a giant cottonwood to enjoy a hot meal.

But now they stopped. For some reason unapparent to her, he just slipped from the saddle and stretched his arms, taking his time. They'd just climbed a ridge and dropped behind an outcropping of rock. There was nothing except juniper trees and blue-bellied lizards basking lazily in the sun with unblinking eyes. A fly buzzed by. Heat waves danced across the far away flat. A small, tiny plume of dust rose and drifted slowly with the currents of air. Dust devils.

Beyond, the Sierra Nevada mountains climbed into the sky, broken, raw, and barren. They were partially obscured in a murky haze, dimly outlined by tall white clouds that towered tens of thousands of feet into the sky. At the top of the ridge, Jacob Hannon laid down, belly flat on shale rock, glasses to his eyes, staring out over the desert floor. Su Lin watched him and wondered what kept his attention--especially in the dry, baking heat where nothing stretched forever into more nothing. Su Lin dismounted, dropping the reins to the bay horse, and crept up beside him.

"Five or ten miles," he said.

It was a statement. Su Lin didn't know how to respond. Apparently it was an answer to a question she hadn't asked. She said nothing. Instead she knelt on the hard, rocky ground and gazed through the dancing heat waves. Off and away gusts of wind picked up small clouds of swirling dust.

Lowering the glasses, Jacob Hannon turned his head, looked at her, breathing out slow and easy, seeing her through dark blue eyes. She glanced at him to see what he wanted. Three weeks now and she had discovered that was the way with him. He'd look at her without saying anything, thinking who knows what. Then she'd look at him as if to say "What?" and he'd tell her.

"What do you see?" he said. "What's out there?"

Su Lin squinted in the bright desert sun, trying to see what was important, wondering what "important" would be. "I see land rolling from us . . . away, much land," she said. "I see . . . I feel heat. I see smoke . . . dust, waves of air . . . dancing. I see nothing."

"What do you reckon caused that dust you're seein'?"

Incredulous, Su Lin stared at him. "I cannot know," she said. "It is far. Maybe the wind. Maybe it is a . . . you know . . . " She moved her hand in a circle. ". . . a dust devil."

"It's a dust devil all right." Hannon handed her the glasses. "Take a gander."

The binoculars were heavier than she'd thought they'd be. Holding them to her eyes, she tried to find the swirling dust devil. Instantly the land jumped so close she gasped. Right before her eyes, so close she could reach out and touch them, was a line of small horses with grim faced riders slouched over, sitting tiredly in their saddles. Su Lin jumped.

Hannon's hand on her shoulder stopped her from getting up. "Take it easy, girl," he said. "If you're seein' them, they'll be seein' you. Don't give nobody nothin' to see . . . not unless you want them to know you're around. And that ain't likely. Not likely at all." He took the glasses from her and wrapped them in a cotton cloth, seating them into the leather case.

"Are they seeking us, Jacob Hannon?"

"I reckon they know we're around."

"How do you know this?"

"When our trail turned south, they turned south. When our trail turned north . . . they turned north. A couple of days ago, we backtracked a bit, goin' back the way we came. Rode up a draw, out on a flat . . . remember?"

She nodded and wondered if she did remember.

"Those gents are followin' our trail. They ain't lookin' for strays. And they ain't ranchin'. There's no grass, no water here. Sure as hell, they're followin' us."

"Part of the land is gone," she stated, a note of fear rising in her voice.

"What?"

"Part of the land is gone. It does not look at all like where we have been. The trees are gone; there is no stream of water. I do not see the steep hill."

A smile hung on his lips as he stared out across the flat, and casually scratched behind his ear. "Country's deceptive. Just lookin' you'd never know there's a creek and who knows what canyons betwixt here and there. Looks flat, looks five to ten mile, but it's a hell of a lot longer."

Hannon edged away from the cropping of rock, rising to his feet, returning to the horses. Su Lin followed. Behind her the tiny plume of dust rose from the desert floor. It seemed no closer. She thought it deceptive in its progress for they would catch up soon. Today, maybe tomorrow. Not long now. What then? And why was Jacob Hannon so unconcerned? Days ago on the mountain, he had fooled around wading horses in stream beds when they could have been running, escaping their pursuers. That suddenly seemed really stupid.

Hannon glanced at Teddy and Judith sitting their horses. "They're a comin'," he said.

"Jocund?"

"Could be. Maybe they are those folks from China, comin' for Susie here. Maybe they are the folks still hostile about me killin' their captain and first mate. Jocund? Possibly. Maybe all of them. They're comin'."

Neither replied. Judith seemed relaxed. Ordinarily patience was not something readily noticeable in Judith. Heat had parched and cracked her lips, adding to the dark greenish-yellow bruises that still prominently colored her cheeks. Violent blooded splotches still hid the whites of her eyes, giving her a savage, crazy appearance.

Beneath it all she was pretty as white people go. Not that she was altogether white because she sort of wasn't.

"They come for our lives," Su Lin said. "What shall we do?"

Hannon laughed. "Do? Girl, you got it right. They're lookin' for a killin'. I'd say they're set on hangin' the lot of us. If it's Jocund, he found those two boys a roastin' and toastin' in the sun. Imagine that wasn't too pretty. Those two yeller bastards all puffed up. Maggots crawlin' in and out of their eye sockets. Coyotes most likely chewed their faces away, pulled their guts outta their bellies. All that probably upset the old man some, bein' that one was his kin. Poor bastard probably couldn't tell which."

Hannon smoothed the hair down on the bay horse's rump, glancing at Su Lin. "Yep," he said. "I'd say I got all those boys hoppin' mad, and fixin' on havin' themselves a hangin'. No matter the reason."

"They'll catch up soon?" Judith asked.

Hannon nodded and said, "Guess we'd better catch them first. Slow them down." The tone of Hannon's voice was matter of fact, hardly what Su Lin felt.

Judith persisted. "This is serious, Jake. What can we do?" All three looked at him.

"Answerin' your question, Susie, we're goin' to do two things: slow them down, and run like hell."

"And?" Judith asked.

He looked at the three of them. "Can't do a lot of runnin' in this heat," he said.

Judith shook her head. "They're coming, Jake. Heat or no heat."

"True. But if we push too much it'll kill our horses . . . then we're good as dead. Ain't no water for fifty miles. We'll rest here. Ain't got no choice."

"Rest?" Judith exclaimed.

"Yeah, rest."

Hannon walked over to the mule and popped him on the rump. The mule flattened his ears against his head and looked wall-eyed at him. Hannon popped him again. Su Lin wondered about this animal with long ears. The horses he didn't do that to, but the mule he did. Maybe the mule didn't like him or he didn't like the mule. Having been popped on the butt twice, the mule twitched his ears back and forth, and continued eying Hannon suspiciously.

"Ladies, you hold up here," he said as he untied the rigging that secured the pack to the mule's back. "Find some shade, rest the horses. Lay low in those juniper over there. Come nightfall, I want you to pull out and keep goin'. I'll catch up."

Su Lin felt a twinge of apprehension.

"Sip a little water, not much. You'll be needin' it."

Jacob Hannon pulled a Springfield rifle from a slender box that had been carried, tied to the mule's packs. It had belonged to Henry, the gypsy. He set it aside then retied the packs. Going from horse to horse he loosened their cinches. The long, slender box he retied to the back of his saddle.

"What are you going to do with Papa's rifle?" Judith asked.

Reins in hand, he led the spotted-blue horse to where they stood. "Listen, girls," he said. "Here's what I want you to do. Stay here until nightfall. Don't be movin'. Save your strength. Let these horses and mules rest up. At dusk cinch up, ride easy and make your way toward those McCullar peaks. That's what we've been chasin' for the last three days. Keep pointed right at the one on the left. Build no fires . . . no fires at all. Hear me girls . . . no fires."

"We hear you, Jake. And don't be calling us girls," Judith said. "I ain't no girl. Su Lin here ain't no girl. And I ain't so stupid as to build a fire with an army chasing us."

Su Lin looked at Judith in surprise. So--so angry. Should she also be insulted? Over what?

"I reckon you ain't stupid," Hannon said, smiling. "I'm makin' sure you all remember how smart you are." Stepping up into the saddle, he reined in the moving Appaloosa. "Judith, those boys are close but not that close. There are two canyons and a creek between us and them. Come nightfall, you don't stop ridin'. Don't stop 'til daybreak and then hold up. Try to find some shade. If I don't catch you, ride out at sunset again. Sooner or later I'll find you. Do exactly as I'm tellin' you. Those boys out there ain't figurin' on invitin' you to no tea party."

"What are you going to do?" Judith's breath was quicker.

Teddy cut in, his eyes wide. "What are you gonna do? I want to go with you."

"No, boy. You stay here. I'll try to slow them down, feed the buzzards a couple of their horses. Put as many as I can to walkin'." He sat his horse a moment, staring at Judith. "Listen, girl, if I don't come back, those boys will be comin'. Do you understand? If I don't come back--now I'll be back, mind you--but if I ain't, pick your place. Kill them all. Do you hear me? They ain't gonna give you no chances. Don't you be givin' them none." He paused. "If you can, kill the old man first. Maybe that will slow them down."

Judith nodded.

He continued to stare at her. "Kill them all. You hear me?"

Again she nodded.

For a brief instant his eyes rested on Su Lin, then wordlessly he touched the Appaloosa's belly with the heel of his spurred boot. Then he was moving, walking the horse in the direction they had come: back down the draw, riding out across the flats---no hurry, no rush, no ticking of a clock. Half an hour later he was a small speck on the desert floor, a speck that disappeared, reappeared, and disappeared again before he was lost from sight in the waves of heat.

He simply amazed her. For three weeks she'd been with the White man. He hadn't beaten her. He hadn't taken her to his blankets. He hadn't forced her to wash his clothes, to clean his pots, to make his bed, or prepare his food. He had promised to take her home . . . to Oldest Uncle, a place she couldn't go. But he knew that. He knew soldiers--the assassins--were coming. This . . . this White man, who never asked her to do anything, who treated her like she was someone, like she mattered, was a puzzle. He called her priceless. Priceless? He said it meant she had much value. He said so. She'd tried to figure it out. But it was hard.

When she cleaned, or watered the horses, always he said "Thanks," "Thank you," or "Much obliged." He waited on her, got her water to drink, handed her a plate of beans, found her a place to sit. Sometimes he stood when she came into his presence unexpectedly. *And that "damn" hat.* Sometimes he touched the brim of that "damn" hat when he saw her. Now why was that? And what was this "damn" word? It seemed appropriate, whatever it meant.

At dusk Hannon had not returned. As the sun sank, coloring the skies a violent red, Judith and Su Lin tightened the cinches. They climbed in the saddle and started toward the peaks that lay low on the horizon. Su Lin kept looking back, seeing nothing, hearing nothing but the wind drifting through sage and juniper.

Doggedly, they rode until Orion had marched across the night sky and sank in the west. Coyotes kept them company, silently trailing the small cavalcade. Mostly they remained hidden in the ghostly shadows of juniper, and sagebrush. The land steadily rose. Their journey took them past steep bluffs, red rock rims that towered darkly above them, sentinels that stood silent and foreboding guarding unseen gates. The night stretched out before the riders, an endless ocean of darkness.

Water claimed their thoughts. Hannon had always found water, seemed to know where it was. But she didn't know. The horses hadn't had water for a long time. They moved slower. Their canteens were dry.

After midnight, before the first signs of false dawn, the crisp night air was cold on her skin. She shivered. Goose bumps marched up her arms like a swarm of angry ants. Her tongue was swollen and dry. It felt like sandstone and grit, her mouth and throat too dry to even cough. They kept going. At last the light grew in the east outlining the McCullar peaks in hues of yellow and orange. When the sun finally appeared, it popped up, its golden light bathing the country, stretching the shadows long, then chasing them away.

Still there was no Jacob Hannon.

Ahead of her, Judith sat astride her skinny bay horse, her slight shoulders drooped as she hunched over the saddle horn. Riding beside her, Teddy nodded away, his head bobbing with the motion of his horse. An unseen hand kept him from tumbling into the sage brush. They had to stop somewhere. They proceeded off a ridge, horse after horse, then the mule, and last, Su Lin and her pack horse. At the base of the ridge they followed along a dry wash, passed through a clump of juniper trees, and stopped.

Judith waited for Su Lin, her face lined with fatigue. Su Lin dismounted, her legs stiff but no longer sore. She held herself very still and breathed deeply. Judith crawled out of the saddle and leaned up against her horse. Thus the decision to stop there was made.

The shrill cry of the killdeer lost itself in the whisper of wind running through clumps of juniper and bunch grass. There was nothing: no water, no Jacob Hannon, just juniper trees and sagebrush going on forever.

Judith and Su Lin unsaddled the horses and removed the packs from the mule and pack horses. Before they had finished, Teddy had curled up and was fast asleep amid two saddle blankets and a pair of saddles. The women sat down and looked at each other without speaking.

They had to have water. Where was he? Su Lin stared up the draw then rested her head on her arms. She closed her eyes just for a moment.

Someone was shaking her shoulder. She resisted. The voice. Her eyes blinked open.

"Wake up. Wake up. You stopped too soon. Wake up."

Su Lin looked into the face of Jacob Hannon.

"Come on, girl. Get a move on. There is a seep spring up the draw five hundred yards. Get those horses movin'. Get them some water."

Jacob Hannon had returned.

CHAPTER FIFTEEN

The weathered sign read Piedmont, Nevada. The "t" was mostly faded and the "d" looked more like an "a." Those facts didn't matter much. What mattered was they'd reached somewhere, alive. They arrived in the late evening, after three consecutive eighteen-hour days in the saddle. Su Lin, travel worn, hungry, saddle sore, short tempered, thirsty--in short, a bundle of raw, aching nerves--wasn't speaking to anyone. No one was.

Piedmont, Nevada didn't look like much compared to a San Francisco or a New York but it looked like a paradise to these saddle-worn travelers. It had a dusty main street, several store front buildings with false fronts on either side, log houses built along the creek and down a gentle rise. Yellow lamp light dimly glowed from several windows. Horses were standing in small corrals eating sun-dried hay. A milk cow bawled for her calf. Dogs barked incessantly at shadow. Smoke columns curled slowly up amid pine trees and aspen. Somewhere someone yelled at a bratty kid, but mostly it was quiet. Certainly nothing looked or smelled better.

In the fading twilight they made camp on a creek bottom at the northwestern edge of the settlement. Su Lin fell onto her bedroll, hiding her head under her blankets. She took refuge, too tired to eat, too tired to think, too tired to care, thankful for a blanket, for hard ground, for the forgetfulness of exhausted sleep.

Daylight came early. Awake at first light, Su Lin lay in her warm blankets feeling the depths of her empty stomach. There was nothing left to eat. Lifeless sacks, once full of Oldest Uncle's jerked meat and dried berries, were folded and empty. Even the weevil had left the flour container for better pickings. The coffee can hadn't seen a bean in days.

Su Lin wasn't alone in her thinking for no one slept; everyone was awake. They staked all but one of the horses on new grass, then walked into town, a small, dusty cavalcade of travelers, slowly moving down the street. Mostly the windows were dark and lifeless. No one was about; it was too early. The only sign of life was a mangy black dog trotting up the center of the street ahead of them, head down, tail wagging vigorously. A rooster crowed. The milk cow was still bawling for her calf.

They walked past a saloon. Five horses were tied to the rail in front. From the churned up ground and the mounds of horse manure, it looked like they'd been there all night. Two hundred yards up the street another two horses stood in front of a hitching rail. It seemed a ghost town.

Hannon led the sorrel horse. He'd said something about the left front shoe being gone and another loose. He wanted it fixed. "No shoe, no horse," he said.

No shoe, no horse? Su Lin idly wondered how horse meat tasted and what happened to a horse if it had no shoes. To Su Lin's delight, the two horses stood in front of a small eating establishment. Through the window she could see nine or ten tables with chairs of various sizes: some handmade, some store bought. It was a café, not very big by Oldest Uncle's standards, but a café. Immediately she wanted to go inside, smell the aromas, sit down, and eat food prepared by someone else.

It was still early. The sun wasn't up when Hannon opened the door and held it for Judith, Su Lin, and Teddy. The smell of fresh coffee boiling, bacon frying, and pine wood smoke permeated the atmosphere, assaulting Su Lin's nose. *Oh the smell of it. So wonderful.* Breathing deeply, Su Lin followed the others to a table near the front window.

Hannon pulled a chair from the table and looked at Su Lin. When she didn't sit down he said, "Have yourself a chair." Su Lin sat in the chair he'd pulled from the table thinking the act was silly, never having seen it done before. Hannon did the same for Judith. She seemed to like it. *What kind of ritual was this? Holding a chair for her! For me?* Certainly she could seat herself. She needed no help. Judith said, "Thank you." She'd even smiled. *Was Judith so helpless she couldn't get her own chair and sit on it? I don't think so.*

Down the counter toward the back, two men sat, dressed in rough, coarse clothing, talking and laughing loudly. A rifle lay on the counter within easy reach. Both wore gun belts hitched around their waists. In the far back corner two men and a woman were eating, their faces hidden from Su Lin.

The café was warm, a marketplace of smells and aromas. It didn't take long to forget and forgive

Jacob Hannon for the chair. It didn't matter. Eating was much more important. Still, it was something to think about.

Only White man fare was served: bacon, baking powder biscuits, hen's eggs, pancakes, sliced potatoes fried in bacon grease, and scalding coffee. She could smell what was there and what wasn't. There was no rice, no baked fish, but that didn't matter as long as she could eat.

The cook came to their table, wiping his hands on a greasy, stained apron, looking from one to another. There was something peculiar about him. His eyes fell on Su Lin. He shook his head slightly. Su Lin noticed. *Why?* Had Judith noticed? If Jacob Hannon had, he didn't show it. Surely this man didn't recognize Su Lin. He wasn't anybody she'd seen before. Yet she felt uneasy.

"Mornin' folks. Coffee?"

They all ordered the same thing . . . some of everything he was cooking.

Having taken their order, the cook returned to the kitchen.

From where she was sitting, Su Lin could see into the back of the frame building, into a room filled with a large black kitchen stove, a kettle of boiling water. She saw counters covered with loaves of rising dough, and fresh meat not yet cut into steaks. Overhead, the high ceiling was stained dark from smoke and rain water. In the corners and along the edges, drooping cobwebs, choked with old dust, hung down, moving back and forth ever so slightly as air circulated about the ceiling. It was not very clean, not like Oldest Uncle would want. The cook, oblivious to the abandoned spider webs, seemed lost in his work.

Soon they ate. A stomach full of White man's food, followed by a slowly sipped cup of hot coffee made Su Lin drowsy, warm, and tired. It surprised her that she couldn't eat much. In less than twenty minutes it had become difficult to move. She really wanted to clean her plate but her stomach protested, oddly smaller than it had ever been. There was much on her plate that she hadn't eaten. Her eyes had betrayed her.

Hot food, as much as she wanted, bright, warm sunlight, people, buildings--what a relief. She didn't want to leave the table. She wanted to remain where she was, sitting without moving, with no dishes to wash or pots to scrub. Certainly she did not want to climb onto the back of another horse, swat another horse fly, or brush away another gnat. This was the way every morning ought to be.

Rising from the rickety white chair, Hannon motioned to the others to remain seated.

Where was he going? Please, can't we just sit a while longer? Please.

"Finish your breakfast," he said. "I'll find a smith to look at that horse's hoof. Get him fixed up. Be back as soon as I can. Judith, you and Su Lin buy supplies. We can pick them up on the way through town." Hannon paused and handed Judith some gold coins. "I wish we could stay longer, ladies, and rest up a bit. We all need it. But we're three days from the Coulee and that's a good place to disappear. As you well know . . . we need to do a little disappearin'." Before he turned to leave, he looked at Teddy. "Ted, if you would, help the ladies get squared away. Get the horses ready. We'll be movin' soon as I get back to the creek."

Teddy nodded.

Jacob Hannon walked to the front door. Su Lin listened to it squeak on its oil starved hinges as it opened and closed. *Why so soon? Couldn't we wait just an hour longer? What difference would it possibly make?*

Judith sipped at her coffee and stared past Su Lin through the front window. They ate slowly in a pleasant silence.

"Store's open!" Judith exclaimed.

Su Lin and Teddy turned to see. Across the street a man was sweeping the boardwalk in front of two large windows. Behind him a door was open wide.

"Tell you what, Su Lin," Judith said, "I'll get the supplies. You and Teddy rest here. Finish your coffee. I'll give you some of Jake's money. Pay the man. It'll only take me a minute. So you two take it easy."

Who could turn down that offer? Another moment just to sit without moving!

"Here's a ten-dollar gold piece. That'll more than cover it. Pay the man when you are through."

Su Lin took the coin. Was she missing something by sitting? Not likely. Before she could decide whether it'd be better to stay or go, Judith was out the door. Absently, Su Lin turned and watched Judith walk across the street, and step up on the board walk. The storekeeper, wearing a white apron and a hat, paused and spoke to her before she disappeared through the open door of the general store.

Su Lin sipped the dark coffee feeling the warmth of it creeping through her stomach, melting her belly. She idly nursed the cup until there was nothing left. How wonderful it was not to think, not to fight with a horse, just to exist in a comfortable chair with a full stomach. It was absolutely wonderful.

The cook looked their way again and then again. *He must want money*, she thought. After her coffee cup was empty and the chair began to grow hard she thought about paying him.

"Well, Teddy," she said, "I suppose . . ."

Immediately, Teddy stood up.

Regretfully, Su Lin followed his example and took the cook the gold coin, studiously avoiding the thought of horses, bridles, saddles, packs, horseshoes, and saddle sores. Over the cook's shoulder she saw bread ready for baking, a pot of beans boiling, bacon frying. The smells hung in the air. She handed him the coin. To her surprise, he put the small piece of metal in his mouth and bit it. *Why would he bite a gold coin?*

"Can't be too careful," he said to her. Reaching into his pocket, he handed her several coins of different sizes and shapes. She stared at the coins, realizing she didn't know what he had given her.

"Ain't that right?" he said.

"Yes. Yes. Thank you. Your food is . . . is most delicious. We hope to return."

Grunting, the old man smiled a yellow, toothy grin and nodded his thanks. "Glad ye liked it," he said. Turning away, he moved back into his kitchen, muttering to himself as he limped toward his pots, pans, and skillets.

Su Lin, Teddy walking beside her, passed through the front door onto the board sidewalk, leaving the grisly cook and the smells tucked inside. If she never did anything else in her life, she was coming back to that place to sit in that chair, drink that man's coffee, eat his bacon, his eggs, his pancakes, and his fried potatoes. He made it easy to forget rice and fish.

A sun-bleached buckboard rolled up the street. Another wagon passed, followed by a horseman. There was no dew to keep the red dust from billowing up, thus a dust cloud followed the wagon as its wheels churned up the street. The dust drifted and died covering the board walks.

"Let us find Judith," Sun Lin said.

"I don't think so."

Su Lin looked at Teddy, puzzled.

"Why do you say that?"

"She likes to store shop by herself. We'd be in the way. Papa just stayed outside. Said it was best."

"She does not need help?"

"Not likely. She's good at buying stuff, haggling."

"What should we do?"

"I don't wanna work. I don't wanna go back to camp."

"All right," Su Lin said. "Let us sit down right here. Wait for Judith. That is not too much work."

Teddy promptly sat down on the edge of the boardwalk, followed by Su Lin. They dangled their feet off the boardwalk and watched the occasional pedestrians, a horse, and several more wagons move past. The sun felt warm and bright on her face. The moment felt so good, the air so crisp.

CHAPTER SIXTEEN

"Well, younger brother, how are you?" Su Lin asked Teddy.

"I ain't your brother, Su Lin. But I kind of wish I was."

"Thank you, I think," she laughed. "I do have a younger brother--Kai Chung. He is older than you. Not much though. Why do you wish you were my brother?"

"Well,'cause. . . for a girl you're all right."

Su Lin nodded. "Thanks."

"You're welcome."

A buckboard came up the street pulled by a pair of blacks. It turned at the corner of the street and disappeared from view. Teddy was staring down the street.

"Look at that," Teddy said. "See those folks. See them? They're blind drunk and it ain't barely breakfast," Teddy explained. "See?"

Su Lin turned in the direction Teddy pointed. Down the street two hundred yards or so, four men staggered about, soon joined by another. Their loud laughter carried on the morning air as they slapped each other on the back, holding each other up. One man fell to the boardwalk. His companions proceeded to assist him to his feet. Drunks. They looked harmless, if not comical.

From the opposite direction she heard a horn blow. Moments later a stagecoach rounded the bend. The lead horses shook their harnesses as they trotted down the street. Behind Su Lin the café door opened. Two men and a woman stepped into the bright sunshine and walked toward the approaching stagecoach. Neither Teddy nor Su Lin said anything while the six horse team was changed and the passengers boarded. A few minutes later the driver and the stage rolled past them, moving down the street, then out of sight.

Diagonally across the street, a Chinese woman opened a door and stepped out onto the boardwalk. The sight startled Su Lin. Kin? Not likely. But Chinese. It was a laundry. The woman glanced at her from across the street. Their eyes met. Immediately the woman retreated inside. Soon a man appeared. He, too, was Chinese. He, too, stared at her before going back inside, closing the door behind him.

"Hey, they're just like you," Teddy said. "Do you know them?"

"No."

"Except they ain't near as pretty," he continued.

"What do you know about pretty?"

"I ain't blind. You gots all them curves, long hair and stuff."

"Teddy. What do you know about girls? You are too young."

"Not that young."

"Yes, that young."

She mussed his hair. Where was Judith? She should be finished making her purchases by now. Su Lin glanced across the street at the open door of the general store. No one came out and she couldn't see inside. A dog barked.

"Oh, oh," Teddy said looking past her. "We gots trouble." He stood, backing away from the edge of the boardwalk. He was staring at the drunk cowboys who'd made it up the street to where they were sitting. Standing on the boardwalk, they towered above them.

"Boys, would ye take . . . say, take a look at this here."

Su Lin turned to the voice. Before her she saw five, staggering, drunk, red-faced, bleary-eyed, men. They were so close she wanted to get up and retreat. Each stared down at her like cats looking at a live rat. They smelled sour and were only standing by the questionable assistance from one another. Instantly she remembered the White men, the village street, the rice wine bottles, the cries of her sister, and Oldest Uncle leaning on his battle sword. She sprang to her feet, backing into the street. Teddy was on her left beside her.

"Did you ever see . . . say did you ever see such a yeller chink gal in all your worthless lives? A picture. She's a picture." A big man with a red flannel shirt spoke, running his words together, pointing at her with an unsteady arm.

"Wouldn't ya like to get hold of that, Hank?"

" . . . damn right . . . get hold that . . ."

"Ah, get sober . . . you horn dog rooster. She'd throw you quicker than ol' Snake, that wicked, worthless, son of a bitch."

"He ain't old."

"Ain't got no teeth."

"Don't need no teeth."

"Well, you ain't got no teeth neither. So pull it in Hank, old boy. Stone sober you couldn't pour piss out of a boot with a hole in the toe, instructions done burnt in the heel."

"Hell, ya say, he can't even read nothin'."

The first speaker erupted in laughter, hooting like a drunken fiend, hilariously stamping his foot. It wasn't funny. His companions joined him. Together they nearly collapsed on the board walk. Supported by another collective effort, somehow they remained upright. Once gaining an unsteady equilibrium, they stared down at her again, suddenly church mute.

"Lordie," one whispered.

" Almighty . . . " said another.

"Ah, shut up. Both of you. Pull in them claws. Neither one of you knows what to do."

Teddy grabbed her arm and Su Lin spoke to him. "Come on, Teddy," she said backing farther away. "Let us find Judith. Let us get away from here."

The cowhand wearing the plaid shirt reached out toward her. Someone grabbed at his arm, but he was too late.

To avoid him, Su Lin stepped further back, almost tripping on Teddy.

"Say you're fast, girlie," the plaid shirt said. Waving his hand, he beckoned to her. "Come here so I can get a look at you . . . you girl, you." He stumbled, teetering out over the boardwalk.

Teddy and Su Lin retreated farther into the street. A team of horses pulling a wagon passed close behind them.

Someone cussed.

Off balance the drunk lunged at her, and fell, collapsing face first into the street, a cloud of dust exploding about him. Caught between the falling drunk, Teddy, and the wagon behind her, Su Lin tripped, falling backwards herself, knocking the air from her lungs. Powdery dust enveloped her in a cloud, filling her mouth, coating her nose, face, lungs and clothing. It clung to every strand of her hair. She spit. Coughed. Gagged. She convulsed, fighting for air.

Disoriented, she tried to sit up, tried to get her feet under her, tried to blink the fine dust from her eyes. Her eyes watered. Wet, beading mud balls clung to her eyelids and eyelashes, growing bigger until she was blind, unable to focus, unable to see anything but oblique shadows, dark moving forms. She was aware of Teddy at her side tugging fiercely at her arm.

"Come on, Su Lin. Come on. Get up," he screamed. "Let's get out of here. Come on. Come on."

But she couldn't breathe. Faces milled around her, shadows in a finger play. Someone pulled at her arm. Laughter rose and fell in waves. Her eyes were saturated in fire, ablaze with grains of dust grinding delicate membranes. Teddy's high pitched voice screeched, filling her ears. Her body strained for air, fought for it, but choking dust clung to the back of her throat, to her lungs. She couldn't breathe.

The drunken white beast who'd fallen beside her struggled to his hands and knees, cursed his companions, cursed his father, his mother. He cursed the day he was born, the dust he breathed, the street that moved under him.

Somewhere, someone--then everyone around her--started kicking street dust. It billowed up, hiding her. She was kicked and then multiple hands held her fast in the street. Teddy yelled her name. Squirming for her life, she fought to get up but their hands held her down, pushing against her, flattening her body to the ground. *Father! Oh Father, help me.*

Teddy was pulled from her, his grip broken. He flew through the air like a rag doll, struck the earth and rolled. She reached after him but the hands held her, pushing, shoving her onto her back. Horse manure, sticky, smelly horse manure splattered onto her face. A putrid, sour taste spread in her mouth. Her mouth, her blouse, her pants were filled with the sticky, clammy substance. The hands rubbed and mashed it into her skin, her face, her clothing. Hands groped at her body as she struggled to turn over, to get to her knees. But she couldn't move. She couldn't cry out.

Peals of laughter echoed up and down the street. A crowd of gawkers gathered, watching, saying nothing, doing nothing. In the rolling tumble of her struggle, she could barely see. She wanted to die, thought she was soon dead. The plaid shirt grabbed Su Lin's arm. Teddy jumped on his back and was thrown, rolling beneath a horse's belly. She thought he'd be killed, tromped to death. Air bursting from tortured lungs, she screamed--gagged--and screamed again, vaguely aware of Teddy still trying to reach her and again being thrown brutally to the ground.

"Teddy," Su Lin choked. "Get help. Get help."

A hand clamped over her mouth . . . her eyes. Laughter.

"Yeah, boy. Get help. We could sure use it. This here chink gal is a handful. And we're too damn drunk to know what to do."

More laughter. Her blouse ripped, buttons flew. The world reeled. Against the constant pushing and shoving, she managed to turn herself over, pulling her knees under her. Someone kicked her as she tried to crawl onto the boardwalk. The blow stunned her. A hand grabbed her foot and held her back, dragging her back into the street. Her torn shirt, her eyes, her ears, her mouth, the legs of her trousers were all filled with dust and dirt. Frantically, she kicked at the hand. Her brother's shoe came off. She heard their laughter. It filled the streets, echoing over and over again. "Help me. Help me. Help me," she screamed.

CHAPTER SEVENTEEN

An explosion banged in her head like the ringing of a gong in the night. Everything stopped. No hands held her. No one tugged at her. In the silence a hand seized her by the arm. She started to resist, violently shrinking away but the grip was unrelenting.

"Easy, girl." The horse voice. The hand lifted her slowly, carefully, to her feet and held her against him. There was no reservation, no hesitation in him. Every fiber in her body shook and trembled. Her knees buckled but the arm held her, not letting her fall. "Easy, girl, I got you. Take her easy."

His arm tightened around her waist. Her chest heaved. Sobs bubbled from her mouth; a helpless anger twisted her insides. Street laughter again chased her sanity. Angrily, she grabbed a fist full of the coarse cloth that was Jacob Hannon's shirt, her hands and fingers white knots. She held onto him, burying her head in his chest, hiding her face, shutting out the grating, clashing voices. His arm tightened. *Oh, please make them go away. Please . . .*

A hand brushed dust from her torn shirt, gently wiping her face, smoothing her hair, pulling it out of her eyes. She blinked, felt a hand patting her back, heard the muffled, soothing voice echo in her head.

From somewhere she heard her name screamed out but Su Lin didn't turn to the new voice. Seconds later she was conscious of Judith, of hands and arms pulling her from Jacob Hannon.

"My Gawd, what have they done?" Judith murmured. "You poor, poor girl. What have they done to you?"

Guffaws, little comments, and digs were passed back and forth between the drunks. They laughed. They giggled. Judith's voice erupted in Su Lin's ears. "You bastards," she screamed. "I'm going to kill you. You worthless . . . "

"Judith. Judith . . ." Hannon's free hand grabbed Judith, the other was on Su Lin's shoulder, pulling her around, moving her away, pushing both women out of the street toward the boardwalk. "Judith, I'll handle this."

His voice was ice cold, a freezing calm. The sound of it, measured. Everything stopped.

No. No. No. Su Lin couldn't stand it. *Oh but, yes. Yes. Yes. Kill them all.* She wanted to scream, to peel the living skin from their faces, to pluck their mocking eyes from their sockets, to stomp them under her heels--forever and ever, until they were absolutely blind and dead.

"Judith . . . get Su Lin off the street," he said. "Now, Judith," he said, his hand steady on her shoulders. "Get her off the street."

The voice. She could barely hear him. Jeers and mocking laughter grew in volume. Su Lin tried to see him, tried to locate the voice, but he was behind her. The pressure on her shoulder increased.

"Judith . . . " he said.

The pressure was gone. Jacob Hannon was gone. He had turned his back, but Judith was with her. She leaned on her and thought she would call him back but the words wouldn't come out; her mouth wouldn't move, her voice was too weak.

Judith started moving, pulling her by the shoulders, taking a step. Su Lin collapsed into the street. Judith dropped to her knees, holding Su Lin like a helpless child, crying, sobbing with her, trying in vain to clean the dirt, dust, and manure from her face, her blouse. "What have they done to you? Oh, what have they done?" she whispered.

Su Lin blinked. Bleary eyed, like seeing through frosted glass in winter, she made out the shadow that was Jacob Hannon. He stood but a few feet away, his back to her, five men before him. Desperately, she wanted him to come to her, to lift her to her feet and take her away from those White men, from this awful place.

Her tormentors, grins painted across their faces, their mouths full of yellow, tobacco stained teeth and mocking lips, were restive. Something tight built up inside Su Lin as she listened and watched, something ugly. The tormentors laughed the deep gut laugh and guffawed, amused at their own cleverness, pleased with their silly words.

"Hot horse turds," they mimicked. "Served sunny face up, cooked in their own gravy . . . you'll like it." Their raucous laughter filled the street, clinging to the store fronts, echoing, returning, echoing again as they relived their exploits, talking the whiskey talk. Su Lin struggled to get up. Judith helped.

"Boys . . ." Jacob Hannon paused.

Su Lin heard a magpie squawking quietly to itself, muttering its complaints to the cottonwood leaves. Her fingers tingled. She felt so cold. She shivered, then began shaking. The odds didn't look good. Jacob Hannon against so many. Suddenly she feared for his life.

"You boys got less sense than God gave a dead mule."

They're going to kill him. He's going to die.

Judith's grip on her shoulders relaxed.

"Easy, Mister," the tall, lean man drawled. "We were just having a little fun with that chink gal. Didn't mean no harm. Thought she'd like to try some hot horse biscuits." His companions laughed then their incessant snickering grew quiet and stopped altogether.

"Too bad she has to remember you boys havin' so much fun . . . seein' your ugly faces. Reckon you boys won't be mindin' me havin' a little fun myself."

"What's that supposed to mean? You're talkin' a little fresh, ain't ya?" The tall, lanky man next to the plaid shirt spoke, his thumb hooked in his belt, raising slightly on the toes of his feet, his head cocked off to the side.

Unconsciously, Su Lin rubbed her eyes as she worked to clear her vision.

"It means I'm goin' to have a little fun with you all. Maybe I'll just gut shoot you, the yellow, hairless dogs you are. You boys surely know better . . . pickin' on a defenseless woman."

"You ain't doin' shit, mister." The tall man was suddenly sober, the laughter lines disappeared, his head no longer cocked off to the side. A tinge of wariness colored his speech.

"That's what I like to hear. An ignorant, yellow sack of green cow shit, tellin' me what I'm doin'. You got yourself a gun, Buster?" Hannon paused. "Use it. Use it before I shove it down your throat. Go on, use it, friend. Show those with you just how big and tough green cowshit is."

"Hellsfire, mister," the man stammered, half laughing, "We was just havin' a little fun with that Chink gal. How's we to know if it'd bother nobody. She's a Chink. No need gettin' yourself all het up."

"Showin' yellow." Hannon flung the words like a club, scoffing. "All this--for fun. Well, just for fun each one of you can tell the lady how sorry you are. Sorry for your mothers' raisin' yellow sacks of green cowshit."

The cowhand turned his head slightly, squinting his eyes at Hannon. "I ain't doin' it. And you better be backin' off, mister. And right now. Back off before you get yourself kilt. We ain't in no mood, you Chink lovin' son of a bitch." The cowhand extended his hand over his pistol butt, his fingers stretching. "This ain't none of your affair," he said. "You ain't got no call insultin' us. Not for no goddamn Chinese chippy."

As if pushed by a wind, or an unseen hand, people ran for cover, disappearing through doorways, into alleys, clearing the street. The man grabbed for his pistol, his long fingers wrapping around the butt. Su Lin tried to cry out, tried to shout, but it happened too fast. Before a word escaped her lips the morning air exploded with pistol fire and the man was shoved violently backwards, knocked flat against the ground, his pistol barely out of the holster. The percussion stung her ears. But the tall man would not stay down.

Su Lin wanted him to; he did not. Disbelief registered on his face; a patch of blood grew on his abdomen. He tried to get up, tried to regain his balance and get his legs back under him. Staring at Jacob Hannon, he struggled for balance, his pistol wavering in his hand.

Another explosion of sound: a small hole appeared magically on the man's forehead. Su Lin grabbed her ears, the percussion sounding loud, tigers roaring in the forests of the night. He collapsed backwards, a dust storm erupting around his body, his head lolling to the side, his eyes open to the morning sun. On his left and right his bewildered companions stared, paralyzed with shock.

Su Lin, too, stared at the body and then at Jacob Hannon. *The man was only trying to . . .* What was wrong with her? *He deserved to be dead . . . he . . .* Su Lin started to cry, clutching her face with her hands.

"Now, boys which one of you yellow bastards is next? Who wants to die this mornin'? Who's tellin' the lady just how sorry you are for bein' a yeller sack of green cow shit?"

The leg of the cooling corpse twitched.

"You." Jacob Hannon pointed the pistol at the abdomen of the plaid shirt. "Tell her or go for your gun."

Glancing toward Su Lin, the man hastily repeated Hannon's words. "Ma'am, I'm right sorry that my ma raised such a yellow sack a shit for a son. I'm right sorry, Ma'am."

Hannon nodded. "You're next," he said.

"I ain't doin' it, mister."

"Then use your gun."

"I ain't doin' that neither. I ain't dyin' today except you're gonna shoot me in the back. I'm ridin' out of here."

"You yellow son of a bitch."

"Maybe," he said. He started walking up the middle of the street.

Jacob Hannon pulled back the hammer but the man didn't stop and he didn't turn around. The plaid shirt didn't move. Neither did the two on his left.

"And you boys?"

"We're leavin'," they said almost in unison.

The leg of the dead man twitched again, warm air rattling in his throat, escaping his chest. The plaid shirt started to walk in a drunken sway, moving cautiously away from Hannon, keeping his hands well away from this gun belt. His two companions followed him. Neither seemed as drunk as they had been. The four reached the hitching rail in front of the bar, milling about as they pulled the reins of five horses off the rail. The plaid shirt mounted. He sat in the middle of his horse staring at Hannon. Someone handed him the reins of a horse. The remaining three mounted. People reappeared, cautiously at first, then in numbers. Turning, the horsemen rode away, moving down the center of the street, their horses breaking into a trot at the edge of town.

Somehow Su Lin knew they'd be back. Trouble never really goes away. Hannon picked up the dead man's pistol, removing it from the man's limp fingers. He flung it down the street. It landed with a plop and slid under the carpet of pale red dust.

From out of nowhere a black streak of alley dog rushed out to smell it, to fetch it, to play the game.

The dog held Su Lin's attention, its dark nose blowing dust as he vigorously searched the street. Suddenly, he stopped, turned his head and looked at Hannon as if to say, "Do you want this thing?"

That dog is the winner today, Su Lin thought. *The dog takes the prize: the black mangy dog, not the dead man, just the dog, standing in the street, whining, wagging its tail.*

Blinking her eyes she sniffled thinking she'd lost her mind. A dark, ugly, foreboding feeling hung heavy in her stomach. She glanced at Jacob Hannon and wondered where Teddy was, whether he was safe.

A short, squat man, wearing a dirty shirt, buttons pulling desperately at the strained cloth, bulled his way through the crowd, past Su Lin, past Judith. A metal star was pinned to his shirt pocket, an item insignificantly small in the great expanse of chest. Without saying a word, he glanced at the corpse and then at Hannon. Finally he spoke, addressing no one in particular.

"What happened here? Who kilt this fellow?"

Hannon answered him, his words clipped and precise. "The cowardly son of a bitch drew on me. I shot him dead."

"Well," the bulky man stated, "there will have to be an inquest."

"Have it."

Looking uneasily at Hannon, he hesitated.

Hannon continued talking, giving the man no time. "Now," he stated emphatically. "Now, would be good."

"What's an inquest?" Su Lin whispered in Judith's ear.

"It's sort of a meeting to see how a man died."

Su Lin watched, listening. *Why would they need such a meeting? The dead one had two bullet holes in him.*

Nonplused, the sheriff turned to the thickening crowd, "Anybody see this shootin'?" No one had; at least no one said anything.

"There was five of them, one of me," Hannon stated succinctly. "This here dead son of a bitch drew his gun. I shot him. That's all you need to know. The other skunks left town, tails tucked between their legs. That's your inquest. Anythin' else?"

"Who are you?"

"Hannon. Jake Hannon."

There was a murmur in the crowd. If the name meant anything to the lawman, he didn't show it. Squinting his eyes, the sheriff stared at Hannon. He pursed his lips, his eyes hanging on the pistol in Hannon's hand. Abruptly, he turned and pushed his way back through the crowd. Just as he had arrived, he disappeared, the crowd closing in behind him.

Four or five men gathered to inspect the cooling body, pointing to the holes in his head and chest, remarking about someone called Bill Hitchcock and another called Earp. The others, the street gawkers, the store keepers, the barber, the Chinese laundry matron, and the cook from the café began to disperse, slowly at first, one, then another, moving away.

When Hannon came to her Su Lin started to cry, sobbing into her stained hands, holding her rent clothing together. The smell of fresh horse dung clung to her hair, face, and arms, to her torn blouse. "Where's Teddy?" she blubbered. No one answered. An utterly useless feeling washed over her.

"I'll find Ted," Jacob Hannon said to her. "Don't you worry. Judith, take Su Lin. Go over to that hotel yonder and get her a bath. She'll need some new clothes."

"Jake, to the hotel? Su Lin . . . she's . . .? They won't even let a gypsy in there. Don't tell me you ain't been here before?"

Hannon looked at Judith, and at Su Lin, and waited.

"She's Chinese, Jake. She's Chinese. Why do you think this happened? Do you think those . . . those men would do that to a white woman? They'd all be dead if they tried. Every man."

Finally, he nodded, the stare softening as his eyes rested on Su Lin. Squinting against the sun, he looked down the street. Methodically, he hefted his pistol and flipped open the magazine with his thumb. Spent cartridges fell into the dust and were replaced. He snapped the cylinder shut and turned his attention to Judith.

"Judith, go tell the son of a bitch that runs the place, if he ain't got any hot water for this girl, I'm comin' over there and I'm burnin' the place to the ground! Tell him that."

Hannon seated the revolver lightly in its holster, deliberately not hooking the leather thong that normally rested over the trigger. Su Lin's eyes locked on Jacob Hannon. There was something irrational about him . . . even a little crazy. He was hot. She could feel it. It occurred to her that he meant exactly what he had said--that he'd burn the place down. But what good would that do just because they had no hot water . . . because . . . ? Then she realized, then she understood. It was because she was Chinese and because . . . Now that made no sense. Nothing made sense. *Just what was evil here? Who was the dragon down from the mountains? Who was the tiger that came for children in the night?*

Agitated, Judith responded to his directive. "Jake Hannon, I know you're angry," she said. "I know it. I'll tell him. I will. Damn you." She paused. "Don't you go using that tone of voice on me. I ain't no slave." Judith stopped, regaining her composure. "Besides burning the hotel, is there anything else we can do announcing us all being here? Shall we build ourselves a little sign?"

Hannon smiled. A second later that, too, was gone and the man who had handed Su Lin a plate of beans two weeks ago returned. It was as if nothing had happened, as if everything was good in the world. Killing the drunk? What drunk? Never happened.

"I apologize. Forgot myself. Judith, if you'd be so kind, get Susie here a nice hot bath . . . and a shirt or somethin'. I reckon she's due for a change. I'll go look for Ted."

Then he spoke to Su Lin. "I'm awful sorry, Susie girl. Really I am. If I'd . . . I should a know'd . . ." Jacob Hannon paused as if he were struggling to find the right words. "Judith'll help you get yourself cleaned up, squared away. Get you some clean clothes." The words trailed off again and Jacob Hannon stood looking at her.

"Judith . . .?" he said.

"All right," Judith said. "All right. You find Teddy. I'll take care of Su Lin." Dismissing him with the shake of her head, Judith turned Su Lin away holding her by the arm, her other hand around her waist, and walked her toward the hotel.

Turning her head, Su Lin looked back and caught a glimpse of Jacob Hannon as he stood in the street, seeming so lost, so abandoned, so all alone. So like her. What was wrong with her mind? He wasn't lost. He wasn't alone. He'd never been alone a day in his life. He had himself. No. No. For him alone was good, very good. The very fabric of being alone was part of him.

For a moment she wanted to rush back to him, hold him tightly in her arms, tell him that everything would be all right, that somehow everything would work out . . . tell him that the black alley dog wasn't the only winner.

No. No. No. Her head was mixed up. She was mixed up. She'd pull herself together. She'd wash herself; she'd change her clothes, rest a while. She felt so tired and drained, she could hardly lift a foot. *No shoes.* She had no shoes on her feet. *No.* She was leaving. She was getting out of here. She was getting just as far away from Piedmont, Nevada as she could get and just as quickly as possible.

CHAPTER EIGHTEEN

The walk to the hotel helped. Each step seemed to clear her head, but not her eyes and not her mouth. She repeatedly spat dust and blood. The hotel loomed large, a rectangular, two story building with windows that faced the street. Soon they were in the shadows of the upper story. Climbing the steps, they walked past glass windows that reflected the street, her disheveled appearance, and Judith's passive face. She really didn't want to be here. Together they stepped to the door. *Judith, let's just get out of here,* she thought. *I don't know if I can stand anymore. Tell her.*

One step and they were inside. From the open doorway, she heard a magpie squawking and muttering to itself. What she wanted was to go back to the creek, back to their camp, and clean up, to get the manure smell from her clothing, out of her hair. How pleasant it would be just to take a deep breath and forget the round, bearded faces, the smell of whiskey breath, the laughter, the dead man, his body twitching in the sun-baked street.

But Judith drew her across the foyer, past the chairs in the waiting room, through the shadows of the dark lobby, the echo of Judith's boots striking the hardwood floor in her ears. From behind a varnished counter a clerk looked up from a book with a smile that quickly vanished. A lattice work of pigeon holes, most with key fobs hanging out, and the large face of a clock occupied the wall behind him. The large hand pointed at the three, while the small hand clung resolutely to the nine.

"We would like a room with a tub," Judith announced to the skinny, drawn up, little man. Her voice was a little shrill, pointed, and tinged with a distinct lack of patience.

From behind the wire frames of a pair of spectacles, the clerk looked from Judith to Su Lin and back to Judith. He snorted, not impressed by her demeanor, clearly not inclined to be of any service. His spitting on the floor behind the counter made that absolutely clear. "There ain't no rooms here for the likes of you." Condescension coated his voice. He smacked his lips, words falling off his tongue. "Ma'am, it's the policy of this here hotel not ta rent ta no Chinks, no Injins, no Irish, no Niggers, and no Gypsies. There ain't no rooms and there ain't no exceptions and that includes you. So you all get yourselves out the way you got in--and now!" He spat again. "This here conversation, it is closed."

Su Lin turned to leave but Judith stopped her. *Oh, no,* she thought.

Judith cleared her throat. Nodding, she smiled ever so daintily, innocently blinking her eyes as she spoke. "Sir, Mr. Jake Hannon asked me to tell you that if'n you ain't gots a room, with a tub and buckets and buckets of hot water and he does mean hot, he's coming right over here and he's going to burn this here place to the ground. Now, Sir," Judith paused, leaning forward, still smiling but no longer blinking her eyes, "Do you gots a room or am I smelling smoke?"

The skinny clerk snorted and wiped his nose. Anger, disgust, and bigotry registered on his face. He locked his eyes on Judith, looking at her as though she had some disease and was an insect to be stomped. Taking his time, he spat into an unseen spittoon, gathering himself like a plucked rooster. "You little Gypsy hussy," he hissed. "You turn yourself around and you get your bustle out of here and right now. Take this stinkin' Chinese chippy with you." His voice rose. "Do it before I forget my manners. And I ain't tellin' you twice, lady. Jake Hannon, good . . ." He shook his head. "What kind of fool do you take me for? The man's dead, lady. Now get out of here." His lips smacked together full of satisfaction.

Behind her another voice interrupted the conversation. Su Lin turned to see yet another man. "If this fellow Hannon's dead . . . if he ain't showing up, I'll burn the `damn' place down for him."

The voice came from a tall man, wearing worn range clothes, packing a saddle in one hand and a Winchester carbine in the other. A wide brimmed hat shaded half his face. The rifle came up; the man's thumb drew the hammer back; the metallic click sounded in the room. The barrel was pointing at a lamp well full of oil, wick up, flickering dimly in the now silent room.

Su Lin saw only the rifle, felt her heart thudding deep in her chest.

The voice said, "You know better, Charlie. Talking to ladies like that. Now get them a room or I'm accidently going to put a round through the well of that oil lamp."

The hotel clerk swallowed. His Adam's apple bobbed nervously. "Ben, I didn't know these . . . I didn't know they was with you. I didn't." He hesitated. "But, Ben, they don't look like no ladies to me."

"They ain't with me, Charlie. They's just women needing a place to sleep, and a bath," he said. "So get them fixed up, Charlie. Don't you let me be asking again. There ain't no rules against ladies . . . not that I know. You sure as hell better not be inventing such a rule."

For the space of a heartbeat the clerk was silent.

"And they'll be wantin' a good room," he added. "They don't want no ticky mattress."

The clerk hurriedly pushed the registry book across the counter toward Judith. Su Lin noted that the rifle barrel never wavered, that Ben never smiled. There were no whiskers on his face, not like Jacob Hannon.

Judith stared at him. "I thank you," she stated, then glanced back at the clerk.

Pulling the register toward her, she took the pencil, and carefully formed an "X" in the space and line allotted, then handed the instrument to Su Lin who carefully placed three Chinese characters next to Judith's "X". Finished she set the pencil down and noticed the green stain of horse manure on the back of her hand.

The clerk paid no attention. His face full of apprehension, he stood behind the counter and said nothing, smacking his lips, a small trickle of tobacco juice leaking from the corner of his mouth.

"Our room?" Judith said to him.

"Down the hall, to your left," he answered.

"Bath water?"

"I'll have hot water down there. Right soon." The voice trailed off; the smacking lips grew silent.

"I wish to leave a message," Judith said. "In a short while, Jake Hannon will come by. Please give him my most sorrowful regrets over his untimely death. I did so want to attend the services–to pay my respects. Be so kind, would you? Give him that message?"

"Jake Hannon?"

"Yes."

The clerk stared at her.

Judith took Su Lin by the arm and they proceeded toward the hallway. Su Lin glanced back at the clerk. What had Judith meant? *Jacob Hannon's services? Pay respects?*

Behind her, the clerk had regained control of his voice. She heard the click of a hammer eased down, the sound of a rifle laid on a counter, a cleared throat, the ticking of a clock. "Damn your worthless soul, Ben."

"Easy, Charlie. Just saved your worthless hide. Hannon ain't so dead. He just shot a fellow full of holes down the street. Where you been? You need to get out more."

"You're just sayin' that to scare the shit outta of me."

"No, Charlie, I ain't just saying it. Besides that's a piss poor way to treat fine-looking women. We sure as hell ain't got enough of them and you running them off like that. Someone ought to put you outta of my misery."

"Oh, shut it off. I don't want to hear it no more."

"Take it easy, Charlie. I just kept that Hannon fellow from burning down this here wreck. Keeping you working. I get my usual room?"

"I shouldn't."

"Yeah, you should. You know what's good for you."

"Ain't you with them?" the clerk asked.

"No, I ain't. You know better. Wish I was but I ain't with nobody."

"Well, who's gonna pay for them?"

"How the hell do I know, Charlie? You rent the rooms around here, not me."

CHAPTER NINETEEN

Su Lin's second morning in Piedmont, Nevada for the second time came very early. It started with a loud bang on the door. Afterwards everyone was awake, even if they didn't want to be. Jacob Hannon spoke loudly in the hallway telling everyone in the building that he'd be waiting outside. Moments later Su Lin emerged completely awake, leaving Judith and Teddy to pull themselves together. She hurried down the hall and through the foyer. Outside she found their horses packed, saddled, and waiting. Out on the porch resting in a large chair just where he said he'd be was Jacob Hannon. He sat talking to two old, old men, appearing not to have a care in the world, leaning back in his chair. *How does he do that?*

"Mornin'," he said to her. "Hungry? Why don't you get Ted and Judith and get down to that café and get a bite?" It wasn't a question as much as an instruction.

Su Lin looked at him hesitating, wondering if she dared.

"Don't worry. You'll be fine. There ain't a mother's son livin' that won't just be dyin' to make sure you're treated like the Queen of England, herself." He pushed his hat back on his head, reached in his pocket, and handed her a gold coin. "Here," he said. The coin was a dull yellow lying in the palm of her hand.

Judith and Teddy appeared in the doorway and looked from Su Lin to Jacob Hannon.

"He says we should eat first. Before we go."

Judith stared at Hannon.

"Go ahead," he said. "No one will bother you."

All three were a little hesitant.

"Go ahead. I'll be right there, you have any problems."

Jacob Hannon was correct. No one gave either woman more than a glance. The same man took their breakfast order. It was the same fare only not as good. All three had had enough of Piedmont, Nevada. Once finished, they returned to the front steps of the hotel and their horses.

Jacob Hannon was still on the porch with the old men. They sat in their unwashed clothes, their uncombed hair, tobacco juice on their shirts. They talked about Easterners "buyin'" land and "throwin' their weight around." Su Lin tried to follow the conversation and got hung up on "Easterners" and "throwin' weight." *If you go far enough east everyone becomes an easterner*, she thought. *Maybe Chinese people were buying land.* But "throwin' their weight around" puzzled her. The grizzled old men, with hoary white, tobacco stained beards, spoke about the land east and the land west, the Coulee and the country beyond the mesa. Hannon listened, asking questions as they talked.

It was still early morning when they rode out of Piedmont, Nevada: a man, two women, and a boy. They led four pack horses and a long-eared mule. Main

Street took them outside of town and past the stone and wooden markers of the cemetery. Beyond lay a rugged raw land, broken up with bare mountains, distant peaks--and another desert. Seeing it, Su Lin rechecked her canteens making sure they were full.

Several men stood amid the markers, looking into an open grave. Nearby, a new coffin, made of fresh-cut pine wood, lay in the back of a buckboard. Two horses stood in harness. The grave looked deep. She could hardly see the hat on the head of the man who threw dirt from the hole. It suddenly occurred to her that they were burying the drunk, the cowboy--the dead one, the one Jacob Hannon had killed. Su Lin did not look again.

CHAPTER TWENTY

The first day after leaving Piedmont was uneventful. Night passed. The second day disappeared. Evening clung like a dark cloak to branch and thistle, hiding the long-eared jack rabbit, the lynx cat, and the hunting coyote that slinks through the underbrush. In that dwindling twilight of the second day Jacob Hannon announced, "We're close," and nudged his sorrel horse forward. Su Lin knew what "we're close" meant. It meant they kept riding, riding by starlight, riding past midnight, riding after Orion had settled in the tops of mountains behind them and the big dipper had rotated, following its short path around the North star.

Somewhere in the night the gods of mercy found them and Jacob Hannon stopped. Without warning he dismounted next to a clump of sagebrush that stood as high as the shoulders on his saddle. There was no moon, not even the promise of a new day, just starlight and the aching song of crickets. Su Lin followed his example and slid out of the saddle. She stood numbly in the dark by her horse, feeling the heat from its body. Seeing Jacob Hannon releasing the cinch strap on his horse she loosened the cinch strap on hers. That's how she knew they were stopping.

In the middle of this mechanical ritual he appeared at her side. "Shuck the saddles and stake them horses out," he said. "There's grass yonder. This is as far as we go." Having said that, he disappeared into the dark shadows that surrounded them, the silhouette of his hat a vague momentary impression against the starry sky.

She did as he asked and stripped the other horses as well as the mule of saddles and packs. Judith helped. Thirty minutes later Judith and Teddy laid themselves down amidst the equipment and were fast asleep, lost in their blankets. But there was no sleep in Su Lin. Instead she sat, leaning back against her saddle, Hank's old Remington rifle across her knees, and waited for Jacob Hannon. Nearby she heard a rat scurry through dry leaves; a small stick cracked and popped. She jumped, holding the rifle tight in her white, bloodless fingers. Her mind conjured up visions of tigers slinking through the sage brush on padded feet, the smell of death on their breath, the rush of the black wind in their nostrils.

Anxiously, she glanced at the heavy rifle. What good was it? She didn't even know if it was loaded, or how to use it. *I'll beat them to death with it. Club whatever it is until they can't move.*

In the middle of these thoughts the wraithlike Jacob Hannon returned. His hand touched her shoulder and her heart caught in her throat. She could hardly breathe.

"You all right?"

"Yes," she whispered. "All right. You frightened me a little."

He waited. "What's wrong?"

"Nothing. Bad feelings. I have bad feelings."

"Yeah, well, I got them, too."

"You do? You have bad feelings?"

"I got the jitters. Can't shake them. Get some sleep. Hard tellin' what tomorrow will bring."

He walked away from her, heading toward the horses. Drugged from fatigue, Su Lin wished she were asleep. Instead she followed him, stopping to remove dried venison, and some hardtack from one of the packs. By the time she caught up, he had already checked the horse's tethers and hobbled the Appaloosa, testing the stakes on the others. She could see the white of his teeth, his eyes. She could smell the fresh sage scent in his clothes.

Handing him some dried jerky, she said, "Here. Take this. Eat."

"Thank you," he said, taking the jerky, rolling the hard, salty meat in his mouth.

The cool snap in the night air chilled her.

"Just jumpy," he confessed, taking a deep breath. "A little on the edge."

"Jacob Hannon," she said, "you sleep. I watch. You lie down. You rest."

For a moment he looked at her, then turned his head and stared into the darkness, listening. There was a hoot owl, coyotes, night birds, crickets, frogs: all ordinary sounds, nothing unusual, nothing out of place. For an instant it seemed that time stood still and held its breath. She was more aware of this man than of any other person or creature she had ever encountered in her life. He nodded. His arm encircled her about the shoulders, he hugged her, gave her a pat on the arm. An electric shock raced through her body.

She couldn't think.

"Susie girl, you're all right," he said. "I'll do just that. You take first watch. Wake me if you hear anythn' . Don't hesitate . . . you understand? Wake me in a couple of hours, no matter what. You need sleep yourself. Do you hear me, girl?"

"I hear."

"Good."

He paused. "I meant, 'do you understand me.'"

"I do."

He released her. His hand was on the small of her back as they walked back to where Judith and Teddy slept. Su Lin couldn't talk. She couldn't breathe. He stopped. *What is wrong with me?*

"You all right?" he asked.

"Yes . . . yes. I think so."

"You think so?" She heard worry in his voice.

"Yes. I am well."

"All right. But wake me if anythn' , and I mean anythn' , happens. Anythn' at all." He paused, looking at her. "You damn well better be well. You ain't tellin' me no stories are you?"

"Stories? I do not know any stories. No tell stories."

"All right," he said. "Two hours. You wake me."

"All right," she answered. But her voice--it didn't sound all right, not even to her. As if by magic they were standing by the packs and saddles, his hand no longer touching the small of her back. He reached for his bed roll and Su Lin picked up the Remington rifle, cradling it in her arms. By the glow of starlight she made her way to the edge of camp knowing his eyes followed her.

Unspeakably tired, yet very much awake, exhausted, yet absolutely sleepless, she found a large rock and wedged herself down between it and a dead tree stump. From her perch she could see the outline of dark trees that seemed to follow a creek. Beyond that a monolithic mountain rose violently against the eastern sky. The frogs and crickets sang their ceaseless, aching song. Far away a nest of hoot owls spoke into the night, a lost and lonely sound. Younger Brother was probably asleep in the room next to Oldest Uncle's. She imagined he had finished his studies, helped wash dishes, had cleared tables--maybe he even wound the clock. What would he think if he could see her now, a rifle cradled snugly in her arms, listening to the night? Even if she didn't know how to use it.

The stars shifted slowly. A partial moon made a ghostly specter of the bluffs and mountain on the east. Several times Su Lin found a new place to sit. She listened, watched, and waited. Three head of deer walked across the clearing; their large ears twitched back and forth as they sniffed the air.

Fatigue made her bones and muscles ache; her mind felt flat as a rock. She caught herself nodding off. She got up and walked, the night air cool and fresh on her skin, at times cold. She could tell it had rained nearby. Goose bumps crawled up her arms like a mad rush of angry ants. She again reinserted herself between rock and tree stump, holding the rifle close to her bosom.

She dozed. For a moment she thought of the White man's clock on Oldest Uncle's wall, the broken minute hand that dangled, the hour hand that slowly moved. Vaguely she was aware that it was becoming morning, of a small dim line of light in the east. Before she realized it, sunlight had crept down the slopes of the west mountains, casting a yellow light on canyon and draw.

Below her in the cottonwood trees was a spring and beyond that, sitting in a clearing on a gentle slope, she saw a collection of buildings: a house, corrals behind the house a hundred yards, a barn. Staring at the scene, she waited, more asleep than awake. A steady, warm sunlight fell on her face, warming the skin on her neck. Stillness borne of early morning seeped into her soul along with the forgetfulness of rest.

Jacob Hannon appeared beside her, setting his long frame on the rock where she kept watch. "You didn't wake me."

"No. I am sorry," she said, blinking her eyes, sitting up. Stretching her arms, she tried to get the blood pumping and fresh air in her lungs.

"That's good. I was tired, needed to sleep. You sleep well?" He was smiling at her.

"I did not think there was danger," Su Lin said. I did not mean to . . . "

"You didn't? And it don't matter if you did."

Hannon studied the house, the pole corrals, the horses standing behind the pole fence basking in the sunlight, and the trees that followed the creek.

"No? I . . . well the birds, they chirp in the cottonwood trees. Two deer walk across the clearing waving their ears. The horses in the corral, they stand, looking at nothing in particular. Smoke raises from the house chimney. A woman, she came out, waved her towel, looked at the morning, standing with her hands on her hips. She went back inside. Nothing moves quickly. Nothing. I see no danger."

Jacob Hannon nodded. "I see," he said.

"Do you think expecting trouble keeps us from feeling peace? Last night I felt evil was everywhere, waiting. Waiting for something to grab me, to reach out from the dark. Today, sitting in the sunlight, a new day . . . it is nothing. The world is at peace. Trouble seems far away."

Jacob Hannon sat beside her without moving. He said, "I reckon expectin' trouble keeps us from bein' surprised by it." He paused, pulling the brim of his hat down over his eyes. "Trouble . . . that sort of thinkin' colors my thoughts. Sometimes that's all I see. That what you mean?"

Su Lin nodded, looking at the man sitting beside her. "Should we go down there?" she said. "Where the woman waves her towel? I would really like to remember something different, Jacob Hannon, something good, something not covered in blood."

They were joined by Teddy. Behind him came Judith, rubbing the sleep from her eyes.

"Just in time," Hannon said, "We're 'bout ready to find some peace, if there is any to be found." He turned his attention back to Su Lin. "Well, girl, let's go have a look. Maybe we'll find somethin' good, somethin' not covered in blood." He hesitated. "Remember, Su Lin, good never lasts and trouble never stops comin'. Never. If we find somethin' good, peaceful, we best hang onto it. It sure as hell ain't lastin' long."

"What are you talking about, Jake?" Judith asked.

Su Lin pushed herself to her feet. "Ok," she said, thinking it ironic. *Trouble, anger, revenge, always chasing peace, keeping it at bay. Why not invite peace in? Why not bask in it, ignore its opposite? Couldn't it happen*? Jacob Hannon thought it a counterfeit of reality: not to be believed, to be distrusted, perhaps feared for its illusion. *Distrust peace? What about that?*

"Ok, what?" Judith said but no one answered her question.

Together the four walked down the hill across the flat, with Teddy scurrying, bringing up the rear. Su Lin listened and watched, taking comfort in the Remington she cradled in her arms, the man walking at her side, a gun stuck in his waistband, a pistol belt girded about his waist, a Winchester in his hand. She savored the warm, delightful sunlight on her face. *We sure don't look peaceful. We look like we expect a war.*

Jacob Hannon did not knock. He walked through the open door without hesitation. Su Lin followed behind Judith. The inside of the building was large, dark, surprisingly cool, and so spacious that Su Lin wanted to stop a moment just to feel the way it felt.

In the center of the room a baby was playing, holding onto a chair as he circled it on wobbly legs, babbling to himself. The woman was busy, bent over the wood cook stove, stirring up the coals, removing clinkers, her back to them. The baby looked up, immediately stuck out his lower lip, and began to whimper. Within seconds he was crying.

The woman turned to see what was causing the disturbance. Seeing Jake she screamed. Her hands went to her chest, to her face; her eyes watered. She launched herself across the room, yelling, "Papa, Papa, Papa." She threw her arms around Jake's neck, standing tiptoe, leaning against him, sobbing into his shirt. He picked her up, hugging her, turning a full circle with her in his arms, the woman joyfully crying. Even Jake was smiling.

Perhaps this was peace. Su Lin hoped so. It felt so good.

Even with the baby crying, the woman refused to release her grip around Jake's neck. There was no reticence. Jacob Hannon drank it all in, winking at Su Lin from over the woman's head, enjoying his daughter's reception.

Perhaps his happiness was from standing in his kitchen in his house, Su Lin thought.

The baby stood on unsteady legs, leaning against the chair and looking up at the adults' embrace, sobbing.

"Sis," Hannon said, "you'd best be lookin' after that little howler. He ain't lookin' all that happy."

The woman turned in Jake's arms to look at the baby. "Papa," she said, "this is Henry. He's your grandson. Isn't he beautiful? So pretty."

"Well, I'll be damned," Jake said, releasing the woman to pick up the baby. Little Henry stopped crying, staring suspiciously at this new person whose face was darkened with three days' growth of beard and a hat so big it seemed to shelter the baby under its brim.

Hannon was amused. "Well, Henry," he said, "let's you and I take a look at those critters standin' in the corral, give them a bite to eat. We'll get ourselves acquainted and see just what's what." Hannon walked out of the kitchen through the front door, talking to the baby. The baby wasn't too sure, not knowing whether to cry or laugh.

The daughter looked from her father to the two women. "Judith," she cried. The two women hugged, patting each other on the back. "It is so good to see you. It's been so long"

Awkwardly, Su Lin stood in the kitchen doorway looking at the room. It was big. Against the far wall was a black kitchen stove. Between the stove and the doorway was a long table that could seat upwards of sixteen people. Cupboards and counter tops extended from the stove in both directions. Blackened pots and pans hung on hooks just under the cupboards. A huge rock fireplace dominated the entire wall adjacent to the stove and cupboards. The immensity of the room caused her to wonder where the maids were. And the slave girls?

Judith hugged the woman, saying, "Gin, Gin, Gin," over and over again.

Su Lin gazed at the cooking stove, the black chimney rising through the ceiling, noting there were no cobwebs collecting dust hanging from the rafters. The women's embrace broke and the stranger's gaze fell on Su Lin and Teddy.

"Who's that?" she asked Judith.

"Excuse my manners. I'm Virginia. Nobody calls me that, but that's who I am."

Judith laughed. "Gin," turning to Su Lin, "this is Su Lin. And Teddy. 'Course you know that. But he's grown since last time you saw him. And Su Lin, this is Virginia. Jake's big little girl."

The woman's eyes rested on Su Lin.

"Does . . . does Henrik have a new wife? Where is he?"

"Papa? No, Gin. This here ain't no mother of mine. I guess you could say she's yours."

Virginia blinked her eyes.

"What? Papa? Papa . . . he's married? She's so young!"

"Sort of. You see, Su Lin's Uncle thought Jake was a little lonely so he gave her to Jake. Figured he needed a wife. And here she is! Your new mother."

"Papa's got a wife?"

"Sort of," Judith said.

"Sort of? How do you get sort of married?" Virginia looked over at Su Lin. "I'm so sorry," she said. "I apologize for talking like you were not in the room. My manners are terrible. As I said, I'm Virginia. You are most welcome. I am just so surprised. Papa getting married! I hardly know what to say."

Judith smiled suddenly very serious, her voice low and confidential. "Virginia, I didn't want to tell you, not so soon, you being surprised by us barging in like we owned this place. But you asked and I ain't lying to you. You see, Jake . . . well, Jake . . . he ain't married before God or nothing like that,'cause. . . well, the preacher said something nasty about him marrying and Jake . . . being a little drunk and all . . . well, he shot the Preacher dead. Put a round right betwixt and between the lookers, he did."

Virginia was shaking her head, listening.

Judith continued. "I'm sorry but all your little brothers and your little sisters are going to be rotten little bastards and Jake . . . he's going to hell. That's the good news."

Judith's face suddenly brightened. "Now girl, tell us about you. Such a pretty baby. Where's Joe? And what's burnin' on the cookin' stove?"

Virginia didn't move. She just stared at Judith, starting to smile.

"Oh, Judith, I'm having a morning," she said. "How could you say those things?"

"'Cause they are true . . . 'cause I just couldn't lie. I swear, I couldn't," Judith replied. "You just asked. I swear, this is the latest Mrs. Jake Hannon." She grinned at Su Lin. "Ain't she a looker"? Judith paused, looked at Virginia then the stove. "Ah, sister, I think you're burnin' the biscuits."

"Oh my . . . " Virginia ran to the stove. She moved pans and potatoes, flipped pancakes. After she finished she turned to Judith.

"All right," she said, "get some plates. Sit down. I need to get more butter and side pork. I wasn't expecting company. And I need to know the real truth."

"And lizards love snow," Judith said, smiling at her. "You'll have to ask your Papa. Where's Joe? Where's everybody?"

Virginia's face clouded up. "That's a long story," she said. "It's not so happy."

Jacob Hannon appeared in the doorway, the baby in his arms. Henry squealed as he tickled him, waving his arms and legs, creating an armful of commotion.

"Susie, this here is Henry. As you can see, he's all about peace." He looked from Virginia to Judith then back to Su Lin. "Hold him, would you? I'll see to what's burnin' on the stove."

"Oh . . . " Virginia exclaimed again, turning back to the pancakes and side pork.

Su Lin took the baby from Hannon's arms, not sure what to do with him. She ending up setting him on the floor. He wasn't too excited at being held by yet another new person. Hannon went to the stove where Virginia was standing.

"Papa?" she said to him. "I can do it. I am just so excited."

Hannon turned to his daughter, a pancake rolled up in his hand.

"Besides," Virginia said, "you haven't introduced me to your new wife."

"What?"

"Introductions? You know. Your wife?"

"My wife?" Jacob Hannon looked at Judith. A wry smile held the edges of her lips.

Judith said to him, "I just told how Su Lin's uncle gave you a wife. I was explaining that to your lovely daughter."

"Well, thanks, Judith," he drawled.

"Oh, you're very welcome, Jake."

"Let's eat," Hannon said. "Pancakes anyone? Side pork? Teddy, help set the table. These ladies are catchn' up on gossip." He glanced at Judith, then at Virginia, shaking his head.

"Papa? Tell me."

"Oh, I'll tell you but let's eat. Where is everyone? Where's Joe?"

"He ain't here, Papa. He's gone."

"Slick?"

"Joe fired him, Papa. He ain't been here for months. Joe's angry at me and little Henry. He won't even pick him up when he's crying. He don't stick around much."

Hannon glanced at Su Lin. She smiled knowingly at him, he at her. "Right peaceful around here. Let's eat," he said. "Where's Slick? I'll be needin' to hire him. He still around? He gone far?"

"Last I saw, he was heading for Clearwater and pretty mad. It's been six months, Papa. Everyone thought you were . . . not coming back. That you were dead somewheres."

CHAPTER TWENTY-ONE

Su Lin was surprised. The house was actually made of mud and straw. Who would have known that? Teddy told her. The mud and straw were hidden behind smooth, white plaster walls, inside and out; it had something to do with lime. The roof consisted of logs that extended from one end of each room to the other, overlaid with rough, hewn cut lumber, overlaid again with large tile shingles.

Teddy called it adobe. It was marvelous. In the heat of day it was cool inside. There were regular rectangular slits in the walls, maybe four inches wide and eight inches tall. These rectangular holes in the exterior walls could be closed by inserting an adobe brick. As windows they seemed extra small to Su Lin, something for her to wonder about.

The inside opened up on an expansive courtyard with inside trees. The courtyard walls of the adobe had windows and larger openings for doorways but no doors. The smoke stained ceilings and the lack of sunlight made it dark, particularly in the kitchen. A fifteen foot wide porch encircled the adobe's exterior. Except in the very early mornings or late evenings sunlight never touched the exterior walls. The roof of the house extended a few feet over the courtyard's interior, shading the inner courtyard walls. Virginia had planted a garden. Plants, trees, flower boxes and several large cactus grew inside the interior walls.

After breakfast Su Lin helped Judith and Teddy retrieve their horses and packs. That morning the house was filled with laughter. Everyone ate dinner and supper at the kitchen table. There was no lack of talk. Jake did get to the questions Virginia didn't want asked. He did it after supper. He did it while Su Lin watched him as she cleared the table and Judith washed the dishes. It started innocently enough. He asked how long she'd been alone.

Virginia answered him without meeting his eyes. "It must be ten days."

"Good . . . Good Gawd," he said. "You alone that long!"

"Papa, it ain't like it's the first time or nothin'."

"No? There shouldn't ever have been a 'first' time. Or any time."

"No. Sometimes Joe's gone days, weeks. He don't like stayin' around, like I said."

"And no one was here?"

"No one. He let everyone go. I suspect he don't like ranchin'. He don't like cows."

"He don't like cows in cow country? Where is he?"

"I don't know. Town, I guess. I ain't been followin' him, Papa. Maybe he went to their home. He's got a mother and a father, you know. Maybe he went home."

"That's clear up in the foothills. I'm surprised they'd have him!"

Virginia looked directly at her father. "Papa, it's been hell around here. That's why I wrote you like I did. I needed help bad."

"You wrote me?"

"Yes. Didn't you get my letters?"

Jacob Hannon ignored her question. Virginia started crying, tears running down her face. The room got quiet. In the midmorning heat, with cows bawling in the fields below the house, Su Lin drying knifes and forks, and Judith washing plates, peace did seem a liar, a counterfeit. Jacob Hannon held his daughter in his arms and patted her on the shoulders, his face drawn and unpleasant, colored by dark words, dark thoughts. For a moment nothing was heard beyond Virginia's sobs and little Henry's babbling on the tile floor.

"Papa? Papa, promise me. Please don't . . . "

Jacob Hannon's soothing horse voice interrupted her. "Virginia, now don't you go frettin'. Don't you be worryin' yourself about nothin' except little Henry. You see to this baby. He's a sight. Little Henry? Now that's a damn good name. Name him after Hank?"

She nodded.

"I'm sure glad for that. He'd be right proud. Lost Hank, you know. He'd be right proud of that boy. That's a fine name."

"Papa . . . ?"

"Now, Gin, don't you go frettin' none. I'll see to this problem. Do like I told you. You hear me, girl?"

"We lost Hank?"

"We did. Let's not talk about it now. We've had enough grief. I'm goin' to have a look around," he said standing up. Then he was gone. He left the kitchen, walked out through the entryway past Judith who was holding the baby, and through the outside doorway.

Come evening Su Lin left the adobe to see if she could see him but there was no sign of Jacob Hannon. If he was about, he was swallowed up in the long shadows of dusk, concealed by the growing darkness that enshrouded the mountainside and the far reaches of the Coulee.

Virginia found a place for everyone to sleep: a room for Judith, two blankets, a pillow: the bunkhouse for Teddy: and a room with a four-poster bed for Su Lin. There were blankets, feather pillows, mattresses, and springs that didn't squeak. Su Lin's room was large. Multicolored rag rugs covered the tile floor. There were no windows in the thick, smooth walls. A doorway arch opened onto the court yard. No door.

Jacob Hannon still hadn't returned.

Su Lin, worried about where he might be, couldn't sleep. Her restlessness could have been caused by a dozen things. The room was too hot, too confining, too stuffy, the bed too soft, the floor too hard, the adobe too quiet. Finally she got up and walked outside under the starry night, listening to the aching sound of crickets and a host of frogs that lived in the creek. A dry breeze cooled her skin. She felt very much alive and very tired. She filled her lungs with fresh air and breathed out.

Standing by the tongue of an empty wagon, she watched lightning flash from a thunder head too far away to hear the roll of thunder. She listened to the quiet hooting of owls, the swift, silent keening of the hunted and the hunter, the coyote, and the baby-like scream of a rabbit caught and dying.

She smelled grass drying in the hay meadows, the sage and juniper from the hills, and the fresh washed smell of rain cleansed air, remnants of a cloudburst beyond the far mountains.

Lightning continued to dance along a dark unseen ridge--flashing brilliant against the underbelly of a thunder head that marched resolutely up the valley toward her. This wasn't a time to be inside, but it was a time to be alive, to be outside the adobe, to be part of the life around her and feel its sweetness. A cloud drifted overhead, casting its shadow from the hard pack yard to the cottonwood trees and the Big Spring.

She returned to the room that Virginia had given her and removed her blankets, gathering them in her arms. Outside she made a bed on the floorboards of the empty wagon box. Before crawling under her blanket she leaned against the sideboards of the wagon, wrapped her arms around her knees, feeling the evening breeze cool on her face.

The far away thunder head rumbled a deep-throated growl. *Must be closer now,* she thought. A light breeze brought the fresh smell of rain. Su Lin laid down pulling the blanket over her. Stars twinkled against the dark velvet sky, a sparkling jeweled belt strung across the length and breadth of the heavens. During the night she thought she heard Jacob Hannon return. It was such a small noise, so small she paid it no attention. She slept.

A face loomed dark above her. She was asleep. She knew she was asleep. But he . . . it . . . was so real, so ugly and twisted, a gargoyle face full of wrinkles. A sticky wetness dripped from its beard and fell onto her skin. She heard a scream, followed by a shout. A warning gong sounded. The air was alive with the sound of running feet. In the cacophony of sound she heard her father's warning voice. It filled her mind, her ears. Her father? What was he doing--in Nevada? Or was it Arizona? Where was she?

"Run, Su Lin, run!" he shouted. "Be quick. Run for your life!"

No. No, this couldn't be Father. It was her father's voice. He yelled at her, "Run, run, run." The urgency choked his words. Where? She wanted to run to him and throw her arms around his neck. What was he doing here? Where was he? She looked. She could hear his voice, but . . .

"Run, run, run," he screamed again.

Su Lin ran. Springing from her bedding, leaving the mat, her sandals, her clothing, leaving everything, she ran. Through the garden she fled, past the lamps and the statues that adorned the fountains and marked the well. Su Lin ran, pulling the darkness with her, pulling the stars from the night skies.

Behind her the face, beard wet and silver gray, chased after her. His outstretched hands reached, his voice shrieked; he laughed an ungodly wail. Inside Su Lin's exploding chest her lungs screamed for air. Her fatigued heart thundered but she ran stumbling in the dark, moving, then hardly moving, lost. She was lost. All was lost. Lost. Lost.

"Run, Su Lin, run."

"Father?"

Where? How? This wasn't right. It wasn't logical. She ran past him but Father did not look at her. Instead he focused on the man, the beast that chased after her. In his hands he clutched the mighty war blade of the House of Kou. Its steel gleamed cold in the dark, so bright it took on a light and life of its own. It sang the song of war, the song of death, of bloody heroic battle.

Su Lin stared, transfixed in its hypnotic light. The blade sliced through the air and the bearded man was no more; just pieces of flesh severed, cut and hacked asunder. Her father bowed to the fallen enemy and taking the sword, walked past her as if he hadn't seen her, as if she weren't there. But the severed head talked. Its lips moved. Its tongue wagged.

"She is mine," the bloodless lips roared. "I will have her. I will have her living heart beating in my hands."

"No," she screamed. "No. No. No. This cannot be."

Before her very eyes the dead man gathered himself: his head to his body, his arms, his legs. Knife in hand, lifted and raised above its torso, the corpse ran after her father. Su Lin tried to raise a voice of warning. She wanted to scream. She tried to shout. But it was too late. The knife blade sank into Father's back, buried between his shoulders. Again and again the hand raised and fell.

"Ha, ha, ha, ha! She's mine, mine, mine! Ha, ha, ha, ha!"

Su Lin screamed and screamed.

CHAPTER TWENTY-TWO

Hands, hard hands, seized her and, like a steel vise, held her. She tried to fight against the grip, wanting to escape the talking head. She had to get away.

"Susie, Susie . . .? What's wrong? What's wrong, Susie?"

Her eyes flashed open. It was dark. It was so dark, so very dark. The man gripping her--Jacob Hannon--not a gargoyle! Raising herself from the floor of the wagon box, she flung her arms around his neck. "He killed him. He killed him," she wailed.

"Killed who? What are you talkin' about, girl?"

"My Father . . . ?"

"Take her easy, girl. I think you've been dreamin'. Everythin' is all right. Nobody's dead. Nobody's been killed. You've just had yourself one hell of a nightmare."

His arms were around her and he held her.

Su Lin kept herself very still, her heart pounding wildly. *Just don't move,* she thought. *Everything will be all right. Everything was all right. Just don't move.* Tears flowed freely down her cheeks. The hand of Jacob Hannon patted her gently--like a little child. The smell of juniper and sage was in his clothing, in everything about him. *What am I doing?*

Su Lin started to relax and loosened her grip from around his neck. But Jacob Hannon did not.

"You all right now, girl? You were screamin' . . . I thought an Apache had you by the hair. Lordie . . . "

"I am sorry . . . I . . . " Su Lin closed her eyes. For a moment she felt as if her father's arms were around her, hugging her to him. She felt safe and secure. It had been so long since she had felt that way. "I thought someone killed my father," she mumbled into his shirt. "It was so real, I . . . "

"It's all right now, girl. You sure scared the hell out of me." Jacob Hannon laughed.

Awkwardly, Su Lin removed her arms from around his neck. How forward she was. How could she have possibly done this?

"You're awake now," Jacob said. "Figure everyone else is."

"I think so."

"It's a little early. Why don't you lie down, relax. I'm goin' to have a look around, check on the horses. I won't be far . . . if you need me. All right?"

"Yes. All right."

Jacob Hannon walked toward the corrals, disappearing around the side of the barn-like building. For a time she watched but did not see him again. Finally, she laid down and covered herself with the jumbled blankets but she didn't sleep. Her nose was full of the smell of his clothing--of juniper and sage, of drying grass and curing timothy hay. All around her the Coulee lay cool and damp in the darkness of early morning, hidden in the predawn mist like a shadow of some lost, forgotten memory. Jacob Hannon's presence held itself on the edge of her thoughts, tantalizing, not quite there but very near.

Lying in her blankets, Su Lin waited for the sun to begin its climb from behind the red butte, to warm the wings of the dragonfly, remove the chill from the honey bee, and melt the dew from the timothy grass. It was growing light when he returned. She heard his feet moving across the ground before he stuck his face over the edge of the wagon box and looked in at her.

"How're you gettin' along?" he asked.

"Fine." Su Lin sat up, holding the blanket around her.

"Sleepin' inside don't suit you?"

"Yes. But it was hot. I was hot."

He nodded and looked past her toward the spring, listening. Morning doves cooed from their roosts in the vented eves of the barn. Several owls were hooting. Blackbirds, sparrows, meadowlarks and some other bird that she couldn't place flew about. Suddenly she remembered the bird's name. It was a robin. This she had learned in the last two weeks and it pleased her. Su Lin stood up, shook her hair loose, and folded her blanket.

Jacob Hannon started to walk toward the creek and turned to her. "Goin' for a walk. Want to come?"

"I . . . "

"Don't have to if you don't want. You could go inside if you're cold."

"I . . . I want."

"Good. Let's go."

Laying the folded blanket over the edge of the wagon box, she climbed down. She need not have hurried for he waited for her. That always amused her. Men didn't wait, not for a woman. But this one did.

Everything seemed so clear in the early morning. Her father liked such a thing. She hoped he was safe and imagined him strolling in his own dew-laden garden. It had been so long since she had seen him, held his hand, felt his arm around her shoulders. Jacob Hannon was silent. She cast a glance at him. Stuck in the waistband of his pants was a forty-four colt revolver, a heavy reminder of the dangers of Jacob Hannon's garden. There was another in his gun-belt. Father had never carried so much as a dagger in his garden. Maybe he did now. She remembered the face in her dream. *He'd better*, she thought.

Jacob Hannon knelt by the stream and swished his fingers in the running water.

Su Lin asked him, "Why is it that Virginia is all alone?"

A whimsical expression crossed his face. "Wish I knew," he answered. "I'm wonderin' where that damn husband of hers ran off to. I don't know. Seems I don't know a hell of a lot." Rising, he wiped his hands on his pants.

Su Lin glanced toward the adobe, taking in the barn and horse corrals. The sun was barely poking its head above the red butte that towered behind the buildings, making the buildings seem small. She watched Teddy come out the front door of the adobe, look around and finally spy Jacob Hannon and herself. Waving his hand, he ran toward them. He seemed so small dwarfed by the red cliffs. By the time he reached them his pant legs also were wet.

"How are you?" she asked, greeting him.

Teddy laughed. "How are you?" he mimicked, speaking stilted English. They all chuckled.

"Teddy, I am fine," she said.

"Me, too."

Su Lin looked over the waves of grass. She imagined herself, standing with the boy, small dots of life lost in the wide expanse of blue sky. Gazing at the distant mountains, she saw the white clouds circling their craggy peaks, hiding the deep canyons, the rushing streams. She was getting hungry. Fortunately no one spoke. Silence was good.

Finally Teddy broke the silence. "We staying here, Jake? This sure looks like a nice place to me."

"Yeah. Home always looks nice."

"That's good. I sure do like it."

Su Lin watched Jacob Hannon, listening to the way they spoke, watching the way he held himself. He seemed so different, not the same man that stood in the streets of Piedmont, Nevada, a killing rage burning in his eyes and a dead man laying at his feet. *Maybe, we are different people at different times*, she thought. But she didn't feel any different.

"What about you?" Hannon was looking at her. She'd been caught thinking how different he was. Thinking about him embarrassed her especially when she was caught. How could he know? Yet she did it all of the time.

"Fine," she answered. "I am fine."

"I know you're fine," he said. "I can see that but a young woman like you, where do you want to end up? Got the whole world starin' at you fat as a plum just waitin' to be picked. Where do you want to spend your life?"

The thought flashed through her mind, *I want to stay with you . . . be where you are.* Almost choking, she quickly shoved that idea aside. That simply wasn't true. She certainly didn't want to do anything like that. That was something Oldest Uncle wanted, not her. *Oh my, maybe it's happening to me! Maybe I'm going crazy.*

Teddy was watching her, listening.

Composing herself, she smiled and said, "This is beautiful. It is like heaven."

Nodding in unison, they agreed with her.

"You're right about that," Hannon said. "Becky and me used to come down here in the evenin' to watch the sunset. We'd bring us a bottle of rye and we'd set down here on a log . . . talk a little treason. We'd sip a bit. Get nice and warm inside. We'd talk and dream together. I tell ya, Susie, those were the best days of my life."

He turned to look at her, smiling. "If I were you, and I ain't, but if I were, I'd look for some young fellow. The kind you can sip a little rye with and talk about things--good things like babies and birthdays, ribbons in a little girl's hair, curtains in the windows." Jacob Hannon laughed. "I didn't use to think that way. But fact is that's what it's all about."

As she listened to his words, a lump started to grow in her throat. Swallowing, she tried to make the hurt go away. But it only grew more painful. *I want to talk with you,* she thought. *I want to talk about your babies. Hold your hand. Listen to your voice. I want to be with you. I do not want to live my life without you being part of it.* Then, *what? Out of the question. Very unreasonable. That is not for me. Be reasonable, not mindless.*

A warm, glowing feeling washed over her. The pores in her skin tingled with an energy of their own. A pleasant burning grew within her stomach leaving her indescribably light, happy with herself, her life, things as they were and could become. *This is too much. Much too much. This is absolutely ridiculous. No, this isn't just too much. It is absurd. My life is absurd. Shoved into a carriage, a dream . . . a horrible dream. Birds tearing the flesh from dead men. Wild thoughts, uncontrolled thoughts. My father.*

She turned away from Jacob Hannon, looked toward the adobe and remembered the morning, the iron hands that seized her by the shoulders as she lay in the wagon box. *That had felt . . . no, no that wasn't good. Not at all.* A dark feeling rushed over her.

"What is going to happen?" she asked. "When are they coming for us?" *This question. That's where we really are. That is what we wait for.*

"Don't know. We'll have to wait and see. Maybe they'll get themselves all tuckered out." Watching her, Hannon asked, "What? What are you thinkin'?"

"We must leave, Jacob Hannon. We must leave now. Bad things come."

"Bad things are always comin', Susie. That can't be helped. It's what you do about them that matters."

Su Lin looked at Jacob Hannon, involuntarily bringing her right hand to her heart, the dark feeling growing stronger. "I feel them," she said. She heard another magpie. "Someone will die. Many will die." The shadow on her heart was so strong she could hardly speak.

Hannon glanced toward the adobe. "I believe you, Su Lin. But leavin' ain't it."

"Why?"

"Why, what?"

"Why cannot we all just leave? Run. Go somewhere where no one seeks to end our lives?"

Hannon looked at her for a long time. Finally he shook his head, pursing his lips. "Where'd that be? This place, I mean, where no one seeks our lives? Runnin' don't solve no problems, Su Lin. It just gives them time to fester, get bigger. Runnin' makes things worse."

"But Jacob Hannon, I am running. I run from the men in black boots. Why is it all right if I run and not you? Teddy's father is dead; we run. What is the difference? Why is this running good for me and not for you?"

"Good question, Susie. Your askin' makes me look like I am speakin' out of both sides of my mouth. Doin' double talk. Sayin' one thing, doin' another. When I left this place three, four years ago, I was never comin' back. I was lyin' because I was always comin' back. No matter how far I traveled I couldn't get it out of me."

"But Jacob Hannon, if I go back, I die."

"Listen, girl, you and me are different. If you go back all that your father gave up for you is wasted. It is gone. I get that. It is all gone. No offense, but it'd be like you spittin' on your Grandfather's grave."

"So I should run to honor my father and you should not run because it makes problems bigger? Does not my problem grow? Am I not putting off what will happen anyway?"

"Hell's fire, girl. You sure make things hard where they don't need to be."

"Yes?"

"I'll tell you what. We run no more. Both of us. We draw the line in the sand. We run no more."

"But where do I go? This place is not home. Where am I going? What am I doing? Am I just waiting to die? If I am waiting to die why should not I go to my home and die with those who care for me? Perhaps my death can make my Father's life good again. Perhaps living is selfish. Perhaps dying has meaning and living does not." Su Lin looked at him. She wiped away the moisture that had grown on the edges of her eyelids.

"Listen, Susie, I ain't got all the answers. I ain't sure that the ones I got are right. I suppose I could be wrong. Frankly, I doubt it. Leastwise I ain't lettin' on. But you, girl, are standin' on the edge of life. You're just beginnin'. Ahead of you is a husband, a nice little house, babies, grand babies, love, laughter, and Juniper nuts. You'll find someone. Takes time. Things have a way of workin' themselves out. It took me twenty years to find Rebecca. I didn't think I ever would. It just happened one day. Give it a chance. Good things will happen for you."

He paused, looking at her with that knowing look. "One more thing, Susie, and this most of all. If there is anythin' I know . . . live every minute, every second that God gives you and love it for the gift that it is. Suck the juices right out of it. Hang onto it like tomorrow will never get here. Get that dyin' foolishness out of your head. Get to the livin'. Taste it, roll life around in your mouth like it was buffalo berries. And make no excuses for it. You got the right to live. To be here right now. Let troubles come. Line them up. Let's get after them. No regrets. No lookin' back."

"What about you, Jacob Hannon? Oldest Uncle said you needed me. That you did not know this. He said you would know. Do you need me? Do you know?"

"Need you?"

Shaking his head slowly he studied her. "Girl, I'm forty-two years old. I'm more than twice your age. My saddle is older than you." Hannon smiled and shook his head. "Come to think of it, I got saddles older than me. I ain't the man for you. You need one of those youngsters that's full of buckwheat and honey, someone to grow old with, someone . . . you know, fresher, not so set in his ways. And girl, it's right here for the takin'. Look around you. Life's all whirlin' and swirlin' and ready to pop. It's your time in the sun. Don't you be wastin' it. All right?"

"I guess. I do not know."

"You guess? Don't you be guessin', girl."

"But I did not know."

"You do now."

Su Lin smiled at him. "All right," she said. "I will not guess."

In the afternoon of the second day he came for Su Lin with two pistols and a wet towel.

"Come with me," he said.

They went down by the big spring up against the hill. He laid the towel and one of the pistols down on the bare surface of a fallen tree trunk. At ten foot intervals he had stacked cans and glass bottles, four stacks going as far as forty feet away.

Turning to her, he handed her a pistol. "This is a Navy pistol. I figure you ought to learn to use it." Su Lin just stared at him then at the pistol in his hands. "Here," he said.

She took it from him. It was so heavy she almost dropped it. "But . . . "

"But what?"

"Nothing."

"Now the secret, girl, is to make the pistol part of you. Imagine it as an extension of your finger. Point your finger. Squeeze the trigger. Now that squeezin' part is a bit tricky." He handed her the wet towel. "You take this towel in your shootin' hand and you squeeze the water from it. That's the squeeze you're lookin' for. Do it til you can't stand it then do it some more. You'll get the hang of it." He stared at her for a moment as if he doubted his sanity. A smile started to form around his mouth then disappeared. "Let's give it a try. We're burnin' daylight."

All afternoon they "gave it a try." The cans and bottles were safe that day. But Su Lin was not safe from Jacob Hannon. Practice did not stop. Over and over and over again, shot after shot, it was squeeze, squeeze, squeeze, and "now, do it again."

The next day and the next they did it more, again, again and again. Point. Point. Point. Squeeze. Squeeze. Squeeze. Two hours. When they quit shooting, he taught her to load, to oil her gun. He showed her how to move: to line up her body, her arm, to bring the pistol down on the subject without hesitating, squeezing the shot, pointing her finger, concentrating. Over and over again, until her ears rang from the percussions and her muscles ached from holding the weapon steady.

That was the beginning.

CHAPTER TWENTY-THREE

On the evening of the fifth day the bruises on Virginia's neck and arms became a topic of discussion between Judith and Jake. Most had faded. They were hidden from view most of the time, except when she bathed. Then Su Lin saw more.

"Her husband," Su Lin said to them.

"What?" Judith asked. Both Judith and Hannon stared at her.

"Her husband . . . he beats her."

"What makes you think that?" There was no humor in Jacob Hannon's voice. It was sort of edgy, tinged with anger. It was so ominous to Su Lin that she wanted to back up, put distance between herself and him, escape to the courtyard.

"Her back. It is beaten with a staff, a switch, like bamboo. The marks, they are long."

The silence was thick.

He said, "What marks?"

"On her back," Su Lin replied.

Jacob Hannon looked at her. "You've seen this? You've seen this before?"

Su Lin nodded. "I've seen Virginia when she washes herself. I have a mother," she said. "Once my father beat her with a bamboo staff."

"My God," Judith's clapped her hand to her mouth.

"My mother . . . she asked him. I was small."

"I find that hard to believe," Judith replied.

Su Lin stared at Judith. The words of distrust made her a little angry. "I do not lie. I was small. My father . . . he did not want to. He said no. But my mother . . . "

"Easy, ladies . . . " Hannon said.

"I was small," Su Lin repeated. "I do not lie."

"Nobody is sayin' you weren't small, Susie. We know you don't lie. I'm just a little irritated. This sort of thing sets a man's teeth on edge. Thinkin' someone would do this to a woman grinds hard. To make it worse, he ain't here takin' care of her, his wife, his baby. It ain't right." He looked at Su Lin the way he did sometimes. "And it's hard," he said, "to believe that someone--your mother--would ask someone to do this to her. It's even harder to believe that your father would do it."

"My mother . . . she asked for this."

"I heard you. I heard you and I believe you."

"Husbands beat their wives," Su Lin said.

Jacob Hannon stared at her. "I suppose it happens," he said. "But I ain't seein' it."

"In my home far way it happens."

"Maybe . . . here, too, but it ain't right . . . men beatin' their women."

Su Lin looked at Jacob Hannon. "Women are punished. It is permitted. It is expected. A husband is slothful that does not take care of his family. Did you not care for your wife?"

"I cared for her. But I didn't knock her around. I never did this to her. I make mistakes all the time. Lord knows, I probably make one every five or six minutes whether I'm needin' to or not. It was a lucky mistake for her to marry me. I was just lucky. I'd be in a hell of a shape if I beat the hell out of her for marryin' me."

"Lucky? What does this have to do with luck?"

"Nothin,'" Hannon said. "Rebecca and I just fell in love."

"I think it was her husband," Su Lin said again.

"I think you're right. And I think I'm goin' to kill the son of a bitch."

Su Lin looked at Jacob Hannon, astonished. "You . . . you think I am right?"

"Unfortunately, yes," he said.

"You be taking care, Jake," Judith warned. "Killing might not be the thing to do. Killing her husband is killing that baby's Papa. That ain't right either. He only has one even if he ain't here."

Hannon wasn't persuaded.

"Besides you don't know he's done nothing," Judith argued. "You're just guessing, Jake. It ain't right killing that baby's father just guessing and you know it. The truth of it? Killing him ain't right no matter how worthless, good for nothing at all, and . . . and ugly he is."

Hannon let his breath out slowly, adjusted his hat, fingered the brim. Finally he shook his head and walked outside into the courtyard heat, disappearing in the garden scrubs.

Su Lin looked at Judith and discovered her looking at her.

It was Judith who broke the silence. "Made his day, don't you think?"

"What do you mean?" Su Lin said. It exasperated her. *White people speak in riddles,* Su Lin thought. *Lots of riddles. Why not just say it---what it is. No one made his day. It was made. No one brought the sun up. It just happened. No one, least not me, not you had anything to do with day making.* Su Lin stared at her, waiting, knowing more was coming.

"My guess?" Judith said. Judith tossed a wet rag onto the table then slumped into a chair. "My guess . . . you're probably right. That Joe did this. But I ain't saying it. No I ain't. If it was him--if it was that damn Joe--Jake'll skin the little bastard, break every bone in his worthless body, probably shoot him full of holes, and, if there's anything left, . . . hang him. That'll make it pretty hard on this family don't you think?" Judith eyed the doorway and then looked at Su Lin. "You see what I mean? Shooting that baby's father ain't considered real good manners."

Su Lin said, "Because her husband--he beats her---he would be shot?"

"Shooting him ain't good manners, neither. You want something to eat? I got a craving for something sweet. Wonder if Gin's got any sugar. I'd like some sugar. Might bake some sugar cookies." Judith smiled at Su Lin.

"Problem that Joe gots is beating on Jake's baby girl. And leaving her and the baby all alone. Don't take no brain to figure that out. And what's that Joe expect? A `thank you'? He has beans for brains, I tell you. And they ain't good beans neither. I can't really blame Jake none," Judith said. "Somebody beating on his women folk--can't expect him to be right friendly. Know what I mean?"

Su Lin did. *Finally something that wasn't a riddle.*

"I'm gonna have a look for sugar. Come with me, okay?"

Su Lin nodded.

"Great, I'll hustle us something real good to eat. You ever have bear sign?"

CHAPTER TWENTY-FOUR

Shooting practice continued. There was a lot of it to do. Everywhere she went, she carried the wet towel, squeezing it over and over again. The pistol was too heavy to lug around but not the towel.

The riddle of Virginia's husband was not solved. The days were so hot, the nights so cold. It was a place without rhythm, where the weather couldn't make up its mind, a place where rain fell but nothing got wet, a place of grasshoppers and crickets, dry wind and cloudless skies.

In the late afternoons through a smoky haze, sheets of rain fell, outlined against dark clouds. Often it was followed with the sweet smell of rain-washed air, sometimes the smell of electricity. Then nothing. No rain, just dark foreboding clouds that hesitated then drifted away on the hot, afternoon air, leaving a dry barren land, chapped lips that cracked and bled, and a growing restlessness that seemed to have a painful, agitated life of its own.

Three weeks passed, still nothing. She tried to figure out what she expected, what she wanted. Jacob Hannon expected her to shoot. But there had to be more than that. Su Lin expected bad things to happen. She couldn't help it.

There were more men about. At first there were only a few. But as the word got out that Jacob Hannon was hiring, there were more and more. At last count there were sixteen: some old and toothless, some young with bright eyes full of mischief and wonder. There were those that watched her appreciatively and those that didn't. It bothered her not knowing whether to be glad or irritated.

Cattle were gathered in the long grass pastures that extended for miles south of the adobe, thousands of them. In the mornings she heard their lowing. Sometimes the still air was filled with the tortured smoke of branding, the frustrated shouts of cowboys, the bawling of summer calves looking for their mothers, of mother cows looking for their calves.

Why this was done wasn't explained. According to Virginia this "gather" hadn't been done in a long time, not since Jake had left four years ago. Apparently it should have been done each year. That was the best Su Lin could conclude. Afterwards the bawling beasts, herds of steers, and aged cows were separated and taken somewhere to the east.

The word among those hired, those men who came to the water barrel to drink wearing shotgun chaps, carrying braided riatas, with high leather boots, and spurs that jingled as they walked, was that Virginia's husband had left her for another woman, that he beat Virginia without reason, at times slapping her senseless, knocking her unconscious. That was said among the "hands" as they ate beans, steak, and tortillas at noon and in the evenings sitting on the stoop, leaning against the wagon beds and pole corrals.

The dog days of August came and the long valley turned golden brown. In the late morning Su Lin hung damp dish towels from the clothesline and stared into the distance, feeling the heat bake her skin, smelling the curing grass, listening to the rattle of cottonwood leaves as the breeze picked up and died.

CHAPTER TWENTY-FIVE

Toward evening Hannon returned from one of his many trips. Su Lin found him with Teddy. He had been on her mind ever since the day he left. "You know," Su Lin said to him. "You are not as bad as you think. You do not place the heads of those you kill on staffs for all to see. You do not make examples of Joe in this way."

"I suppose you've seen this?" Jacob Hannon said.

"I have seen this, yes."

Both Teddy and Hannon turned and looked at her. "You've seen that?" Hannon asked again.

"I have seen heads on wooden staffs--on stakes."

"Where did you see that?" Hannon was watching her.

"At my home. Where I lived. Oldest Uncle, he took the heads of seven White men."

"The hell, you say," he said. "Were they alive?"

Su Lin looked at Jacob Hannon, puzzled. "Men do not live without a head."

"No. No. Were they alive when he hacked their heads off?"

"Yes. They were very much alive. There was much blood . . . much example."

"I'll be damned. And I thought I . . . Why'd he go do that?"

Su Lin hesitated. Telling felt like giving something of herself, something that was inside, private and all hers, no one's business. But Hannon looked at her and she felt a need to tell him. Suddenly, she wanted to tell him. She wanted him to understand her.

"My sister, the one with whom I was born," she said, "White men came and took my sister--her voice, herself, her body. They drink the rice wine. My sister . . . " Her voice fell away. "They killed youngest brother. He tried to stop them. They cut him like a melon."

Hannon shifted his weight and nodded. "Bet your Oldest Uncle didn't bury none of them bastards," he said.

"No. Their bodies were thrown in the river. Their heads were stuck on staffs outside of the village. Grandfather, he was very, very angry."

"I'll bet he was. Had every right to be."

For a moment she was silent. She said, "At the wagons of your friend, is that what happened? Did the dogs . . . ?"

"My friend?"

"Yes."

"You mean the Gypsy?"

"Yes."

"I reckon. Except it weren't dogs. Coyote, I imagine. Probably chewed them up right nasty."

"They themselves, their family will not be happy. The dead will not take the long journey to the land of spirits."

"Well, seein' how they're goin' straight to hell it ain't gonna make much difference how happy they are."

"Their family will come to make death of sons right, to free dead to take the long journey?"

At first Jacob Hannon did not answer. Instead he nodded, watching the horse flies buzz about his horse. He swatted a mosquito. "You're right, Susie," he finally said. "They'll be comin'. No matter how those bastards died or what they were doin' that got themselves killed. They'll be comin'. Sure as hell. And it ain't to free their spirits either. They'll be lookin' for blood, an eye for an eye, with a little Bible thumpin' vengeance chewin' at their craw."

Su Lin looked straight at Jacob Hannon. "This is not good. Too many men seek you dead."

"Seems likely. Rebecca, she most likely would agree. She'd say `this ain't none too good.'"

"Rebecca is your wife?"

"Yes, my wife. Well--was my wife. Virginia's mother. Got her buried down there beneath that cottonwood."

Su Lin had noticed the graveyard before. It rested in the shade of gnarled cottonwood limbs, enclosed by a short pole fence. She remembered several wood crosses for the most part hidden in long grass. She glanced toward the creek. A red-winged blackbird rested on a bare limb that was leafless and dead. The bird flew. Su Lin watched it disappear into the trees. "Soldiers will come for me soon, Jacob Hannon."

"Think so?"

"Yes."

"Su Lin, how will they know where to find you? Girl, you yourself ain't got a clue where you are and you're in the middle of nowhere."

"They will know."

"Think so? Even in this God forsaken place?"

"Yes."

"Well, I told you we'd solve that problem. I meant it."

"They will not be one. There will be many. Soldiers. Warriors. In matters of death they are skilled. They do not fail for they cannot fail and live." Su Lin looked at the man, Jacob Hannon, and a shiver went up her spine. "It is not me they want, Jacob Hannon. It is my head . . . for the staff outside the village of Tinian. For the example."

Jacob Hannon did not seem impressed. Instead he pulled at his nose, rubbing it with the back of his hand. Removing his hat, he wiped his white forehead and stood there as if he hadn't heard her. After a while he reseated his hat and turned his dark blue eyes on her. "Don't worry yourself, Su Lin. Nobody's takin' your head anywhere. Not today," he said.

"You? You can solve this? Solve an army? Are you so strong?"

"An army? How many do you think really?"

Su Lin hesitated. "Two or three. Maybe five. I do not know."

"Two or three, maybe five. Well they ain't here. We ain't got to deal with them until . . . until we got to."

"There are not enough bullets, Jacob Hannon."

"We'll see, Su Lin. Maybe those sons-ta-bitches will decide the price of a killin' is a little high. I tell you there is a hell of difference in this place and some half-baked, half-horse settlement ten thousand miles from here. This is my backyard. It's where I live. There is a difference. The rules are the same but the fight's different." Jacob Hannon again tugged at the brim of his hat, pulling it down further over his eyes. "If we take care of the two, three or five . . . can you go home then? Will that end it?"

"No, it will not and more will come."

"Not out of sight, out of mind?"

"What?"

"You know. After awhile, they might just forget you."

"It is possible. But they have long memories . . . remembering what they want when they want."

"Dead men don't remember anythin'."

Su Lin looked at Jacob Hannon. "My Father once said that dead men do not forget."

A smile crept over his lips. "Lordie, Su Lin, you got me there." He shook his head. "Right now give that head of yours a break. What'd that fellow say about elephants?"

Su Lin looked at Jacob Hannon, puzzled.

"You know. You know. How do you eat an elephant?"

"I . . . I do not." And she didn't. Who would eat elephant? She'd heard that the meat was tough, tasteless, to be avoided.

"No . . . no. Susie. You eat him one bite at a time, girl. One bite at a time. Surprised you ain't heard that. It's some sort of wise saying. I reckon you'll tell me that that's a hell of a lot of eatin'. We'll just have to wait and see. Nothin' we can do about it now except set the table, get out the knives and forks, and bib up. That damn elephant . . . he'll be along soon enough if he comes at all."

Su Lin nodded, unsure. She looked at the improbable man standing beside her, his arms folded across his chest as he gazed across the narrow valley. He sure didn't look like much. The valley didn't look like much either though it was pretty. And yes, the soldiers would come. There would be much blood: hers, Jacob Hannon's, maybe Teddy's, Judith's. She had to do something. *But what?*

She remembered the white fish, a mud-sucker left to die in a depression of mud, surrounded by a diminishing pool, all but abandoned by the receding river. Things were beyond its control. No matter what it did it was wrong. A flip of its tail only made muddy water. It swam in a murky soup in which it soon could not breathe, back and forth, back and forth. No control. Truly, she was the fish. Around her the water vanished, evaporating in the heat of the day, slowly, almost visibly sinking into the sand. She starved for air in a valley of air: around and around, flipping, flopping, her dry back raw, burnt by the noonday sun, dying a little more with each gulp of mud.

"Jacob Hannon, I am not sure I understand elephants. But are these the reasons I practice with the pistol? Are these the reasons?" She looked at him.

"Yes," he said. "Yes. It is. You're plannin' for peace and preparin' for war."

CHAPTER TWENTY-SIX

"What are you thinking? Give you a pretty penny and a plug nickel for your thoughts."

Su Lin started and turned at the sound of Judith's voice.

"Nothing." Su Lin smiled. "Just looking at the men who come riding."

"Who comes riding?"

Su Lin pointed down the long valley beyond the milling cattle herds, south along the creek bottom. A band of six or, maybe even, ten riders forded the creek and rode out to the edge of the prairie grass. She couldn't tell how many. They kept in a tight group just beyond the timber. Maybe three miles away, maybe more, they were small figures that disappeared among the cottonwoods then reappeared.

"Ah, it's nothing," Judith said. "Just more riders. More to feed. Wonder what Jake wants with all these men. He's gathered half of the stock. You'd think he's raising an army. When's he got enough?" Judith took a breath, her fingers playing with the pleats in her skirt. "Say, would you get some more wood? Gin's fixing to bake bread. We'll need more." Judith stared across the waves of grass at the approaching riders. "We'll be needing to fill the wood box more than once to feed this outfit."

Su Lin nodded and glanced at the woodpile beyond the barn. The wood had already been chopped and split. She decided to carry it inside and fill the box by the stove. Maybe she'd watch the baby. The riders came slowly. Su Lin made three trips before they reached the bend where the creek turned south and the wagon road crossed it. It occurred to her they hadn't come by the road.

Something else was odd but she couldn't place it. She stood, her arms full of wood, a gentle breeze tugging at her skirts, and watched. The riders rode strung out single file. There were eleven. Shouldering the firewood, she walked toward the house.

Something was different. She heard a door shut, a dog bark, a rooster crow. The man who cleaned his rifle on the steps of the bunkhouse had disappeared. The skinny one who was leaning on the pitchfork in the barn, the one who kept the corral poles in place, who made the gates swing, was gone. Starting toward the adobe, Su Lin thought of Jacob Hannon. She hadn't seen him all morning. That wasn't unusual for he was seldom around.

A flock of laying hens had gathered in the shade out of the sun. They dusted themselves, their wings spread loosely about them, beaks open breathing the hot air. Overhead a magpie silently flew toward the cottonwoods down by the spring. Su Lin shook the foreboding feeling from her shoulders like dust. It was nothing, she told herself.

Inside she dropped the firewood in the wood box and brushed the dirt from her blouse. Virginia was kneading bread dough at the table and singing softly to herself. Judith was in Virginia's bedroom sitting on the floor with the boy child, making faces and laughing.

"Hi, ya," she said when Su Lin came inside. "I was going to the smokehouse but this one was stinky. So I fixed him up." She poked at the baby's belly. "Yes I did," she crooned. He laughed and giggled at her menacing finger. "Oh!" Judith rolled her eyes. "I gotta get that meat. Stay here with Bright Eyes, would you?"

Su Lin nodded and Judith disappeared out the door. Su Lin sat on the floor, cross-legged. Now she was a nanny, which was sure different from having one. How things changed. Smiling, she poked the baby in the belly with her finger and was rewarded with peals and squeals of laugher. He rolled on his belly, got to his knees, and stood up waiting for her to follow him, to get him, to play the game of grab, poke and clutch.

Turning, he glanced up at her then struck off, mounting the stairs on the south side of the garden, hesitating to make sure she chased after him. Discovering her, he took off again, laughing, giggling, waddling his way toward the kitchen door. Once she had caught up to him he stopped and lifted his arms up to her. She picked him up, whirling him around, then held him in her arms thinking she'd get him a drink, a piece of bread and butter, loving his arms clasped around her neck. He patted her on the head as she entered the kitchen.

It was quiet. Too quiet. Inside the front door stood a man she'd never seen before. Several more strangers bearing rifles were just outside peering in. Virginia and Judith were across the room, the distance between them reeling with miles of unspoken words. The baby's hand stopped waving, no longer patting at her face, his attention seized by the man's presence. The baby stared and started to whimper, his lower lip curling as he puckered up.

"That damn kid ain't changed none. The little horse turd." The man walked across the room and dropped his hat on the table. "Got yourself a maid, I see." His eyes rested on Su Lin and hung there wandering up and down her frame. "How you payin' her?"

The child started to cry, squirming in her arms. "Get that little shit outta here," he ordered. "I don't want to hear that whinin'. Go on. Get him outta here." He slumped into a kitchen chair. "I'll be needin' breakfast. Got ten out there to feed. Throw on some extra eggs and griddle cakes."

The baby was beside himself, wanting to get down.

The stranger fastened his gaze on Su Lin. "Did you hear me? I said get that kid outta here. Understand? Get that little son of a bitch outta here and I mean now."

"No, Joe. She isn't leaving. The baby is just fine where he is."

"No?"

Every eye turned toward Virginia. The man stood slowly. "No? Did I hear you right? Did you tell me, no?" The chair fell backwards, its back cracking against the stone floor. The child screamed. "Did I hear you right?" He paused. "Get over here, woman. I'll slap you down right now. What's got into you?" He stopped, staring at Virginia, his eyes momentarily coming to rest on Judith. "Who you got gatherin'? I ain't told you to do no gatherin'. Who you got out there?" He came around the table toward Virginia.

The baby slipped in Su Lin's arms. She grabbed at him as his feet reached the floor. Immediately he ran toward his mother, screaming at the top of his lungs. The baby grabbed his mother's leg. As Virginia reached for him, Joe seized her arm, practically lifting her from the floor.

"You're hurting me," she cried, her voice mostly lost in the baby's wails. "You're hurting me."

"I'll bet I am . . . " Sarcasm dripped from his words. Impatiently he looked at Su Lin. "Thought I told you to get that snivelin' kid outta here." He paused. "Do you know who I am?" His eyes bored into her, his hands squeezing Virginia's arm. "I run this place. I ask you to do somethin' you do it. Understand me?"

Virginia pulled away, frantically trying to break his grasp. Judith sprang to her assistance inserting herself between them. The baby fell backwards, knocked to the floor by surging adults.

"What the . . . you little . . . " Angrily, he swung his free arm at Judith but Judith ducked, slapping his hand away.

"You little bitch," he exclaimed. "I'll get . . . " He had Virginia's hair in his hand and yanked it down, pulling her to her knees.

The doorway darkened. Su Lin glanced toward it as she grabbed for the child, scooping the bawling baby up into her arms, cradling him against her body.

"Don't, don't," Virginia screamed, reaching for the hand clutching her hair. "Let go. Let go. You're hurting me."

"Damn right, I am. What'd you think I was gonna do?"

Judith leaped to her feet, seizing a butcher knife from the kitchen counter, turning furiously toward the man. Spurs jingled; rowels scraped across the doorsill and stopped. Su Lin stared. Judith advanced. Jacob Hannon stood inside the kitchen door taking in the scene: his whimpering, crying daughter, the bawling baby, Joe's back turned toward him. The terrified and angry Judith stood menacingly, the long blade of the butcher knife in her hand.

"Judith . . . " Though Jacob Hannon's voice was but a whisper everyone heard it.

Judith stopped.

The stranger whirled to the sound of the new voice to find Jacob Hannon watching him.

"Let her go, Joe," he said.

"Who the hell do-- ?"

"I said 'Let her go,' Joe!"

Joe pulled Virginia around by the hair of her head as he faced Hannon. "You ain't givin' no orders, Jake. And I ain't lettin' this bitch go. She's my woman."

"Bitch?"

"You heard me. Bitch. She's mine and I'm tellin' you to get the hell out before I kill you." Joe paused. "Naw," he said, "I'm goin' to kill you and get it over with. You're too damn stupid to know you're dead."

"You ain't killin' no one."

"Who's gonna stop me?"

Su Lin watched in fascination as the man's hand came out of nowhere full of pistol, holding Virginia, hair, head, and body, in front of him like a shield. Hannon didn't move. The stricken woman screamed, falling to her knees, her arms flailing, catching herself when her hands struck the floor. Suddenly she turned and struck her husband squarely in the groin with a clenched fist. The pistol discharged in the confines of the kitchen walls. Virginia struck him again, her fist guided up the inside of his thigh like a ball on a string.

Joe's face was a twisted contortion. He tried to hit her in the head with his pistol and missed. The pistol discharged again, the slug slamming off the stove into the wall, the recoil knocking the weapon from his hand. Frantically, he leaped for it. But Jacob Hannon reached Joe first. As Joe grabbed for the gun, Jacob Hannon kicked the scrambling man in the head, the rowels of his spurs slicing the side of Joe's face like a dull can opener. Joe jerked Hannon's foot out from under him. Both men sprawled on the floor, slugging at each other, rolling under the table, breaking one of the legs, sending a chair flying. More flour flew up into the air. Bread dough plopped onto the floor.

During the melee the outside door was flung wide open and a shaft of sunlight framed Stetsons, rifles, and the shadowed faces of men peering inside. These faces were familiar. A pistol shot exploded in the room followed by another. Joe was caught in mid-strike, his fist plummeting down, half turned, a look of incredulity spreading across his face. A third shot shoved him backwards across Hannon's legs.

Virginia stood in the middle of smoke and flour, in a room of broken furniture and smatterings of blood, Joe's pistol held in both hands, shaking uncontrollably. Her dress was powdered in flour and stained with bacon grease. She crumpled onto the tile floor, the pistol clattering at her feet, a broken chair leg partially hidden beneath her skirts, her head striking the edge of the over turned table.

Silence reigned in a kitchen filled with the acidic smell of burnt gun powder. It was interrupted by the cries of a frightened child, Hannon's cursing, and the sound of spurs jingling as men pushed their way into the kitchen. A very large room grew much smaller.

Astonished, Su Lin stared at the fallen Virginia. She'd shot her husband! He looked dead. He was dead. Blood spread over the front of his shirt where three bullets had exited. His sphincter muscles relaxed. The smell was horrible. Judith threw up her breakfast.

Su Lin picked the baby up. His cries diminished. She was conscious of Jacob Hannon close to her.

"You all right?" he asked.

She nodded.

He glanced at the baby then at her, peering into her eyes like he was studying the bottom of a dark well. Without explanation he patted her on the shoulder, then squeezed the baby's hand, touching his cheek with knuckles and fingernails. "Give Judith a hand," he whispered then turned his attention from her to his daughter.

Reality is a heavy burden, she thought. *Virginia has killed her husband.* For an instant the horrible vision of the slain, headless corpses filled Su Lin's head: White men, Oldest Uncle standing with the bright sword of the House of Kou dripping in blood, Youngest Uncle, his disemboweled body in the marketplace, her sister rocking slowly back and forth, cooing to herself, her mind in some distant place, never returning.

Judith threw up again.

No. This couldn't happen, Su Lin thought. *Why did this have to happen?* Virginia had killed her husband. She'd shot him dead. Now his people would come. They'd seek her head: for the example, for the pikes, for retribution, to force the final payment. What value would be placed on the loss of a son? Even a worthless one?

The whimpering child rested quietly in Su Lin's arms, his head on her shoulder, his fingers playing with the buttons on her blouse. Somehow Su Lin got Judith out of the kitchen and into the garden. She made her sit. Su Lin sat beside her, the child still clinging to her neck. With some effort she moved him onto her lap, then put her arm around Judith, holding her close. Neither spoke.

Be strong, she told herself. *Strong? Oh, poor Virginia. What horrible things had happened. And what choice did she have? What would become of the baby?*

Judith was staring at her. "You don't look so good," she said. "Worse than I feel. You okay? What's wrong?" Alarm rose in her voice.

Su Lin just stared at her, unable to speak.

"Jeez, sister. It's okay. You're crying. Do you know you're crying? What's wrong? It'll be all right. Everything's going to be fine. That bastard, Joe, he's got to be dead."

Judith put her arms around her. Both women held each other, the child balanced on the edge of Su Lin's lap, his lower lip stuck out. He climbed off, holding onto her skirts.

"Will they hurt her?" Su Lin stammered, sniffling and trying to dry her tears. "For her husband . . . will they hurt her?"

"Gin, hurt?" Judith jumped up and ran toward the kitchen doorway, lifting her skirts to keep from stepping on them. Mounting the steps, two at a time, she disappeared inside. Clutching her arms about herself, Su Lin bent over and sobbed. The baby had his hand on her thigh, patting her slowly. A moment later, Judith returned.

"No. No, Su Lin. She's all right. She's okay. You don't have to cry. It's not even her blood. She ain't hurt at all." Then it was Judith who held Su Lin in her arms so close Su Lin could smell the coffee on her breath, smell the vomit on her blouse. "No. No," Judith whispered. "She's fine. Not hurt at all."

Suddenly Judith stopped talking, staring at Su Lin, studying her face. A realization registered. Abruptly she hugged Su Lin even more. "Oh no, Su Lin. No. No. No. Not at all. No one is going to hurt her, not Virginia. It's okay. Everything's okay. That bastard Joe . . . he's dead. Good riddance. No loss there. He deserved killing."

The words were far from consoling. What did Judith know? She was a woman. Didn't she know? Virginia had killed her husband. There was no doubt what would happen. His family would come. It was just a matter of time.

Judith turned to the doorway, her arm still around Su Lin. "Jake, get over here. Explain this. Su Lin's got it in her head that someone's gonna hurt Virginia for killing that worthless bastard. Get over here and tell her it ain't so. "

Jacob Hannon appeared in front of her. His arms lifted her, pulling her close, so close she could smell dry grass and sage, branding smoke, and the sweat of horses in his clothes. It only made things worse. She couldn't stop crying. She just couldn't. *Oh, Virginia, Virginia*, she thought. No matter how she tried, she couldn't talk. Her throat hurt too much.

"Now listen," Hannon said, "don't you be frettin' none." He whispered using that horse voice, the "everythin's goin' to be all right" voice.

Su Lin just looked up at Jacob Hannon. In a shaky voice she asked, "Will his father come for her? Will he make an example of her?"

Hannon stared. "Su Lin," he said, "that ain't the way it's done. There ain't gonna be no example. Understand? None of that. Gin, she's as safe as a baby on her mother's lap. There ain't gonna be no father and there ain't gonna be no mother. Understand? It's over. There's just one dyin' and a buryin'. That's it. That's all she wrote. Now, girl, you go inside and help the ladies make some sense of that mess in there. Workin' will take the sting out of a killin'. Get your mind on somethin' else. All that damn thinkin' will just get you in trouble."

Su Lin nodded.

Tips of his calloused fingers wiped the tears from her eyes and dried her cheeks. He was so close. "Thank you, Susie, for all you've been doin'. Sorry that things have been so tough. This ain't China. Understand? Ain't nothin' gonna happen to Virginia. Nothin' at all."

He held her hand in his. "Think you'll be all right?"

She nodded.

"Good," he said. "I'll be around, girl, if you're needin' anythin'. I'm right close. So don't be frettin' none. Understand?"

She nodded again and watched his back as he walked away, watched as he climbed the three sets of pine plank steps, crossed the porch, and disappeared into the kitchen.

Judith came to her. "That was something," she said.

Su Lin didn't reply.

"Jake set you straight? What'd he tell you? Tell ya everything was gonna be just fine?"

"He said that . . . said he'd be around if I needed anything."

"He said what?"

Su Lin just looked at her.

Judith stood the baby up on his legs but he wouldn't stand. He wanted to sit. "Maybe your uncle was right," she said.

Su Lin wondered what she meant.

CHAPTER TWENTY-SEVEN

By Saturday most of the excitement that had arisen over the killing of Joe had subsided. If anything, Virginia was a hero and Joe was just another marker in the family burial ground. He had no status because he was buried off to the side. No example was made of Virginia. No one came for her head. Su Lin rose early to help the skinny man water the saddle horses and feed them oats and timothy hay. He wore a new red plaid shirt.

When they finished, Judith had breakfast ready and they walked across the hard pack to the adobe. They were greeted by a stack of pancakes, buffalo berry syrup, and fresh cow's milk.

She thought of her Grandmother. Sometimes the old woman felt so close she could feel her aged hand patting her on the head. "I have good feelings for you," GrandMaMa had said. That was long ago. Su Lin had been small. It surprised her that she remembered her so clearly. The feeling was so real her scalp tingled from the mere thought. But GrandMaMa was dead and so very far, far away in another world.

"Today is my birthday," Jacob Hannon announced. "I'm goin' to Clearwater . . . gonna celebrate. I'll get Sam to take the buckboard. We'll bring back supplies. Be back tomorrow sometime."

He left Saturday morning, August 13, 1877, riding the Appaloosa, walking him beside the buckboard. Su Lin stood on the knoll and watched them moving slowly across the Coulee then disappear into the cottonwood trees along the creek. She watched until he was gone from sight.

Judith had wanted to take a walk and Su Lin had agreed to go with her. They went to the cottonwood tree down on the creek where Rebecca was buried, where the fence kept the grass inside high, where the wild flowers bloomed in reds and blues. The wood marker was hard to read, the markings weathered and cracked. White bird droppings ran down the sides. Lichen had grown on the south face of the weathered wood. Timothy grass grew almost as high as the marker.

Midmorning they watched as six riders stopped at the adobe. Su Lin and Judith had been busy laughing and talking but the sight of the riders put an end to their conversation. The riders' horses stood heads down and drooping. The riders did not dismount. Still, they were riders and strangers made her extra anxious especially after the 'Joe' experience.

For a brief moment Virginia stood in the doorway with little Henry hanging onto her skirts. There seemed to be hands and guns wherever Su Lin looked. The skinny one, wearing his red shirt, was smoking a cigarette, leaning against the rails of the horse corral a rifle at hand, a pistol stuck in his belt. Su Lin imagined young Johnny Cutler standing inside the adobe staring over Virginia's shoulder. Mike, the old one needing a haircut, was a hundred feet away in the bunkhouse doorway, a shotgun cradled in his arms, finger on the trigger guard. Things had changed.

Both Judith and Su Lin looked at each other. Abruptly the horsemen wheeled their mounts and rode in the direction of Clearwater. Su Lin breathed. Lately strange riders brought trouble. A dark feeling washed over her. Now six riders who never even attempted to dismount. It might be nothing. But who would start a fight with Johnny, Mike and that skinny one cradling double barrel shotguns, armed with Winchester rifles and pistols? Su Lin was frightened.

"What's the matter?" Judith asked.

"I don't know. Let's see who those men were . . . what they wanted."

"All right."

Both women glanced down the Coulee at the retreating riders, and watched as the small cavalcade crossed the creek and disappeared into the cottonwoods.

"Do you think they're trouble?" Judith asked.

"Yes. But they are leaving, so no. It must be nothing. But I have thoughts of my GrandMaMa."

"What?" Judith looked at her, quizzically. "Your Grandmother? What on earth?"

"It is nothing," Su Lin replied, "except I was thinking of my GrandMaMa when those last men came with Joe. I am troubled. No, I expect trouble."

Judith and Su Lin walked toward the adobe. Virginia came outside as they approached. Neither spoke.

"You seen Henry?" she asked.

"He's not out here," Judith said. "Who were those men?"

Su Lin fidgeted, nervously.

"Don't know. Said they'd come from California. Said they were looking for four, maybe five Gypsies with a string of horses and a mule. I didn't tell them anything. Nothing I could tell them. Sort of a cold bunch. Showed them the road to Clearwater. So, what are you two up to?"

Su Lin stared at Judith, suddenly alarmed. Judith asked Virginia, "Was there an old man? He'd be big with a grey mustache, grey hair, a scar across his nose, and a little squinty eyed. He rides hunched over the saddle horn like his butt is sore. Was there somebody like that? Did you notice an old man like that?" Judith asked.

"There was an old man. He did all the talking." Virginia, seeing Henry toddle out of the house, bent over and picked him up, patting him on the butt. "Had a big old beaver hat so I couldn't see his hair. What I could see was grey around the edges. Mean looking." Virginia placed Henry back on the ground. "I couldn't see his eyes very well," she said. "Why? Something wrong?"

"Did anyone mention any names?" Judith asked.

"Seems like one of the others called the old man Mister something or other. I can't remember. Why? Do you know those men? Are they trouble?"

"Was it Jocund? Did he call him Jocund?"

"May have been. It was something like that. What's wrong?"

Judith glanced at Su Lin. "They'll find him, Su Lin. When they reach Clearwater they'll find him. It won't be hard. He'll be in the Boundary Saloon drinking, maybe even drunk. That's where he'll be and that's where they'll find him."

Virginia interrupted. "But Papa's not a Gypsy."

"No, he's not but they don't know that." Judith started to say something else but Su Lin didn't wait. She was running for the horse corral and saddle horses.

Su Lin caught up a bay, threw the stirrup over the saddle and tightened the cinch. She was in the saddle by the time Judith arrived. A dust devil whirled about her and across the corral.

Judith followed her out of the corral, closing the gate. Skinny was shouting from across the yard but Su Lin did not slow down, belting the bay horse in the sides with the heels of her shoes, slapping him with the reins. Both horses broke into a trot heading for the open expanse of the Coulee, down the winding road to Clearwater.

"They gots maybe a half hour head start," Judith yelled. "We have to be riding hard or we'll never catch them. Clearwater's two hours from here."

Su Lin heard her but didn't reply, wondering what they'd do when they got there without a weapon between them, and whether they'd be so late that it wouldn't matter.

CHAPTER TWENTY-EIGHT

Two hours later a sorrel with one white stocking and a bay horse entered Clearwater, Nevada at a fast trot. Their withers were soaked white in sweat, their nostrils flaring, blowing air, a frothy foam dripping from their mouths. The gypsy girl rode standing in the stirrups, peering over her horse's head. Su Lin's horse ran beside hers, matching strides with the sorrel. Jacob Hannon could be anywhere. Both women were searching the street and hitching rails.

"There," Judith pointed. "His horse."

In front of a saloon stood Jacob Hannon's Appaloosa, its reins draped around the cedar rail. Next to it stood the six trail-worn horses. White alkali dust caked their shoulders and flanks. Old sweat and dried lather, the desert itself, hung on them like the pall of death.

Su Lin glanced at Judith. She was looking across the street at another horse soaking up sunlight. A very thin layer of dust had begun to form on saddle and rump. A democrat, pulled by a pair of black horses, moved jauntily up the street past the two women, its bells jingling merrily. Su Lin held the bay in to let it pass.

"Over here," Judith said. "Let's see the Sheriff."

Slapping her horse's flanks with the reins, Su Lin followed Judith across the street. They dismounted, hitching their horses next to the dusty bay. *What good is a sheriff?* Su Lin thought. *We haven't got time for sheriffs.*

Judith dismounted and stepped onto the boardwalk. Hurriedly, Su Lin followed, not wanting to be left behind. Inside the window-lit room the sheriff was playing solitaire with a deck of well-worn cards. He stood up as they entered, nodding in greeting, a wisp of red hair dangling in his eyes. "Mornin', ladies. Fine day, ain't it? What . . . "

Wordlessly, Judith moved toward the gun rack that clung to the wall. "We'll be needing two shotguns," she said.

"What?"

"I don't have time to jaw with you, Sheriff. I need a shotgun. Where do you keep the shells?" Judith reached for a double barrel, pulling it from the rifle rack. Deftly, she broke it open, hefting it, glancing into the breech. What she saw must have satisfied her for she closed it. The sheriff dropped the several cards he'd held in his hand onto the desk top. One fell to the floor, turning over and over before lying on the floor: an ace of spades. He started around the desk, stumbling when his foot struck the corner leg.

Judith re-engaged hammer and barrel. The metallic click of the barrels seating brought him up short. Warily, he looked at her, hesitating as he backed up against the desk. The barrels were pointed directly at his chest. Su Lin moved behind Judith and picked up the other shotgun and likewise broke open the breech.

The butts of two rounded ends of two shells stared back at her. This Remington twelve gauge was fully loaded.

"Now ladies, put the shotguns down," the Sheriff stammered, his fingers outstretched, his feet stationary, his butt secure against the desk.

If Judith heard the sheriff, it was not obvious to Su Lin. Already she was moving toward the open door, her feet a whisper as she crossed the bare floor. Su Lin hesitated. The clock in her head ticked loudly, so loudly that she could not hold still.

As she reached the doorway, Judith abruptly turned on her heel and addressed the man and badge still supported by the edge of the desk. "Sheriff, I'll be needing some extra shells," Judith said. Her shotgun was leveled at the bottom buttons on his shirt. "Where you keep them?" Judith asked.

The sheriff did not answer her question.

"Where?" Judith insisted, loudly.

"Behind you. On the shelf. Who you gunnin' for?"

Judith glanced in the direction he pointed, walked across the floor and seized a square cartridge box from a shelf above the now empty rifle rack. Cartridges in hand, she made her way toward the door and the open street. "The question is who's gunning for me, Sheriff."

The eyes of the two women met as they stepped into the street, their footfalls creating small puffs of dust clouds in the dry, hot air. In front of the Boundary Saloon they climbed up on the boardwalk and stopped. Shotgun in one hand, Judith fumbled with the box of cartridges, tearing at the lid with her teeth.

Several shells dropped to the pine planking as she jerked the cardboard lid off. Neither woman bothered picking them up.

Su Lin stared at the closed door to the Boundary Saloon. The clock in her head had stopped; it had ceased its incessant drive forward. Vaguely, she was aware of Judith handing her additional shotgun shells. She shoved them into her pants pocket and followed Judith inside the saloon pushing the door in front of her. Su Lin never faltered. Without a thought, without waiting for her eyes to adjust to the dark room, she stepped up alongside Judith.

Before her she saw the backs of five men standing, spread across the room, each a tine in an open fan. One turned to look at her. To the rear of the saloon sat two men; one was Jacob Hannon, his hat pulled down in front of his eyes. To her right another leaned against the bar, an old man. Behind the bar another stood wearing an apron; he'd stopped polishing a glass and was setting it down, his right hand reaching under the counter.

Without thinking, Su Lin brought the shotgun stock to her shoulder. Her finger jerked the trigger closest to the palm of her hand. The explosion slammed the shotgun hard into her shoulder and the double-ought buckshot blasted a hole in the hardwood floor at her feet.

The room instantly erupted in the roar of gunfire. All around her weapons discharged, slapping the walls with devastating percussions. Her finger found the second trigger. Beside her Judith's shotgun roared. Something tugged violently at Su Lin's abdomen, lifting her, throwing her backwards across the floor. She fell, her shoulders striking the wall behind her, knocking the air from her lungs. Lights went off in her head. Surprised, she blinked her eyes, suddenly indignant. Her legs gave out and she slumped to the floor, a small patch of red blood fanning out from a dark hole low on her blouse.

I ought to plug it. I ought to stop that bleeding, keep it inside. But she couldn't. As if from a distance she watched the wet, red, liquid spread. *I've been killed. I'm dying.* Her fingers tingled. Across the darkness of the smoke-filled room she saw a man slammed backwards by an unseen hand. It was funny. She smiled. She wanted to laugh but it took too much energy; the roar of gunfire filled her ears. Her arms felt so heavy. Someone was screaming.

In the shadows of her mind she saw him, a pistol in either hand. They spat yellow flame, flame that reached ten inches beyond the barrel, blossoming out. *So pretty,* she thought. He fired across the narrow room at a man, the old man. The grey-haired man jerked backwards. Now he leaned heavily against the bar. Dark blood ran from the side of his mouth as he tried to raise his pistol. It discharged into the floor, then fell from his fingers.

Jacob Hannon moved toward her. He was coming. He fired at another and another. She reached her hand out; it hardly seemed to move. *Just touch him*, she thought. *Just touch him and everything will be all right. I'm dying. This starts the long journey. This is death.*

The room was full of smoke. It was difficult to breathe, and hard to want to. A cough caught in her throat. In his mad dash, Jacob Hannon stumbled, tried to keep his balance only to fall against a table, collapsing it and falling heavily to the floor, rolling. Twisting, he came to a knee, a forty-four pistol still in each hand.

How did he do that? she asked herself. Hannon seemed like a circus clown losing his balance. Maybe he, too, had been shot. Su Lin gave up on the effort to move her leaden hands. They were too far away.

Her eyelids were so heavy that she just closed her eyes and opened them again. Faces were so close. Judith and Jake. Blood had spread like a broken egg across her abdomen, dripping onto the floor. Judith looked lost and bewildered. Tears streamed down her cheeks. Su Lin thought she was smiling at her, wanting to touch her cheeks with her fingers. *She sees I'm dying,* she thought.

The Gypsy woman dropped the shotgun as if it was a fiery hot poker and reached for Su Lin. But Jacob Hannon's voice stopped her.

"Judith, pick up the Greener. Reload it. We got to get this girl outta here damn quick." In front of her, right where she could see him, Jacob Hannon mechanically fed fresh cartridges into one forty-four, then the other. One he shoved into his waist belt, the other into its holster.

He looks so hard at me. Su Lin wanted to reach out and with her fingers touch his face, his nose, his lips, the scar that traced the outline of his jaw, but her body felt so numb, so flat, so indescribably weak.

Judith picked up the shotgun.

Su Lin closed her eyes.

Hannon's voice was loud, so close. "Judith pull back the hammers on that shotgun and lead the way outta here. We've gotta get her a doctor and get these holes plugged before she bleeds to death. Ready?"

Su Lin heard no response. His arms were under her, around her, lifting her off the floor, a feather caught in the breeze. She was moving, floating. The ceiling in the dark room twisted and turned. She heard a rough voice whispering in her ear. "You did yourself right proud, girl. Now you hold on. Hear me. You hold on." Then, "Go, Judith! Now."

Su Lin heard a double click. She imagined that Judith had pulled back the hammers. Vaguely, she was aware of brilliant sunshine, of people standing, crowding closer . . . moving farther away, watching. She closed her eyes . . . not bothering to hate them. Hate was far too much trouble.

They were in the street. She could smell dust. Jacob Hannon was climbing stairs. For a moment Su Lin opened her eyes and watched his face. Then there was no more sun. They were in a room and Jacob Hannon was laying her on a table. Someone looked at her wound. She couldn't see him but she felt her shirt being cut, the cloth being pulled away from her abdomen.

The doctor bent over her. His face loomed large; his nose was so big. He stared at her eyes . . . so very close, holding her eyelids open, his breath . . . sour whiskey. The face disappeared. So, so ugly.

"She's Chink," he exclaimed loudly. "She needs a vet, not a doctor. Absolutely nothing I can do for her. Get her the hell out of here. I do not treat Chinese . . . the yellow, squinty-eyed . . . Get her out of here." The voice stopped, there was silence and then he spoke again. "From the looks of her you can forget the vet. Just take her to a mortician."

From her surreal, fuzzy world, Su Lin heard Judith shriek in dismay. Even the doctor knew she was dying. *Not long now.* The hammer of a pistol being drawn back clicked ominously in the closed room. She heard that. Right above her was an arm, a wrist, and a pistol. Su Lin blinked her eyes, trying to focus. What was this?

Jacob Hannon's face came into her vision, his eyes squinty, drawn tight and narrow. His words were measured, cut precise, each word a sentence in itself.

"Well, Doc . . . " he said, "we got ourselves a real problem here. The way I see it . . . " The bore of the forty-four was pointed right at the bridge of the doctor's nose. The doctor backed away until Su Lin could no longer see him. "You either fix this girl or I blow your brains out the back of your worthless head. Let me make it a little clearer. This here girl lives or you ain't seein' no tomorrow." The arm, the forty-four pistol did not waver.

Jacob Hannon does not like this man. Not very much. It was good to hear his voice, so close.

Suddenly the Doctor's face appeared above her, looked down at her then back at Jacob Hannon. He was perspiring. Su Lin tried to swallow. "A gutshot girl! God help us all." The last phrase was murmured quietly. She could barely hear it. The man stared at Jacob Hannon in alarm. "Do you know what you're asking? I am no God. Do you hear me?"

The world began to move, tilting. Su Lin tried to stop it, tried to will it to stop turning . . . to stay still.

It wouldn't. She let go, wondering if this was death, knowing that it was, embracing it.

In mists of grey, lost in the wanderings of her mind, Su Lin saw Jacob Hannon and Judith and wanted them to come close to her. She motioned to them with her hands again and again. But they would not come. Disappointed, hurting inside, she started to cry. Still, they would not come. Instead, they turned their backs. They walked away and dissolved into fog-like people, amidst crowds made of air and smoke. Darkness closed in on her.

She opened her eyes on a dream, a heavy sadness hanging over her, weighing down on her shoulders, her heart breaking. In this dream she stared at a distant ceiling and in particular at a cobweb weighed down with old dust, long strings waving slowly back and forth. Her stomach ached, a dull pain in the depth of her belly that wouldn't go away. Lying still, watching the dangling web, she wondered where death had taken her and what sort of ghost master failed to clean his ceiling? What sort of dream was this that had dark ceilings and old cobwebs?

Thunderous battle erupted in her ears. Memory flooded her body, screaming at every fiber. Frightened, she started to rise, to throw herself out of the way, but Judith hovered over her and pushed her back, clutching her in her arms bathing her face with tears. In that dream Su Lin wrapped her arms around her sister's neck and shoulders and felt safe and warm.

Hannon's face appeared beside that of Judith. He picked up her hand, holding it in his, patting it. Su Lin closed her eyes. Never had she felt so tired. A voice pierced the quiet, rattled her dream, raking her senses with razors.

"You mule-headed imbeciles," the voice said. "What are you doin'? Put her down. Put her down. You idiots. You'll pull every stitch in her body. Put her down easy. I said easy."

She gasped, realizing that this was no dream. She felt herself being laid back, the doctor towered over her. Tears came to her eyes and she suddenly felt so lonely, so afraid, so helpless, and vulnerable. Her life--all that she'd ever done---so useless, so inconsequential.

Jacob Hannon's face was above her. Judith was pushing him away, yet he remained where she could see him. He was awfully white . . . and so was Judith. And she hurt so badly, her abdomen a bowl of fire. From deep inside her chest a sob welled up and stuck in her throat. The burning pain deep inside her abdomen grew. She had been so wrong, so very, very wrong.

Mercifully, the world began to tilt again and she ran toward the tilting world, thankful for it, taking refuge in the grey fog, disappearing into the mist. But the demons chased her, giving her no rest and the dragon's hot breath burned her skin, singeing her hair as she fled.

In her sifting, changing dreams there was no refuge, no place to hide. Everywhere terror and hate followed her, gazing at her with yellow, bloodshot eyes until she woke and saw the dusty cobwebs hanging from the dirty, smoke-stained ceiling. She wanted to die; she thought that she was dead. But death would be fiery, hot, and sweaty. It was cold; she was cold. First it was the shivers, and then fire and more fire. There was no peace in it.

Hands lifted her, insisting that she swallow hot soup. She didn't want it. But the hands insisted. They kept insisting. She was so hot. Burning hot. But the hands insisted and she swallowed the soup, her clothing damp. It was so cold, a freezing cold, a cold that clung to her, that seized her body and refused to release its grip.

Hot soup was again brought to her lips. Again and again and again until her blouse was soaked with it and the world wanted to tilt and disappear. But it did not. It would not. And the hands insisted that she stay with them. But she wanted to go. She wanted to disappear into the fog. But the hands would not let her. There was more hot broth. Once she thought it was Jacob's hands, and she was in a blanket, his arms wrapped around her, chasing away demons. Once it was Judith, hovering over her like a white dove, touching her burning skin with her fingers, her hands so cool, so refreshing. The images merged and she didn't know whose hands held her.

After many comings and goings, soup and more soup, she became aware of the stained ceiling, and again counted the dusty cobwebs that hung above her. Her body no longer shook. Judith's face appeared and smiled at her. A cool wet rag bathed her skin. Her body felt so limp; she did not move. The smile appeared again, smiling until Su Lin smiled back. And she was alive--very, very weak--but alive.

There came a time when she was moved from the doctor's office, from his study, from the place where he drank corn liquor and rambled about everything and nothing. There came a time when the cobwebs were not on the ceiling and the ceiling was painted white and the woman bending over her frail frame was not always Judith, but another with grey hair, a grey dress, and a pretty nose that hung on a face frosted with freckles. The woman had a scar above her left cheek bone. Su Lin thought about the nose, the scar, the peppering of freckles, and she knew that she was no longer in the doctor's office.

There were others who waited at her bedside: the skinny man who swung gates, who had had her stand on the bottom rung to test its strength against her hundred twenty pounds, and young Johnny who never removed his hat and was going to California someday to see the ocean and throw a rock in it, and there was Mike who hummed the same tune to himself as he sat in the straight-backed chair cleaning his rifle. In all the time she'd known him he'd never said a word to her.

But of them all, Judith was with her most often. She was always talking. One day she stopped suddenly and said "It's your turn."

Su Lin had stared at her. "My turn?" she whispered.

"To say something. Your turn to say something. I'm tired of talking."

"I do not know . . . " Her voice sounded weak, even to her.

"Just what you're thinking. Whatever. You need to talk just so I don't have to."

"What I am thinking?"

"Yes."

"Jacob Hannon says I think too much." Her voice was distant, soft as a feather.

"He's probably right."

Judith sat down in the straight back chair beside her bed and leaned toward her.

"Perhaps," she said, "you think about Jacob Hannon."

"Sometimes," she answered.

Su Lin glanced at Judith's face to see if she was teasing her but there was nothing to read there. "Sometimes I try to consider what I should do," she said. "How I do not belong here. How I do not belong anywhere."

Judith screwed up her face so her lips were tight, her eyes mere slits. She opened her mouth but nothing came out. Finally, "Ah," came off her tongue sticking like honey to the roof of her mouth. "You belong wherever you're at," she said. "Wherever you want to be. There ain't no wrong place. There's just a place. If you're happy, it's the right place. You ought to stay there, if you can find it. There ain't too many of those."

Su Lin stared at her. "What . . . what about belonging?"

"Belonging?"

"I have a far away home."

"Yes and you got a hat, too. I seen it. It's the ugliest thing. But you don't have to wear it. If you get tired of it, you can throw it away. You can buy a new one. You can steal one. If you're of a mind, you can make one out of gingham and lace. You don't belong to that hat. The hat belongs to you. It ain't something you got to keep. Show me a place you can't move away from. Show me a place you can't move to. Show me a home that ain't made."

"Show you?"

"Never mind. You can't. How you feeling? Can I get you something?"

"I hate soup."

Judith laughed. "Don't blame you. I'll see if I can get you something sweet like chocolate, like sugar cookies. You'd like sugar cookies."

Some conversations stuck in her mind. That one did. She reviewed it countless times. And she found out that she did like sugar cookies.

The days passed and Su Lin's strength began to slowly return. At first she couldn't sit up at all. The doctor wouldn't let her. "Too risky" he said. "Might pull a stitch." After he'd said that no one would let her try.

Every day her wounds were cleaned with hot water. Every day she got new bandages. Perhaps it was the drink, but every day the doctor was happy. He'd say, "No infection. Not yet." Then he'd smile and be on his way, closing the windowed door behind him. Later he'd come back, his breath smelling sour, and sit in the room with Judith and talk of the Haggerty baby that came into the world butt first, or the Johnson boy who had broken his arm in three pieces falling out of a Jonathan apple tree. Every day it was a different ailment, a different person. Except for her. Always he said of her, "No infection. Not yet." Su Lin wondered what those words meant.

She discovered that the place she stayed was called a boarding house, a place inhabited by a lot of strange people she'd never seen before. And always, each day, the grey lady with the face full of freckles came to change the sheets, the pillow cases, and the water in the blue pitcher.

The odd group of people who sat with her came and went but Judith was a constant, always laughing and talking. Once she said, "You're moping. What's wrong with you? Moping so much? It sure ain't man trouble. 'Cause there ain't no men around here. Well, there's Mike and Johnny. There's that skinny one. There's Jake. But he ain't no trouble. He's just an old lobo wolf sniffing around. All teeth, no bite, no trouble." Judith had laughed at herself and her giggles had made Su Lin smile.

After the grey lady had come and gone with the changing of the sheets Judith had said, "So, sister, what's on your mind? Tell me." She had persisted. "I don't like being alone with no one to talk to. So spill the beans." Always she'd say this and always Su Lin would think about "beans," picturing in her mind beans all over the floor, beans in the bedding, beans under her pillow, beans rattling around in the chipped water basin. She pictured a lot of beans.

But on Thursday she answered the question and said "Jacob Hannon," staring at the checkered quilt that hid her abdomen from everyone's eyes, speaking softly so there wasn't much to hear. Later Su Lin remembered that. She remembered saying, "I think about Jacob Hannon."

Judith heard her. Su Lin thought that she could hear a mouse tiptoe across a carpeted floor.

"Jake? Good Lord, sister," Judith said. "You're not that hard up. No one is. Things ain't got that bad. Besides he's twice your age. Believe it or not I know'd him when I was a girl. Thirteen or so. He must be forty. Maybe more," she said. "Girl like you could have a dozen beaux knocking at your door . . . bringing you flowers and sweets till you could hardly stand it. You surely don't need no Jake."

"I think no more soup and I think about Jacob Hannon," Su Lin replied.

"Why?" Judith asked incredulously.

"I . . . I do not like soup," Su Lin said. "Soup is for the sick, for old people with no teeth. I do not like being sick. I have teeth."

"No. No. Why do you think about Jacob Hannon?"

"I do not know." Su Lin felt her cheeks turning red. She turned her head to the slip of a woman at her bedside. "Maybe . . . maybe I belong to him," she replied. "I know I do not. But to Oldest Uncle, to Father . . . I do. Sometimes . . . "

"You make it sound like he bought you at some store or something. Where were you standing? With the store-bought dresses or the bolts of cloth? Two for a quarter were you?" Judith laughed and pulled the hair away from Su Lin's eyes. "Come on, girl, I didn't just fall off no turnip wagon. Nobody belongs to nobody. Unless you're married. Then I'm not sure."

"Oldest Uncle gave me to Jacob Hannon for wife. Oldest Uncle thinks I belong to him. That he is my husband."

"Surely you're not serious. You can't be!"

"I speak words that are true," Su Lin said quietly. "I do not speak words that are false."

"Of course not," Judith corrected herself. "Of course not. You don't lie. I know you don't. Your heart is too good for that sort of thing. I wouldn't even think it. It's just . . . well, girl, I gotta explain a few things."

Again Judith screwed her face up, pursed her lips and stared intently at Su Lin. For a long time she said nothing.

"Nobody belongs to nobody," she finally said. "Not like a horse or something. Jake don't own you. He can't sell you. I know'd this man. Know'd him since I was a girl, but I told you that. He doesn't even think it. It ain't never crossed his mind. If you were to say to him 'I'm going,' he'd say all right. Probably help saddle your horse. Sure he might try and talk you out of it . . .'causeit would be a little crazy. But he wouldn't stop you."

Judith stretched her arms toward the ceiling and looked past Su Lin, rocking back and forth. "I don't know how it is where you grow'd up and all, but here--in this country--you got to want to stay with a man to stay with him. Nothing is forcing you. You got to want to, sister. Hear me? You surely got to want to."

Su Lin thought of responding. She knew all that very well. But Oldest Uncle didn't know. Oh, what difference did it make what he knew or didn't know?

"I ain't gonna tell you who to fall in love with. That's entirely up to you. You can fall in love with anyone you choose and God bless you. You can even fall in love with Jake if you're a mind to. It's your choice." Then Judith sat straight in the high-backed chair and looked directly at Su Lin. "Are you in love with him?"

"Love? What is this 'love' word?" Su Lin asked. "What does this mean?" She remembered that the nuns spoke of it. That it was important to them.

Judith laughed. She stopped abruptly, a sheepish grin flooding her face. "I'm sorry. It's just that . . . come on, Su Lin, ain't they got love in China? They got to. You know. Don't you? You were serious?" Judith looked at the young woman. "You were serious."

"All right. I'll explain it to you. Well, I'll try,'causeI ain't sure I can. Love . . . let's see, well, love is that special feeling you have for a feller. You see him and you get all warm and cozy inside 'til you can't stand it. It makes you full of smiles just thinking about him. When you see this special man in a crowd . . . well you don't see the crowd. You just see him and nothing else. You get warmed up inside just looking. And when he sees you and you see each other, your heart, it jumps inside you 'til you feel like dying. Oh, it's a feeling. Is it ever."

Su Lin turned her head and stared at Judith. *What was she talking about? Heart jumping inside?*

"My mother and father were in love," Judith said. "They sat sometimes and talked for hours about nothing special. Just talk. And when they thought they were alone sometimes they'd hug and kiss like tomorrow wasn't coming. Like they were each a tall glass of water and there wasn't enough to get wet. Sometimes my Papa would bring Momma flowers he found somewheres and Momma would light up like a candle. After that I'd catch her smiling. I imagine she was thinking about him. I know he was thinking about her."

Judith's voice wavered and her eyes welled up with tears. "They really had something special. You know what I mean? Something real special. That's love,

Su Lin. Something real special." Neither woman spoke until Judith broke the silence and wiped the tears from her eyes. "So, Su Lin, what do you think? Do you think you're in love with that man? Heaven help you!" Judith smiled, teasing with her eyes, with her voice. "What do you think? Are you a goner?"

Su Lin started to laugh but the muscles tightening caused her abdomen to sting. *In love? A goner? What was that?* "I do not know," she responded. "This love is not important . . . not in China. My mother and father were chosen for each other by their family. They never saw each other until the day they were married. My mother served my father . . . made him happy, gave him pleasure, took care of my father's mother. It was duty. I do not know if she loved him like you say it. She never said. It was her duty, her responsibility. I think maybe . . . there is not much love in China. Maybe it comes after a man and woman spend their entire lives together. I do not know."

"You ain't answered my question. Do you love Jake?" Judith asked again. "Does he make your heart jump up in your throat when you see him?"

"My heart jump . . . ?" Su Lin smiled at the question. "No. My heart does not jump when I see him." She thought before answering further. "You asked . . . and I just think about him. When he's gone . . . I think he is not there. Sometimes I want him to notice me, to see me. Some . . . sometimes I want him to touch me. He never does. Except like my father. I feel heavy inside. I feel bad for thinking about him. I should not. I get confused. I just do not know. The bad feeling I feel . . . it is not love. It is not good, this feeling. It is not what you describe."

"No? Well I think you got it bad, sister . . . real bad. But, why pick him? He's like a crusty old rock . . . all slippery with green moss growing all over it."

Su Lin was confused. "I did not," she exclaimed. "I did not."

"You did not what?"

"I did not pick him. Oldest Uncle picked him."

"Well, your uncle may have picked him but your heart is going along for the ride. It sure ain't saying no. It's not like you don't have a choice . . .'cause you do. You don't have to stay. I don't care what nobody says. You don't have to stay. The man will never ask you to stay. But you're staying. I can see it. I am surprised that I didn't see it before."

"What do you mean? What is it that you see?"

"Listen, sister . . . " Judith leaned over as she began to talk. "When he comes in you're at hand. When he sits down you're handing him a plate of food. It's like you know his thinking and his wants before he does. And you're right there, handy as can be. If'n your heart wasn't in this thing, wanting him, needing him, you'd be hiding somewheres every time he's around. You'd flat disappear. He'd never know you were around. But you're not." Judith paused and smiled. "You sure got it bad, Su Lin, real bad. I am surprised I ain't seen it before."

"What have I got?" Alarm rose in her voice.

Judith ignored Su Lin, ostensibly staring at the wallpaper. "Trouble is . . . " she said, her eyes meeting Su Lin's. "Trouble is he's going to be a real hard nut to crack."

"This is wrong, Judith. I serve him . . . because of duty. You know. I am a woman. He is a man. It is respect to Oldest Uncle. I cannot disappear. I am not without manners. I cannot dishonor Father. It is responsibility." Su Lin looked at Judith. "What does it mean 'cracked nut'?"

"Not 'cracked nut,' silly. A hard nut to crack. I'm saying . . . I don't know what I'm saying. It's not simple. That's what I am saying. It's just not simple. He was married before, you know. A Cinderella sort of thing. Do you know Cinderella?"

"No."

"Well . . . you know Cinderella's a fairy tale. A 'fall in love and live happily ever after' thing. Were they in love! I met her, you know, his wife. Before she got herself killed. The Apache, they done it. I was just a twig of a girl. Maybe I was twelve or something. I don't know. I imagine those 'Pache were sorry they ever harmed that woman. She was so pretty. And so young. She was only twenty-six. She had a baby, you know, Virginia."

"Sorry?"

"Yeah, well maybe more like regret. Like in 'that was a awful mistake.' You know?"

Su Lin didn't know whether she knew or not.

"Jake Hannon went hog-wild crazy: drinking, not eating, not sleeping. He went killing. That's what he did. That blood for blood, eye for an eye, Bible thing. Tracked them down, killed them slow. Liked to cut off an ear, he did. Can you imagine? If they were alive? Cutting off an ear, a nose, poking out an eye. Papa said he'd tie what's left to their ponies and turn them loose. That was eight, ten, fifteen years ago. A long time. Don't know what he's like now. Really not sure I want to know."

Su Lin stared at Judith. It was what--it was exactly what--she had thought. Jacob Hannon was a White man. Just like the others. She had known it. Her suspicion was correct.

"He's still fast to kill. Thank Goodness!" Judith crossed herself. "But he is polite. Sorta kind in an odd way. I don't know. I don't think he's got any heart left to love anybody."

What's she talking about?

"Maybe he's all burnt out inside. Maybe he just can't. Maybe there's nothing left. He's got a mean streak. Remember . . . he left those two rotting in the sun. Don't think he didn't know what would happen. He knew. He knew the old man would see his boy, maggots crawling out of him. Must of been awful. Maybe Jake's got a death wish." Judith turned to Su Lin. "I'll bet that's it. I'll bet he wishes himself dead. And after all this time."

"He takes a lot of time staying alive to wish he were dead," Su Lin replied.

"Yeah. Yeah, he is awful careful. Maybe he just doesn't know he wants to be dead. Maybe he ain't too bright." Judith laughed.

Su Lin measured her words, thinking carefully as she talked. "I do not want him for husband, Judith. I am in awkward position. I cannot go. I cannot stay. Do you understand?"

"Yeah, I do. Sort of. You got to be nice because your uncle told you to be nice. And your Papa expects you to be a good girl. And because you're a little bit scared of what will happen if you ain't nice."

"I think I am afraid," Su Lin said. "Now I thought I was dead. I am alive. I am grateful to live. This is selfish, yes?"

Judith smiled, "Love is selfish . . . sort of," Judith said, pausing before she continued. "It's two people being very selfish. Excluding everyone else from their lives . . . the part they share with each other. Don't sound right, but it sure explains some things, don't it?"

"I do not think you listen. I do not talk this 'love' word. My words speak duty . . . responsibility."

"No, I hear you just fine. I think you tell yourself that it's just a job . . . something you got to do. Maybe its 'cause he's a White. Did you ever think of that? White, black, red, yellow? That's there you know. Tell you one thing . . . " Judith said, "I catch him admiring you. From time to time I do."

"Oh please, Judith . . . you speak without sense. Riddles. Words without truth." Her skin started to tingle. She felt ill at ease and agitated. She didn't want to hear Judith's teasing words, her impossible words, her words for the sake of words: word shells, hollow and empty. This was not the love word. "No . . . " Su Lin said, shaking her head, "no." That's all she could say. Nothing else came out.

But Judith wouldn't stop talking. "Su Lin, it's true," she stated. "Now all we got to do is make him think that admiring is not enough. That he has to do something more than admire. That's what you really want."

Su Lin smiled at Judith in spite of herself. *This is ridiculous.* "No, he does not. This is silly, Judith. You tease me. Besides, he thinks I am too young for wife. I asked him at the very beginning. He does not want wife. His saddle is older than I am old. That's what he said. Besides he promised to take me back to Oldest Uncle but I cannot go."

"Take you back?" Judith looked at Su lin. "Yeah, right. And I'm not . . . no, I'm not teasing you. He thinks he's too old. Too young, you ain't. I'll bet he thinks he's too old for such a young woman."

"Oh, Judith, you make no sense. Old men take young woman for wife many times, often. It is arranged. Why would he think he is too old? He is not dead."

"In China, maybe, they do that. Not so much here. But believe me, sister. This man thinks he's too old. His eyes tell him you're the most beautiful thing they've seen since hot cakes and his head tells him he's too old to make syrup. It is silly, ain't it? But I'll bet you that's what he thinks."

Su Lin smiled, daring not to laugh. "That is not a good wager for you. How do you know what he thinks? Are you going to ask him? What do you think he's going to say, "I am too old to make young woman happy?" I do not think so. What man would say that?" Su Lin really wanted to laugh. But no. No, she wouldn't. She didn't dare.

Three weeks later Jacob Hannon came for her in an old buckboard with a squeaky wheel and a hole in the floor board. It wasn't the one he wanted to bring but it was the one he had. Tied to the end gate was his saddle horse. In anticipation for this planned event, Judith got her ready for the trip home, wrapping a blanket around her shoulders, and getting blankets ready for the floor of the buckboard for Su Lin to lie on. Su Lin waited for Jacob Hannon in an overstuffed chair holding herself upright, not wanting to pull at the wound, not wanting to move. Nausea passed over her in waves--a result of too much lying down, being too weak, too much uncertainty in her heart and mind. Maybe too much Judith.

The door opened and Jacob Hannon filled it. She smiled at him, relieved that he was there, wondering what he was going to do.

"How you doin', girl? Had us worried. Ready to go dancin'?" Without waiting for a response he glanced at Judith. "Ready?" he asked.

Judith nodded.

Hannon knelt by Su Lin's chair, patting her on the knee. "Listen, girl," he said. "I'm gonna pick you up and carry you out to the wagon. If you could stand, it'd make it a might easier for me."

With Jacob Hannon on one side and Judith on the other, she got slowly to her feet, feeling like this was something she didn't want to do. She tensed knowing it was going to hurt. He picked her up, lifting her off her feet, cradling her in his arms. He smiled at her, his face close to hers, talking in that horse voice. It didn't hurt like she thought it would.

"Lordie, girl . . . you really gotta start eatin'. There's nothin' to you but bone and gristle. And not much of that. We'll have to get you on home and fatten you up on steak and beans."

Su Lin stared at him, her right arm around his neck to steady herself, hoping he wouldn't drop her, amazed that he picked her up so easily, like she was goose down feathers.

Judith opened the door. Su Lin found herself staring at white puffs of clouds strewn across an azure sky. Hannon held her effortlessly in his arms. It was comforting. The wagon box had been layered with blanket after blanket, pillow after pillow. Jacob Hannon laid her down in the middle of it. It seemed everyone had come for her. She had drawn quite a crowd: the skinny one, and the heavy man from the barn, and the one who pitched the hay and cleaned the stalls. They smiled at her through yellow coffee stained teeth, The young one called Johnny sat his horse and simply watched. She remembered him leaning against the corral fence watching her as she carried wood into the house and how he said he was going to California to throw a rock in the ocean. They came, eight of them, "just to make sure" that Jake didn't kill her moving too fast. They needn't have been so concerned for Hannon walked the team. Judith sat in the back of the buckboard with Su Lin, the boys riding on either side, two in front and two behind.

"Many came for me," she whispered to Judith.

"Yeah, suckers, ain't they? Jake said he didn't want no jack rabbit spooking the horses. They took him at his word. I hear tell on the way over here they kilt every jackrabbit. That's what I hear tell."

"You tell stories."

"Yes, I do."

The sun was shining so very bright. Jacob Hannon stopped often, saying he "had to rest the horses," that "they weren't in too good of shape." During the ordeal Judith never left her side. Neither did anyone else. It was crowded; that is what it was.

The two-hour ride took all day. To her surprise they even stopped to build a fire and eat at noon. Young Johnny lent her his hat to keep the sun out of her eyes. Su Lin stared up at his white forehead and wondered if he had ever been without it. She started to refuse but he insisted, said it was as good of time as any to burn the lice "offa" his head.

It was a long, long ride home, starting in the morning and lasting until evening. In spite of all the care, she felt each jarring bounce to the bottom of her toes. She found herself praying she'd be home soon, sleeping in her own bed, and that she'd forget each rock, each chuckhole, and each wagon track.

CHAPTER TWENTY-NINE

Su Lin had never felt so weak nor had her body ever been so emaciated. Her skin hung loosely on her frame; her muscles had evaporated. Her eyes appeared recessed. She was a mess. She knew this. A mirror seldom lies.

Out of fear and in the name of a speedy recovery, no one allowed her to lift a thing, not so much as a stick of wood or a dirty plate from the table. She was never left unattended except to sit in the bathtub soaking in hot water and soap. Someone helped her out of bed. Someone walked her to the privy. Someone handed her a wet towel or a spoon for the broth she slurped morning, noon, and night.

One day Jacob Hannon said there'd be no more of that, insisting that she get her own spoon, get out of bed herself, "get to movin' around," and "get to smellin' the wildflowers." The menu changed from beef broth to all-you-can-eat steak, beans, and buttered bread. Sometimes rice replaced beans but there were more beans than rice, so the table saw lots of beans and little rice. Sometimes there were carrots and turnip greens.

Her rack of ribs began to disappear and Su Lin became less of a stick person drying up in the desert heat and more of that slender beauty who had once walked the gardens of her father. The ten-inch scar low on her belly where the doctor's sharp blade had opened up her abdomen became a thin blue line.

No one expected her to live, not gut shot. It was said the doctor counted himself lucky. He was heard telling the people standing around eating rock candy in Miller's general store that the age of miracles had returned, that no one needed doctors, not anymore. After he'd opened Su Lin up, he had confided in the bartender at the Boundary Saloon that he'd cleaned the cavity out with sour rotgut whiskey three times over, stitched the perforated intestine with boiled catgut and prayed to the God of Heaven to keep the girl alive until he could get out of town. It was his intention, he said, to get clear of the entire country before she died and before Jacob Hannon put a forty-four slug through his head, "the crazy son of a bitch."

That wasn't all. Many stories were told while eating at the long table in the adobe. It was said that a day and a morning after the gunfight at the Boundary Saloon, the mortician buried five men, selling their horses and saddles to pay for the interment. On the third day he buried the old man. No one seemed to know who he was or who they were. Strangers, all. Jacob Hannon hadn't volunteered any information without the asking.

"Those boys." he said, "didn't particularly like what he was drinkin'; weren't all that happy with his birthday celebration. 'Course, they couldn't shoot worth a damn."

Getting well with Teddy around was a charm. He always brought her something: an eagle's feather, a bird's nest, a dried flower, rattles from a snake, the bleached white skull of a rock dog he found somewhere–stuff a girl really needed. She tried to think of living without that boy around and that started her crying. She'd get morose. To hide her feelings, she'd walk down to the creek where the pole corral crossed it creating a watering hole for livestock. She'd sit on a lichen-covered rock for hours until the sun dropped below the mountains and the shadows merged in the twilight.

Pistol practice recommenced. Jacob Hannon was adamant. She understood his reasoning but didn't like it. But he insisted. So in the mornings she'd shoot the navy pistols, loading and reloading, dropping the hammer until there were no more explosions, only the clicking of the hammer dropping on empty chambers. Then she'd do it again, hour after hour, until her arm was tired and she had to sit down.

The Navy colts were exchanged for Peacemakers. Brass cartridges were substituted for caps and nitrate papers. Loading was much faster. They were much lighter.

She shot the new pistols until the tin cans were ripped colanders, until the bottles were shards of shattered glass, until the barrel was hot to the touch and she couldn't stand it anymore. Then she'd quit for the day not realizing that she'd practiced more than Jacob Hannon would expect. He never said anything to her about it. She thought it was what she had to do because he said so, and that was that.

Sometimes he came and watched, reminding her to squeeze, telling her to point the pistol like pointing a finger, to feel it with her eyes, and her body, like she and the pistol were one. Point. Point. Point. Squeeze. Squeeze. Squeeze. Slowly the tin can would disappear and he'd be gone. She'd load, shoot and reload until someone called her to dinner, thanking God for the break.

Once she told him the new pistols were still heavy, that her arm grew tired, and the barrel would wobble.

"Let's see," he said. "Shoot it for me."

She did as she was told, firing six rounds then looking at him. *Really what could he do? I just have to get stronger, she thought.*

"Sis," he said, "that colt weighs a little over two pounds and is fourteen inches long. That makes it heavy, especially given your weight and muscle. Here's what I want you to do. Bring the barrel down on what you're shooting at. Pull the trigger just as you line up the shot. It's a little slower but more accurate."

That is what she did. She became more accurate and stronger.

Two weeks later he added a Henry rifle. It was confusing because there was Henry the Gypsy, Henry the baby, and Henry the rifle. It turned out that Henry the Gypsy did not make Henry the rifle, that it wasn't his, that someone else named Henry made the rifle years before. She fired it until her shoulder was black and blue.

Every day he spent an hour with her, refining her techniques, improving her confidence, helping her to make the weapons an extension of herself.

"Why am I shooting these so much?" she asked him. "Do not I know enough?"

He smiled before he answered. "Sooner or later, those boys in the black boots and the sharp razors will come lookin' to trim your locks. Sooner or later. You can figure it. You need to be ready because it's them that will pick their spot, not you. They'll try to put you at a disadvantage and keep you there. You need to be ready. Chances are you'll have to defend yourself. Give help time to get to you and lend a hand. Colonel Colt will make up the difference in size and speed."

"Ok," she replied. "I will prepare to be ready."

"You do that, Susie. I'm hopin' they'll think you're just a girl. Nothin' to worry about. Knowin' how to shoot will give you teeth. That will be your advantage. That and everybody here is waitin' for those boys to show up. It ain't gonna be no walk to the creek. We'll see to that."

Su Lin smiled at Jacob Hannon, picked up the pistol, ejected the brass, and began to reload. She had her answer. This was never going to end.

The evenings grew cooler. She found herself thinking about Youngest Brother, of Father and Oldest Uncle. She resumed washing dishes, bringing in wood for the cook stove, hanging wet clothes to dry in the autumn sun. She'd sit on the top rail of the horse corral with Johnny, listening to him talk of California as if it was right next door. He'd tell her how he was going to fill the ocean up with rocks when he was of a mind. She watched the horse wranglers work the rough string, holding them down by the ears while they climbed on top and turned them loose. And Su Lin waited.

On November 7, 1876, Judith and Virginia took two wagons to Clearwater to purchase winter supplies. Young Johnny and Mike, the Irishman, went with them. The Skinny one stayed behind to insure Su Lin's safety. Su Lin stayed behind to watch after little Hank, to see that he didn't wander afar and "get himself lost."

It was one of those fall days; if you stood in the shade it was cool, even cold, but if you were in sunshine, it was tolerably hot, warm enough to send you looking for a drink of water, or perhaps some lemonade. The crisp air was soaked with the smell of curing grass, the creek bottom a mass of yellow leaves tinged in brilliant reds and purples.

Jacob Hannon had gone to "push" cattle to winter pastures. Teddy was with him. They'd been gone since midmorning and were not expected back before nightfall. Judith, Virginia and the boys hoped to be back from town with the winter's provisions at evening as well.

Su Lin spent the morning and afternoon by the spring in the garden beyond the crosses that marked the final resting places of the dead. Hank wandered about chasing the last grasshoppers of fall, throwing rocks into the creek water, watching water skippers dart across the surface. He talked to himself, laughing and singing as he played. Su Lin sat on the red blanket and read the King James version of the book of the nuns. The nuns had a book in another language that they only talked about. The "begats" and the "begones" were boring. She didn't read it long before setting it down. There had to be something else. "Boring" hardly described it.

There were sandwiches in the basket, a quart jar of lemonade, two apples, and some pinion nuts. And there was the 1873 SAA colt pistol Jacob Hannon thought she ought to have at all times. It was heavy. She hated to carry it. But he'd insisted. "You never know," he said. "The next time might just be that time." She'd spent days wondering what he'd meant.

The baby's song stopped. Su Lin looked up. To her surprise, standing in the shadows of the cottonwood in the clearing beyond the grave markers was a Chinese man. Her heart stopped. Her hand went to her bosom. She held her breath.

For weeks and weeks, for countless hours she'd thought about this one moment in time, the time when they'd come for her. She'd imagined where she'd be, what she'd do. Here it was and all she could do was stare. She saw no others, just this one. Yet intuitively she knew there were others. There had to be for there always were.

She called little Hank to her. He came without hesitation. Perhaps it was her voice. Her executioner hadn't moved. She looked about for the Skinny one but he was nowhere to be seen. *Dead,* she thought. *That'd be the way of it.* She rose from the blanket, Hank clinging to her skirt, wanting to be picked up, to be hugged.

Seeing this assassin was a relief. This whole matter of dying had been so long coming. It was finally here. The thought made her smile. For a fleeting second the irony struck her and was gone. It would be so easy for him to take her and leave her headless body on the ground. She realized what she'd known, that there was no chance for her. This one could move quicker then she could, even if she'd had a head start and knew he was coming. Funny thing, she'd known he was coming. And now she couldn't run, not and carry Hank.

No, she thought. *This isn't over. I'm not dying so easily*. She bent her knees and with both hands she picked up the basket, holding the handle in her left hand, straightening the cloth back with her right. *I will not make this easy. I will not just die. No, I won't. Not now. Not ever.* She stared at the man, her eyes locked on his, a fierce anger rising in her throat.

Her right hand found the pistol grip. She listened for the click of the hammer. Perhaps he would think she had a knife. Not a pistol. What woman was armed with a pistol? He'd soon find out. The baby whimpered, his lower lip curling as he puckered up.

"Hush, little one," she whispered. "Be still."

The baby looked at her, craning his head, raising his arms.

"You should not have run from your duty," the assassin stated in Chinese. "I have come far for you."

"You should not have come after me at all."

"You dishonored your father."

"I dishonor no one. What honor is there for you in killing me, a mere girl?"

"It is the honor of obedience."

"No. It is the honor of money."

"That, too."

He started toward her, his feet soundless in the dry wire grass.

Su Lin did not move, holding the reed basket with her left hand, sheltering the pistol under the folds of cloth, hidden with the slices of bread, the cup to dip water from the spring, the knife for butter and berry jam.

"I will not go with you," she said.

"I come for your head only."

"It will not be easy."

"What could be easier?"

He drew his long battle sword, eliciting the sound of metal against metal. He walked toward her, his steel blade glinting in the sunlight. He held the hilt in both hands and to the side, his face impassive, his eyes locked singularly on hers.

She released the basket. It dropped away from the pistol. Calmly, just as she had done ten thousand times before, she brought it up, leveling the pistol, pulling the barrel down on the approaching man, squeezing. The report split the quiet air. A look of surprise surfaced on the man's otherwise dull facial features. Yet even having been shot, he started to run at her, the war sword held high. She pulled back the hammer and fired again. A tiny hole appeared on his throat. He fell limply to the ground at her very feet, his arm muscles jerking spasmodically, losing the sword in the grass.

Su Lin wondered if she were asleep, if she'd wake up. *When?* The baby howled, hiding his face in the folds of her skirts. Her fingers tingled. This was not sleep. Su Lin looked about her, mentally checking off bunk house, horse corrals, barn, adobe.

Assassins never come alone. So Father had said, warning her. *But where were they?* She listened. There was no sound except for the murmuring of water as it flowed in the creek and the child's whimpering. The trees were silent. There were no birds, no cattle lowing, nothing. A lone magpie flew silently over the adobe toward the corral, then in mid-flight turned abruptly toward her and the cottonwood tree that provided shade for the dead.

The huge body at her feet twitched. It smelled awful. The baby cried loudly. *The others would not be so unsuspecting,* she thought. Her gaze flitted nervously over the barn, past the bunk house, and past the pole corral. Glancing at the adobe, she looked back at the corral. *Where?* The bay horse, the sorrel, and the paint ate grass hay, blowing air nosily, watching her as they chewed. One horse stared across the hard-pack yard toward the adobe. He stamped a foot and kicked at a horse fly on his belly. His ears were pointed at the adobe, his eyes locked on something.

The corrals? The adobe?

Su Lin held still. She patted Hank on the head, staring at the buildings. Waiting. Movement is death. Make the other commit before you do. That's what Jacob said. Little Hank had buried his face in her skirts, his runny nose dampened the hem, making patches of dark spots. He wrapped his arms around her leg. He sniffled, his hand patting her thigh, wanting to be picked up.

Somebody move . . . please.

It was the baby Henry, named for a Gypsy tinker, who moved first. Inexplicably, he released his grip on her leg and started on his three-year-old legs toward the adobe, a familiar building, the last place he'd seen his mother. Su Lin reached out to stop him, grabbed at his arm, missed then ran to grab him. She picked him up. The baby laughed, squirming in her arms. He wanted to get down to run, to play the game of run and be caught, to be kissed, tickled and hugged and released to do it again.

She looked up from the baby and saw a man stepping through the doorway into the sunlight. Teddy stood in front of him, a knife at his throat, a mere whisper away from death.

Oh, Teddy, Teddy, where did you come from? Where is Jacob Hannon?

Around the north edge of the house came another, and from the south yet another. They came as Father had said, "more than two, perhaps three, four." Su Lin let the air whistle through her teeth realizing there would be no Jacob Hannon this time. Still she thought of him, how physically he didn't look like much, not much at all. Not like these grim faced mercenaries, these unshaven soldiers, with fierce, dark, merciless eyes that squinted at her in the noonday sun.

She'd seen too many such men. She'd seen the endless lines of moving soldiers, the smoke of burning villages towering into the dark blue sky, dark columns of grief bending and twisting in the air. And with the marching, shuffling feet, always the moans of the dying, the smell of death, and the bloated swollen bodies of the dead. She remembered the sight of her father through the window of the coach, his eyes damp with tears, and thanked all that was holy that Jacob Hannon was not here, that today he would not die.

Taking the baby by the hand, she walked across the yard toward the adobe, toward the open door where Teddy stood, the knife at his throat. She imagined his fear, the thought of his throat being cut, of bleeding to death in this place in this middle of nowhere. *This isn't over yet*, she thought. They didn't want him. They wanted her. The boy, little Henry, they were nothing, just casualties on the road of death, the road to Tinian.

The SAA pistol felt heavy in her right hand. Four chambers loaded, two empty. Four shots. But they were nothing in the face of her assassins, nothing to the three mercenaries who waited. They watched her approach, making no effort to move until she stood fifteen feet from the grim faced man who held Teddy.

The assassin on her left was thin and wiry. Maybe she could get him. Maybe, but she only had four shots. One shot and Teddy would be dead, choking in his own blood. And the other two? They would be coming for her, for the baby.

The executioner on her right grunted and took one step forward. She pulled back the hammer on the pistol, listening to the clicks as the cylinder rotated and the chamber fell into place. He stopped. His eyes bored in on her. He was a huge man. His sash held a giant war sword, the hilt fashioned from silver and leather straps that sparkled in the sunlight. He had nothing in his hands; that big, that strong, he needed nothing.

I am a woman, she thought. *Why should a big man like you fear me?* Su Lin could barely breathe. The man holding Teddy seemed bigger, bigger and larger than she had imagined. The best had been sent--the very best to bring her head back.

"I am here," she said to the one in the middle, noting the scar above his left eye and the way his hair was pulled straight back and knotted. "Release the boy. Release him. It is me you want."

But the man, an errant strand of stringy hair partially obscuring his eyes, did not move, nor did he respond.

"I am Su Lin Kou. It is me you want. Release him. Release the boy. He is nothing to you."

The man chuckled. It was a guttural sound followed by the smacking of lips. "Drop the weapon."

"I will not. Release him first. Release him. Release the boy. You dishonor yourself making war on children. You should be ashamed."

"Who are you to bargain? I release no one."

"I am a woman. I am the one that so frightens your Master that he sends four. I am Su Lin of the House of Kou. That is who I am. And I am before you. With this piece of metal in my hand I may kill all of you. All three. Already I have killed one. What is three? Three cowards who make war on a child. Three cowards who come for one mere girl. Your weakling master should have come himself, he who fears a girl. Fears me. He is not a man. He is nothing. And you take his orders. You work for one who has no spine, no character. One who trembles in the presence of men. What does that make you?"

Su Lin did not move. It didn't matter. There were three of them. She was nothing. Teddy would be dead. The baby would be dead. All would be killed. No one would be left alive. She knew it just as she knew ice was cold and fire was hot. Talk was as useless as yesterday's wind. It did not matter what she did or did not do, what she said or did not say. A wisp of breeze tugged at a loose strand of black hair. Today was a good day to die.

Su Lin knew then that she wasn't going to put the pistol down. *Not now, not ever.* The thought had barely crossed her mind when without the slightest hesitation Su Lin raised the pistol, brought the sights down on the head of the man in front of her as if it was a tin can or the top of a busted bottle. With the care she'd given to squeezing the last drop of water from ten thousand towels she squeezed the trigger.

Her arm recoiled with the explosion, the pistol flying back. She nearly lost her grip on the gun. A small hole appeared on the forehead of the man in front of her. Turning to her left, she pulled back the hammer, staring at the charging man and brought the pistol to bear, pointing at him as she would point her finger. She felt the explosion in her hands.

The White man's clock on the wall of Oldest Uncle had not ticked twice. She was knocked sprawling, the pistol flying from her hand beyond her reach sliding on the hard pack farther and farther away. On hands and knees she scrambled after it, screaming at the top of her lungs, her legs churning, pushing as she leaped. But her outstretched fingers came up short. There it was eight inches beyond her reach. The last executioner towered above her, his sword held high above her head, the hilt seized by both hands.

Explosions of sound erupted about her: a hammer on an anvil, the crack and roar of thunder that follows streaks of lighting. The sword and man were coming down upon her. She screamed. His weight struck her, smashing her, crushing the air from her lungs. There was nothing she could do. Lights exploded in her head like a thousand shards of glass. Darkness replaced light. And then there was nothing.

A white curtain edged in lace fluttered slowly in the breeze. Soft shadows filled the room. Su Lin eyed the curtain and the shadows distrustfully. She'd been here before in a dream, walking in the world of the dead, walking toward the end of a long, long tunnel. There was no pain. She was warm all over; even her toes were warm. She stretched her arm, watching her fingers and her knuckles bend and flex. The white lace curtain moved slightly. Cool, rain washed air, smelling of sagebrush and juniper, kissed her cheek.

Su Lin turned her head. Suddenly she sat up wondering what had happened and why she was alive. Her eyes found Teddy. He sat in a chair close to the bed and stared at her. This could not be for he should be dead. She was dead, surely. Henry was dead. But the boy who she thought was dead smiled, stood up, and walked out of the room, passing through the doorway and out of sight. She thought she should pinch herself. She did and it hurt.

She looked down and saw her blouse soaked in dried blood. Hers, no doubt.

From the doorway she heard the boy's voice. "She don't look so good," he said.

A petite woman entered through the doorway, a frown on her face.

"How are you?" she asked. "That was a tough one. You had us all worried. It's a wonder . . . " She did not finish the sentence. She bent down and touched Su Lin's cheek.

"Oh, Judith, tell me I'm alive."

"That's the rumor."

"I . . . I thought everyone was killed."

"No."

"What happened? How? No, do not. Do not tell me anything."

Su Lin glanced at her blouse, at the dried, dark blood. The image of herself standing over her brother with clenched fist and blood leaking from his nose flashed through her mind. She remembered him locking her inside the trunk. She remembered wanting to kill him and hitting him as hard as she could, bloodying his nose. She remembered Oldest Uncle saying, "Do you want to kill him?" She had said "yes." And at the time she did. She surely did.

She remembered serving Oldest Uncle and the White man, Jacob Hannon. She remembered how Oldest Uncle had looked at her and said, "I give you to him. You are wife. If you are to live, this is the way it must be. Do not disgrace your father."

"But Oldest Uncle, he does not want me."

"He will."

"But he doesn't."

It seemed a long time ago. Anger suddenly filled her breast: anger at her brother, at Oldest Uncle, at Jacob Hannon. Su Lin closed her eyes. "This must be some trick," she said aloud. "I am so tired of this."

"Tired of what?"

Su Lin fastened Judith in her gaze. "Where is he?"

"Who?"

"Mr. Hannon. Where is he?" No sooner had she said Mr. Hannon than she realized she'd never called him that before.

Judith picked up on the change immediately. "Mr. Hannon? Well, I think he's down in the horse corral working the yearling colts. Been there for an hour. Why?"

Su Lin swung her legs out of the bed and groaned. She was so sore. It was like some thing or someone had run over her. She could barely breathe; it hurt so.

"You better go easy," Judith said. "Three hundred pounds of fat man just fell on top of you. It took three of us just to get him off you."

"Is everyone all right?" Su Lin asked, staring at Judith, holding her breath.

"Everyone except you and those four." Judith smiled. "They surely didn't expect a Chinese girl to be packing a .45. And they certainly didn't expect her to know how to pull the trigger."

"Where is the horse corral?"

"Su Lin, you've been here like forever and you don't know where the horse corral is? Come on."

"Judith, there are four corrals and they all have horses standing in them. Which one is it?"

Judith smiled. "Down by the creek. In the stand of cottonwoods." Judith paused, staring at her, the blood on her blouse, the bruise on her arm and cheek bone. "You going to have a word with 'Mr. Hannon?'"

"Where is my gun?"

Judith pointed to the pistol resting on the side table by the doorway. "You gonna shoot someone?"

"I do not know what is going to happen or who is going to try and stop me."

"I see."

Su Lin stood slowly. "Judith, did I ever tell you about hitting my younger brother, about breaking his nose, and the blood, and kicking him. Did I ever tell you about that?"

"No."

"He put me in a box--a trunk--so very small. I did not fit. He locked the lid. I nearly died. I did not like it. I do not like being put in a trunk. I do not like it. It made me really, really angry. I hit him really hard. Later I felt bad. But I did not like it."

"Oh, I . . . I don't know what to say."

Slowly she made her way to the table and picked up the .45. She checked the loads because she had to, because Jacob Hannon taught her to always do that.

Before she left she turned to Judith. "I will be back," she said. "Maybe we could cook some bread. I am really hungry. I would like baked fish and some rice, but steak will do. Please could you do that for me? Please?"

"I can. I'd love to."

"Thank you."

Su Lin made her way to the creek. The corral had to be the one farthest from the house. The soreness in her muscles made it even farther. The walk, the sun's heat, and moving loosened her muscles. Jacob Hannon saw her from afar off. She knew he was watching for he was always watching. As she moved across the escarpment, she could see him opening the corral gate, leading a two-year-old colt. The pistol in her hand felt heavy, so heavy she wanted to put it down. But she didn't.

As she approached him, she felt his eyes study her body and the pistol in her hand. She didn't want to be limping but she was. Anger washed over her. Again she remembered her brother, blood running down his face.

"Susie, good to see you up and about. How you feelin'?"

"Very angry."

"You figurin' on shootin' someone?"

" I do not know who I am going to meet."

Hannon nodded his head in understanding. "Why are you angry?"

"Oldest Uncle. You."

"Me?"

"Oldest Uncle said I was your wife and that--how you say it?--that is the way of it." She spoke very slowly, fingering the trigger guard.

"Susie . . . "

"I do not like boxes."

"What?"

"I do not like to be put in a box with the lid shut."

"What's that supposed to mean?" The horse colt blew his nose and waited impatiently, shifting his weight from one leg to the other, switching his tail at deer flies. "Is this about your uncle?"

"Yes. It is about you."

"Me?"

"Yes. Oldest Uncle say I am wife. You . . . he . . . you put me in trunk with lid. I cannot go forward. I cannot go backward. I do not like it. I very angry. If you were Younger Brother I would hit you in the nose."

"I see."

"Do you?"

The pistol discharged. How that happened, she did not know. It was a single action. The hammer had to be pulled back in order to fire the weapon, and she didn't remember cocking it. Surprised, Su Lin fell over backwards. Jake Hannon jumped. The horse colt bolted, jerking the lead rope free, running pell mell for the cottonwood trees.

Jake ran to Su Lin. "You hurt, girl? What the hell happened?" He lifted her up. "Jesus, girl. You put the fear of God in me."

Su Lin blinked her eyes in confusion, rallying her thoughts. "This is not about God," she said. "This is not about nuns in black dresses. It is not about me learning English in their house."

"I reckon it's not. It is about you and me."

"Yes."

"I just ain't been proposed to quite this way."

"What is this 'propose?'"

"It's where someone asks you to marry them."

"I am not asking."

"All right, girl. I reckon I can ride that horse, seein' how he's already saddled."

"What is meaning of this?"

Jacob Hannon smiled.

The End.

About the Author

G. R. Howe was born and raised in Northern Wyoming. He graduated from Brigham Young University with a degree in Political Science. He received his law degree from John Marshall Law School in Chicago and became licensed to practice law in 1976. He pursued a career in law for thirty years in Ventura California. He returned to Wyoming to ranch and write western novels. He has written a collection of short stories of his hometown, Kane, a small town erased by flooding by the Yellowtail Dam Reclamation project in 1965, entitled *Short Stories Out of Kane*. *Dragons Of Fire* is the second of several western novels he has written.

Visit his website *Empty Saddles and Rusty Spurs* at www.emptysaddles.com

www.ingramcontent.com/pod-product-compliance
Lightning Source LLC
LaVergne TN
LVHW020658110826
845149LV00012B/2041

9780985040710